W9-BGS-038

THE STARS . . . OR THE STREETS?

Janna had to choose—and soon.

She could go out to the space colony with her closest friends, to a life free of Earth's computerized restrictions. Or she could stay on in the dangerous, frustrating work of a cop, trying to control criminals in the face of hampering laws and partnered with a trigger-happy freak.

The choice was obvious. But there was one last case to clear before she could leave—the problem of how one man could be in two places at the same time . . .

The Doppelgänger Gambit

Lee Killough

A Del Rey Book

BALLANTINE BOOKS • NEW YORK

For Pat, who heard every
word many times and was
always as patient as
his advice was sound.

CHAPTER ONE

The whole world mourned the *Invictus.* People everywhere paused at any news of her, and those who believed in gods and miracles prayed. She was an American-built ramjet, carrying American colonists, but messages from the ships Earth had launched toward the stars over the past twenty years were rare and therefore international events. The *Invictus* became an international tragedy.

The newscanner in the squadroom of the Shawnee County Police Department's Crimes Against Persons squad had been there for so long, no one remembered the set's origin, whether it had been donated or abandoned there or was recovered stolen property someone had "forgotten" to turn in to the property room. It was usually a little-attended but familiar part of the background, and leos—law enforcement officers—on all three watches tossed spare vending tokens into the cup on Lieutenant Hari Vradel's desk so that once a month the burly squad commander could redeem the tokens and have the bankcredit transferred to Newservice, Inc. for the subscription. This morning, however, every eye in the squadroom stared at the set, morning and day watches alike. The only sound in the room was the voice of KTNB's voice-over announcer reading the text that rolled across the screen.

"Her name is the *Invictus,* and in the eternal night of space that covers her, she may be dying. No one aboard knows why. She is a Boeing Starmaster modified 800 ramjet and she was launched from the Glenn Space Platform ten years ago, carrying the nine hundred members of the Laheli Colonial Company. She was bound for a planet seventy-three light-years away. No one expected to hear from her until she sent her tachyon courier capsule to tell Earth she had arrived safely at her destination; however, yesterday the capsule was recovered by workers from the Vladikov Space Platform at 2:53 P.M. Greenwich time, with this voice-only message inside."

The announcer's voice was replaced by another, a calm voice, but one heavy with weariness. "This is Jaes Laurent of the Laheli Company's ramjet *Invictus*. Over the past two weeks, ship's time, we have experienced repeated breakdowns and failures in the life support systems of our sleeper sections. The onboard computer has been able to instruct us how to make only temporary repairs. We have now lost four hundred of our sleepers and face the possibility of losing more. All ten crewmembers are awake and working to repair failures as they occur, but we don't know how well we'll succeed. We realize there's no possibility of you on Earth being able to help us. This message is not a distress call. We just want someone to know what happened to us, and perhaps bring a problem to attention that may save the lives of future colonists."

The voice of the announcer resumed. "When contacted, representatives of Boeing refused to speculate—"

Lieutenant Vradel reached up and turned off the sound. "I'm sorry to interrupt, leos, but the time is now eight thirty on what promises to be another firecracker July day, and a few light years closer to home, in our very own Topeka, murderers and thieves whose activities we just discussed at rollcall deserve our attention as law enforcement officers."

Someone at the back of the room muttered, "Crap."

Vradel regarded the squad with mock solemnity. "No, that's wrong. Crimes Against Property is the crap squad, not Crimes Against Persons." He became serious. "Morning watch, you're all late for debriefing. Dismissed. Day watch, get to work. Everyone in the drugstore stakeout come to this end of the room."

He gave them a few more minutes to sort themselves out. While he waited for the stakeout teams to gather around him, he looked them over, mentally reviewing the assignments. In addition to his own personnel, he had four teams from Crimes Against Property and eight plainjane teams on loan from the Gage division—those sixteen men and women hoping to impress Vradel enough to be permanently promoted to Investigator I. He chewed on his mustache. Twenty teams made an expensive operation. He hoped the stakeout would produce more results today than it had the past week.

His eyes fell on a dark bulldog of a man standing next to a tall smoky-blonde. Sergeant Wim Kiest was wearing a worried frown. Vradel supposed the *Invictus* touched some sharp nerves in him.

Vradel smiled. "Be optimistic, Kiest. That doesn't happen to every colony ship. Yours will be all right."

Beside him, Sergeant Janna Brill hissed. "Don't say that. I've been trying for months to talk him out of this colonial insanity. You see how it's affecting him." She plucked at the sleeve of his shirt, one of the currently popular "neo-pioneer homespun" styles. "It's driven him right off his tick. Don't spoil the best case against his leaving I've found yet."

If Wim Kiest was a bulldog, Janna Brill was a greyhound, one hundred eighty-three centimeters of whipcord sinew. The sleeveless blue romper and matching hip boots she wore set off her pale coloring so well Vradel reflected that with some more meat on her, she could be a very flash bibi. Why did she stay so bony thin?

He glanced at the chrono again. The digital readout said, redly: 8:35. "All right, lions and she-lions; we do it like before, one team at each drugstore in a shopping mall. Same assignments. The computer analog profile of our two jons says they'll continue to hit the Gage area and will prefer to strike soon after opening. Be careful. These deeks are carrying shooters, remember."

"Yes, Daddy," someone called.

One of the janes grimaced. "I wish they'd hit the

3

Highland division for a change, or work evenings so it would be the night watch's problem."

His partner shook her head. "Don't wish it. When the computer starts missing, where will we be?"

Vradel pointed to the door. "Sail. I want to see those deeks' heads here on pikes by high noon."

Another Gage jane tapped Janna Brill's arm. "Did your supervisor take an extra degree, say in dramatics?"

Brill looked back wide-eyed. "I thought Criminal Justice *was* a dramatics degree."

"Sail!" Vradel ordered.

Outside the squadroom, Wim Kiest and Janna Brill separated quickly from the other teams and wound their way down through the labyrinth of the Capitol Division Station toward the basement garage. The station was only three floors high, but it sprawled over an entire city block. They passed clerks, investigators from other squads, a few civilians—looking lost and apprehensive—and uniformed officers from the beta squad coming in off the morning watch. At one point Wim and Janna were surrounded by helmeted and booted leos in iron-gray jumpsuits sidestriped with red from collar to the ends of the short summer sleeves and underarms to boottops. The group swirled around them, yawning and wisecracking, on their way to showers and debriefing—that tick talk session where, it was hoped, the emotional charge of the job stress was discharged—before heading home. The alpha squad would have come in a little after eight and would already be in debriefing.

In the garage, the partners passed rows of watchcars waiting for the day watch beta squad. "Bullet on the half shell" some wit had called the floatcar design, for the way the sleek fiberplastic body poised in the middle of the airfoil's spreading skirt. The vehicles were conspicuously marked with white tops, black bodies, and a light-reflecting red stripe circling the body just below the windows. Wim and Janna passed jane cars, too, unmarked by police insignia but still obviously police vehicles by virtue of being Datsun-Ford Monitors. Everyone knew the Shawnee County PD used D-F's almost exclusively.

Their own car was also a Monitor, painted a bright green. They stepped on the airfoil skirt and climbed in, Wim under the wheel, Janna on the rider side. She switched on the car radio and screwed her personal radio button into her left ear. She activated it with a tap of her finger.

"Indian Thirty to control, requesting a T-check."

"Roger, Indian Thirty." The dispatcher's voice came from both the car radio and her ear button. "T-check positive for three."

For good or ill, the transponders built into the car and their ear buttons were registering on the division map.

Janna looked at Wim. "Your button receiving all right?"

He nodded. He switched on the Monitor. The electric motor hummed. Wim activated the airfoil fans. They whined as they wound up. The car shimmied a moment, then lifted off its parking rollers and rose clear of the floor. Wim floated it backward out of its parking slot and reversed to head for the exit ramp.

Janna relaxed in her seat. "I keep finding myself surprised someone should be jacking drugstores in Gage. I could understand it in Oakland where the government doesn't hand out drug coupons to the poor and needy. Do you suppose the jons are street dealers looking for a way to cut their overhead?"

The car sailed up Van Buren and 'round the corner onto Sixth Street.

"Would you do it?" Wim asked.

Janna blinked. "Do what? Steal drugs or hand out coupons for drugs like the ones for food and housing?"

"Would you really keep talking about the *Invictus* to scare me out of traveling on a ramjet?"

"I'm thinking about it." She trailed her arm out the window of the car. The air was stifling already. It was going to be one of those days when she would wish she had gills to help her breathe. Dear Kansas sauna summers. Then she noticed that Wim's knuckles had turned white around the wheel. She sighed. "Hey, partner, I wouldn't really do it. You ought to know I wouldn't try to keep you from something you want as much as you want to go to Champaign. I just don't understand why you want to go. What in god's name is so attractive about grubbing around on some alien world?"

His hands relaxed. He smiled. "Maybe I have a sense of adventure? Or maybe I just like grubbing."

They had been through this routine dozens of times in the past year. It was like a record. Once the conversation started, it proceeded exactly as the time before, and the time before that.

"I like being outside. I liked being on patrol. I didn't mind Juve and Vice. Since we made Investigator, though . . ." He shook his head.

"You're a good investigator. We're a good team."

"But so much of it is desk work. I want to be outside."

"You've always said you left that farm you grew up on because you were tired of freezing your ass feeding cattle in the winter and being broiled on a tractor all summer."

He shrugged. "I know I said that, but every spring I find myself out digging up the yard for a garden. That reminds me, can you use tomatoes?"

She rolled her eyes. "The August tomato glut is starting."

The radio crackled and muttered in her ear. She noted the calls with one part of her mind, but for the most part she ignored any announcement not preceded by "Indian Thirty."

She and Wim had been partners a long time. They started in an Oakland division watchcar five years before. They had made Sergeant together. Three years ago they had been promoted to Investigator I and been transferred to the Capitol division. Five years working together—there were marriage contracts that did not last that long. She knew he was serious about leaving when he would not take the Investigator II test with her. How could he give up five years for

6

something he had never seen before? She could not imagine working with anyone else.

"Wim." It was almost a wail. "I'll miss you like hell."

"Yeah." He reached over to pat her thigh. "I'll miss you, too, partner."

They rode out Topeka Avenue in silence. Janna watched the traffic glumly. There were few pedestrians as yet. Most of the traffic was bicycles, and tiny runabouts that danced like motes on their air cushions: GMC Vestas and D-F Fireflies, AMC-Renault Sols, some Hitachi Bonsais and Smith Sundowners. The fans of the big transit buses and trailer trucks thrummed deafeningly and left smaller vehicles shuddering in their wakes. There was a scattering of road cars, too—D-F Monitors and Kodiaks, GMC Titans, and the whole pride of Leyland International cats: Jaguars, Panthers, and Cheetahs.

Janna counted twenty-three moving violations. She would have loved to go after one Sundowner. The driver ducked in and out of every traffic lane, including the commercial lane and the bicycle lane. Farther ahead a big Kenworth was trying to crowd runabouts off the road.

"Look at them," she said in disgust. "Who's monitoring the traffic along here? There's never a lion around when you need one."

At the fairgrounds, Wim signaled for a right turn and slid the car sideways. They turned west down Twenty-first Street toward their stakeout assignment at the Fairlawn Plaza. Janna watched more traffic. After counting ten pedestrian violations and fifteen more moving violations, she gave up and watched the passing neighborhoods instead.

It was almost like coming home. She had known these particular streets well when she was going to Washburn University. She had come to know the streets to the south even better. They were in the Highland Park division, where she had spent her probation year. It was a pleasant residential area. There were a few modern semisunken and earth-covered

7

houses, but most featured older architecture, twentieth-century one- and two-floor above-ground houses of stone and wood frame. Many had large windows. Most of the streets were still in good condition, though they were beginning to show some age—potholes and shoots of green coming up around brick and through paving. Airfoils did not need a smooth surface to operate, so street repairs tended to be sporadic. Even so, the streets here were still better than their broken, weed-choked counterparts in Oakland.

At the Washburn View Mall, Janna waved to Investigators Leah Calabrese and Dan Roth. They were just settling themselves with caff and microfiche viewers at the little tables outside a small caff shop next to the drugstore, trying hard to look like students studying for summer school finals.

Wim grinned. "They'll lose their cover if we don't strap these jons before finals are over."

"I wonder if they're learning anything."

They passed the Seabrook Mall. Cardarella and Witt, one of the jane teams, did not appear to have arrived yet. When they reached Fairlawn, Wim set the car down on its parking rollers opposite the drugstore and took out a book to read. Janna stared at it a minute—Wim had some of the most unexpected possessions—then climbed out of the car and went up to rap on the drugstore window.

The clerk inside nodded in recognition and came to let her in. "You look less like a police officer in those clothes than you did in the jumpsuit yesterday," he said.

She decided to treat his remark as a compliment. "Thank you." She slipped on the smock he handed her and prepared to play clerk again. She pitied Wim. The small store smelled of the strange mixed odor of drugs, but it was cool in here. He would cook in the car.

"Isn't it terrible about that colony ship?" the clerk asked. He had a small newscanner on a shelf on the wall behind the counter. He punched it on and switched to one of the stations that rolled text to the accompaniment of background music. "Several years

8

ago the woman I was married to wanted us to join a colonial company. I considered doing so, but—I don't know. I have a nice house and neighbors I think I can trust. I'm thinking of buying a runabout so I won't be dependent on the bus schedule to get to work. That's a lot to give up for—for something unknown. Now after hearing about that colony ship, I don't think I could ever bring myself to get on one, let alone allow someone to put me to sleep for a year or two."

He did not seem to require return comments from her, or even encouragement, so Janna just smiled the way she had been taught and nodded once in a while and tuned him out. She wondered what effect the *Invictus*'s disaster might have on her father. He was a designer for Boeing. Maybe she should give him a call tonight.

The newscanner was rolling a story about another demonstration by the Arabs For a Free Middle East—this time at the United World building in Zurich—against the Israeli domination of Egypt and Syria. *Halt Zionist Imperialism,* their signs read.

She also listened, as always, to the police calls whispering in her ear. Most of them were Gage division calls, with only a few of the Highland Park calls reaching her.

"Beta Gage Twenty, see the woman, 1102 Prairie Road, domestic disturbance."

At nine-thirty, the clerk unlocked the door. The first customer, an attractive young woman, seemed embarrassed as she handed Janna a prescription slip for prostaglandin suppositories. Janna wondered whether the woman was embarrassed about having become pregnant or was sufficiently influenced by Lifest and Bible cultist propaganda to feel guilty about aborting herself.

Janna handed the prescription on to the clerk, who brought a box up from a back shelf.

The woman handed over her card. The Scib Card was a citizen's most important piece of plastic. It was a social care card, ID, and bankcard in one, a universal credit card. The clerk fed the piece of plastic into the credit register and typed in the purchase and price. The woman pressed her left thumb to the ID window of the register and signed her name across the window with a light scriber. The register hummed as it recorded the purchase and relayed the information to her bank's computers. After a minute it spat back the card. The clerk returned it to the woman along with her prescription and purchase receipt.

The woman left. On her way out, she passed Wim coming in. Wim was grinning.

"I just had an idea, Jan. Why don't *you* come out to Champaign with us?"

Janna stared at him. "Come *with* you? Oh, no." She backed away, shaking her head. "I'm a city girl. I need pollution to survive. The Soldier Creek division is east of the sun and west of the moon to me. Besides, even if every passenger aboard your ship weren't already planned for, I couldn't raise the credit for a share in only one month."

"Another ship will be coming out in a year or two. That one isn't full yet."

She rolled her eyes. "Go read your book. I like to look at waving fields of grain, but I'm quite content to let someone else grow them."

Wim headed for the door. "Think about it. There's only so far you can go here. You'll have to get a law degree if you want more rank than Lieutenant. On Champaign you can be anything."

"I can be eaten by a six-legged green wolf." But the door had closed behind him and he did not hear her last remark. She saw the clerk staring at her. "I think it's a fever," she said, "something like Bible cultists' evangelism. Colonists want everyone else to come out and grub in the mud with them."

The clerk looked as if he was unsure if he were supposed to laugh at that remark or not. *Toad,* she thought.

"Alpha Highland Thirteen, Alpha Highland Five, accident on 470 bypass at Gage exit. Two trucks involved."

Go out to that planet with them? Wim was one of her favorite people in this world, but that was the most brain bereft suggestion she had ever heard. Janna and Wim's wife Vada were good friends, but she somehow doubted Vada had ever considered taking Wim's partner to the stars with them. Vada was not the group marriage kind.

"Alpha Gage One, meet Alpha Gage Ten at 1017 Randolph."

The call raised Janna's curiosity. Alpha Gage One would be the alpha squad sergeant. Being asked simply to meet a unit meant the unit was involved in a situation it could not leave and did not care to mention over the radio.

Two young men wandered into the drugstore. Janna smiled at them while she looked them over, checking for weapons bulges.

"What kinds of hallucinogens do you have?" one asked.

"All of them," the clerk replied. "Mescaline, psilocybin, LSD, STP, MDT, ALR."

The jons exchanged looks. "Well, we were looking for something stronger." The first speaker hesitated.

His companion said, "A lot stronger . . . something with a *real* boost."

This time Janna and the clerk exchanged looks. Janna wondered if that were a guilty flush there around the back of the clerk's neck. Could he be doing a little subcounter dealing?

"Trick is illegal," she said.

The two tried to look innocent. "Oh, we certainly didn't mean we wanted any trick."

"It'll cross-wire your brain. Synesthesia. A milligram or two too much will scramble your tick for good. At worst your brain can forget how to make you breathe. Why don't you use something safe, like dreamtime?"

"Dreamtime." Their scorn rasped like a file. "That's just a sleep substitute."

"The hyperdreaming can give a good boost, and better, a safe trip."

"No, thanks."

11

They turned and left the store.

The clerk was trying hard not to frown. "Sergeant." He said it hesitantly. "I would prefer that—you let me handle the sales."

Janna looked at him. "The penalty for selling trick can be heavy. Some dealers go up on manslaughter charges."

The clerk swallowed visibly.

"Alpha Gage Eleven, investigate an abandoned vehicle, Tenth and Fairlawn."

A girl came in. Janna looked her over but was quickly satisfied she could not be one of the deeks they were waiting for. The paint on her depilated head was old and smeared. Her arms were tracked with the scars of a thousand launchings. She was a long-time ulysses making odysseying a lifetime pursuit, the hard way.

She presented her addict's identification and Scib Card to the clerk. The purchase was recorded. The ulysses left hurriedly, clutching her week's ration of heroin.

"Beta Gage Twelve, see the man, neighborhood disturbance, twenty-six hundred block Arrowhead Street."

Janna wished she could hear the replies but the duplex system put replies on a different frequency than the dispatch broadcasts, which was all her ear button received.

"Attention all units, armed robbery in progress, Seabrook Mall."

Janna raced for the door, tearing off the smock. "You can relax," she called back to the clerk. "They picked someone else today."

Wim had the Monitor's fans wrapping up. Janna dived into her seat and slid the door closed behind her. "We're just a straight shot down Twenty-first. Let's sail."

Wim revved the fans. The car bucked up onto its air cushion. Janna slapped the pop-on cherry on the dash and hit the siren. The car shot forward.

"Attention all units," the dispatcher's voice said in

her ear. "Suspects are two males, twenty to twenty-five years old, one Caucasian, one hundred seventy centimeters, eighty kilos, brown hair shoulder length, wearing an orange jumpsuit with sleeves and pantlegs cut off; other suspect is afroam, one hundred eighty centimeters, seventy-five kilos, wearing gray pioneer-style shirt and trousers. Suspects are on foot headed west on Twenty-first Street."

"They're coming our way. Kick her, Wim!"

The fans screamed as the car lunged ahead. The traffic scattered before the *whew-whew-whew* of their siren as if pushed aside by an invisible plow. The siren became a hoarse howl as they rocketed through an intersection.

The radio said, "Suspects have turned north on McAlister."

They had almost reached McAlister. Wim wrenched the wheel, and the car banked so sharply it heeled over halfway on its side. For one fearful moment it seemed they might roll and be driven top-first into the ground by the fans, but then the car slewed around and straightened. They flew up McAlister.

They saw Cardarella and Witt almost immediately, on foot and running. About a block beyond them were two more runners.

"There they are."

Wim passed the Gage janes and started slowing. Opposite the two suspects, he shut off the fans. Then they kicked the doors forward and bailed out of the car before it had even settled to its parking rollers, abandoning it in the middle of the street.

The suspects looked back. Seeing Wim and Janna, one abruptly ducked sideways through a yard. The other cut across the street into another yard.

"I'll take the afroam." Janna charged after him.

The man was fast, she gave him that, and he jumped like a deer. These blocks had no alleys in them. The yards sat back to back, separated by fences. The black man cleared the barrier in one bound and landed racing through the yard beyond. Janna vaulted after him.

Her choice of clothes for the day had been bad after

all, she decided. They were all wrong for running an obstacle course. The romper was fine, but the hip boots were hot and cumbersome. Sweat was already running down her legs inside them. Her gun, holstered down inside one boot, began digging into her thigh.

Damn, that deek was fast. She was one of the top runners in the department but she was barely gaining on her man. He leaped over another fence, through another yard. He almost ran over a small child playing in a sandbox. The child's mother screamed. The black leaped the fence on the far side.

Following him, Janna found herself in a group of children. One had been knocked down by the fleeing man.

Janna's hands itched to pull her gun. A needle would stop that deek fast enough. She could not draw here, though. There were too many children. If she missed, she would either have to come back looking for the spent needle, or trust to luck none of these children found it. A child playing with a needle could prick himself and inject the fifteen milligrams of percurare inside. Fifteen milligrams was enough to paralyze the muscles of an average adult. The drug would paralyze everything in a child, including the diaphragm. Such things had happened before.

So she left the Starke in her boot and cursed herself for not bringing the shotgun from the car.

They pounded across a street and between two houses. There was an alley through the middle of this block and the black turned up it. For the first time she was able to tell she was gaining on him.

They reached the end of the alley. Her quarry crossed the street with Janna close behind. A passing runabout came so close she felt it clip her hip as the driver screamed curses at her. She stumbled but did not go down. In another stride she had the pace back. She was only meters behind her quarry, now. She had a clear, easy shot at him.

She reached for her gun.

He turned around suddenly, a shooter in his hand. "I'll kill you!"

She let go of the gun. No sense needling him now. The four to ten seconds the percurare took to work was time enough for him to empty the shooter at her. Instead she dived to the left as the shooter went off. His aim was bad enough that the bullet did not pass close enough to hear, but it sent a bolt of terror through her, nevertheless. Where, oh, where was that much-rumored stungun R and D kept promising police departments?

The man cocked the hammer for another shot.

Janna dodged again. This time she heard the bullet, a deadly *zit* near her right ear, just audible under the flat popcorn sound of the shot. Before he could fire again, she dived for him. He brought the barrel of the shooter down toward her head. She jerked to the side, then grabbed a handful of his crotch and squeezed with all her strength.

He screamed. As he started to double, she locked on to his shooting arm. She went under it and back, taking the arm with her. She twisted the shooter hard against his thumb. The thumb gave with an audible *pop* and the black screamed again.

Janna felt a ripple of resistance building in him, but before he could translate it into action, she was pushing him toward a power pole. Her hand reached inside her boot for her wrap strap. She put a little more pressure on his arm to keep him moving and shoved him hard against the pole, snapping the wrap strap with a practiced flick of her wrist. The strap circled pole and suspect's neck in one loop and adhered to itself. Janna made sure it was tight, then let go and stepped back, panting hard.

The black pulled, but he was pinned against the pole by the strap. He spat obscenities at her.

Then reaction set in. Janna started shaking. This deek tried to kill her! She hefted the shooter in a trembling hand, fighting a desire to lay the barrel across his jungled scalp. "Shut up, toad." She tapped her ear button. Between gulps of air, she said, "Indian Thirty beta to Gage control."

"Go ahead Indian Thirty."

15

"I have one of the armed robbery suspects in custody. My loc unknown."

"Your T's on the board, Indian Thirty. Wait for a mobile unit."

The unit was there in two minutes, a watchcar driven by a pair of young leos whose uniforms somehow managed to look trim and neat despite the humid heat. Briefly, Janna envied them. Her romper was plastered to her with sweat and the thick curls of her lion's mane lay sodden on her forehead and the back of her neck.

"What about the other suspect?" she asked.

"Beta Gage Seventeen picked him up a few minutes ago. Needled him."

She grinned. The last of her shakes disappeared. That was good news. Vradel would be pleased. Riding back to her own car crowded into the front seat with the Gage leos, she was jubilant.

The mood did not last long. She had expected to find Wim waiting for her by Indian Thirty with Beta Gage Seventeen. He was not there. She frowned at the officers from Beta Gage Seventeen.

"Wasn't my partner behind this jon?" She pointed at the man sprawled motionless on one of the lengthwise seats in the back of the watchcar, head pushed against the laminated wire and plastic screen that separated the control and prisoner sections, feet at the rear door.

The leos shook their heads. "He was all alone when we needled him."

Cardarella and Witt had not seen Wim since he bailed out of Indian Thirty, nor had several other teams that were loitering in the area.

Janna tapped her ear button. "Indian Thirty beta to Gage control, requesting a T-check on Indian Thirty alpha."

The dispatcher came back. "Indian Thirty alpha's T north and west of you and stationary."

Janna's stomach flipped and tightened in a cold knot. The transponders were often despised for betraying officers' whereabouts to supervisors. The "breakage" rate on them was phenomenal. At times they could be useful, though. This was one of those times.

The Gage dispatcher directed the search for Wim, watching all their transponders on the board and guiding them toward Wim's. Babra Cardarella found him first. Her shout brought the rest of them running.

Wim lay in a pool of blood between two abutting backyard storage sheds. He was unconscious but still alive. It looked as if someone had tried to take off the top of his skull. A deep laceration circled his head, amputating the tops of his ears, cutting through the scalp to bone, and sawing through the bridge of his nose so far even his eyelids and eyes were cut.

Janna swore. "Someone get an ambulance. I swear I'll cancel the deek who did this to him."

One of the leos from Beta Gage Seventeen cleared her throat. "We took a monofilament garrote off our man when we searched him."

Garrote! Janna's mouth tightened. The deek must have tried to use it on Wim. Wim saw him and ducked, but not fast enough. She felt sick. He was lucky to be alive. Around his throat, the fine wire would have sliced through to his spine before he even knew what happened.

She wiped the blood from his face. It was a mistake. Clearing the old blood only let her see new blood and fluid leaking out of his slashed eyes.

"Oh, god," someone gasped.

Janna swore. Wim had just two weeks left before he resigned, only a month before his ship left. What a hell of a thing to have happen to him now—a goddam-it-to-hell bitch. That damn deek. That skink toad. Just as well he was locked in the back of the watchcar. She would have gone ahead and canceled him, given a chance, or at the very least broken him in half one bone at a time.

She moved so her shadow fell across Wim, shading him from the sun. Moisture dropped on him. Her sweat? She wiped at her face. She discovered with surprise that the moisture was on her cheeks, flowing from her eyes. She let the tears come. What a rotten job this could be sometimes.

CHAPTER TWO

From the doorway of Jorge Hazlett's office, Andrew Kellener asked, "Did you see the broadcast about the *Invictus?*"

Jorge looked up from the printout he was pretending to read. Indeed he had seen the broadcast. In fact, he had had his newscanner on "replay" and had watched the broadcast six times. Jorge had spent a few terrible minutes on the edge of panic when he first started considering the implications of that message. Calm returned, however, when he realized he had only temporarily lost the game initiative. He was not immediately threatened; there was just the chance of attack. If anything, that thought was exhilarating. He had time to set up his defenses and regain the initiative before his opponents found his weakness.

"I saw it just a few minutes ago," he lied to Andy. "It's too bad, a real tragedy."

"Just too bad?" Andy walked over and sat down in the chair across the desk from Jorge. "Aren't you more concerned than that? Those colonists were our clients. We contracted with Boeing for that ship."

Jorge widened his eyes. *"Our* clients?" He reached for the computer terminal that made an L of his desk. He punched for records of the Laheli Company.

"I tried that a little earlier," Andy said. "The computer wouldn't give me anything."

Sure enough, across the screen appeared: *What's the password?*

Jorge raised brows at Andy. "What's this?"

"I was going to ask you. You handled the account.

You must have coded the records in. Don't you re-member?"

Jorge pretended to think hard. "No, I can't." He opened desk drawers and shuffled through the contents. "I must have written the code down here somewhere, though."

Andy's mouth tightened. "I hope you find it. There'll be a government inquiry, of course. We'll have to have our records ready for inspection."

Andy was aging, Jorge thought. He still wore his hair a fashionable shoulder length, but the fiery mop it had been when they were in law school together was growing thinner and paler every year. It was a washed-out copper now. Jorge took pride in the fact that he had only some gray at the temples to mark his age. Those brown and gray paisley jumpsuits Andy wore were the height of conservatism, too. Something in the line of Jorge's dusty rose and yellow stripes would have been much more modish. Yes, Andy was definitely aging.

"Jorge," Andy's voice sharpened. "Are you listening to me?"

Jorge focused on him again. "Of course. Don't worry. The records will be in order and ready for any-one who wants to see them."

That was no lie, anyway. When the two of them gave up starving in law practice to take up colonial contracting, they had fallen into a feast. Jorge was not about to place himself in a position of having to return to starvation or give up the luxuries for which he had acquired a taste over the years. The records would in-deed be in perfect order for any inquiry.

He kept pawing through his desk. "It will probably be a routine inquiry, just to see if Boeing can be blamed."

"I hope four hundred deaths will rate more than an opportunity for some congressional committee to target-shoot at a corporation."

Jorge paused in his search, then resumed pawing. He frowned. Andy's zealot button had been pushed.

"Are you sure you will be able to remember the release code?" Andy sounded impatient.

Jorge lifted his head and made his smile encouraging. "Of course. I'll have myself hypnotized to get it if necessary. Don't worry. I'll have the facsimiles by tomorrow, or Friday at the latest."

He continued smiling as Andy rose and left. His mouth tightened the moment the door closed behind his partner. Jorge spun his chair back to the computer terminal and punched in: RUY LOPEZ . . . RUN.

The name of the chess opening cleared the query from the screen. The Laheli account promptly appeared on the screen, one page after another, as they had been put into the storage chips. Jorge began to read them. Everything was there: initial communications between the Laheli board of directors and Hazlett and Kellener, the application to the U.S. Colonial Agency for a charter, approval and granting of the charter, contracts with Boeing in Wichita for the ramjet, permits from Forbes Space Center south of Topeka and Schilling in Salina to launch the ramjet sections for assembly in orbit off the Glenn platform, reservations for shuttle lifting of colonists and supplies.

All that was in order. What would raise brows were letters from Boeing expressing doubt over the performance of the modified 800's life-support systems, and his casual replies to those letters. Someone might also wonder when they checked Laheli bank records and found the company had paid for a Starmaster 1000 instead of a modified 800.

The firm, of course, took its six percent from the price of the colonial package based on the modified 800. The rest was Jorge's take.

Six percent. The amount rasped at Jorge even though he was collecting far more than that his own way. Because of that paltry charge he had to resort to fraud. The normal fee for colonial contracting was ten percent. But Andy had to be the altruist, had to give the clients every advantage. Whenever Jorge felt a twinge of guilt about what he was doing, he reminded himself that Andy had driven him to it.

What bothered him most was not the fraud itself—
if the colonists were so blind as to let themselves be
cheated, it was their fault—but the prospect of being
caught. A case like this would not be prosecuted as a
simple fraud. When the knowing and deceitful endan-
gering of human lives was involved, a prosecutor
could invoke the Tescott Act. Under it, actual death
resulting from actions like Jorge's made the offense a
Class A felony, carrying a mandatory death sentence.
Jorge was enraged at the idea of the state of Kansas
injecting him full of T-61 just because one man felt
colonialism was a holy mission and some clients were
too careless to double-check to make sure they were
getting what they needed and paid for.

Jorge cleared the screen and pushed away from the
terminal. He walked to the window and stared out
over the tops of the buildings across the street at the
nearby green dome of the Statehouse rising into the
heat-bleached sky. He frowned at it while he considered his situation.

He had game plans that included alternatives to be
initiated if there were a danger of being caught, but of
course he hoped he would never have to use them.
Best not to come under suspicion at all. All would be
well if Andy would help him cover alterations in the
records.

Twenty years ago there would have been no question about Andy's helping. Back then he was every bit
the gamesman Jorge was. But he had developed this
obsession with colonialism. If anything, it put Andy on
the side of the opposition. Jorge would have to counter
the check by himself.

There were three ways to answer a check: move the
king, capture the attacking piece, or interpose another
piece. Jorge had no intention of running away; and
trying to do something about the agent the government
sent was out of the question. The remaining choice was
to move Andy into the line of attack.

There lay the problem. If there were a threat of
being caught at fraud, there was even more risk involved in offering Andy as a sacrifice in his place. A

living Andy could protest, could possibly defend himself with success. Yet the alternative to that was almost unthinkable. How could he kill a man who had been his friend for nearly thirty years? Besides, it would be almost impossible to do so without being traced to the time and place of the murder.

He pulled his card case out of a breast pocket and took out his Scib Card. He flexed it, wishing he could break it in two. For all the benefits it entitled him to in social care and financial transactions, the card was a curse. In the process of eliminating cash from society, personal freedom had been strangled. By checking bank records, investigators could learn where any particular person had been at a given time. Purchase records were a fatal giveaway.

He slipped his card back into its case and shoved it into his pocket. How could he get around the damned card? No purchases meant no record, but that was also a blank which investigators would hunt for ways to fill. No, what he needed was a record of purchases, all right, but in an area of town away from where he actually was. Jorge smiled wryly. What he needed was to be able to be in two places at the same time. That, unfortunately, was—

He broke off the thought and sat up straight. Wait a minute. There was something in the back of his head about being in two places at once, something he had heard. He remembered thinking at the time that he should remember it for the future. But where had he heard it?

He searched his memory. A party. He remembered a crowd. He doubled his fist and tapped it against his forehead. A party . . . Lawrence! That was it. It had been at the mix-and-match party Colla Hayden gave last year.

There had been a man there, tall and elegant, with a very flash red-haired girl under one arm and a nearly identical boy under the other. Jorge had spent most of the party looking at the women—most wore nothing but their body paint, and even the most liberal clubs in Topeka required that pubic hair and female

22

breasts be covered—but he remembered hearing the man talking to a couple of handsome homosexuals, who were also wearing nothing but body paint.

"Would you believe I'm in two places at once?" he had asked.

The hos had not believed. One of them tugged at the hand of his boyfriend and started to leave.

The man was a bit toxy from liquor or drugs. He seemed to be trying to impress his companions and the hos. "My wife, my very devout Bible cultist wife, thinks I'm in Omaha at a home furnishings show. She's worried I might try to count coup on my assistant, who's with me." He grinned. "She'd never speak to me again if she knew who I'm really counting coup with." He gave the beautiful couple a squeeze.

The couple giggled. "We feel sorry for your poor assistant up there all alone."

The man looked righteous. "Not alone. I'm there. When the bank records come in, the purchase record will prove it."

It was at that point Jorge had started paying close attention. To his unspeakable disappointment, however, the man had changed the subject and drifted off with his beautiful companions.

Jorge had gone straight to Colla. "Who's that man?"

Colla was preoccupied with two male friends. "What man? I don't know. I'll find out later."

He had never gotten back to her about it. Now he could kick himself for not doing so. Why had he let himself be so distracted by that blonde creature— whose most obvious charm was that she wore nothing at all but her glorious hair—that he forgot to find out who the man was?

He returned to the desk in long, determined strides, fishing in his pockets for his memo book. Numbers like Colla's he kept with him. She would be at work now. He looked up her business number, a local one, and punched it into the phone.

Colla answered formally, but broke into a genuine smile when she saw his face on her screen. "Jorgie, honey. How are you?" Her afroam accent made the greeting warm and intimate.

"Never better. When are you going to have another mix-and-match party?"

"When the neighbors stop complaining about the last one. Lonely? You don't need a party to take care of that. I'll be glad to look after you myself."

"And a nova job you'd do, too."

He flirted with her a bit while he considered how best to ask about the man. He did not want to seem too eager. Most of all, if there should be an inquiry at some future time, he did not want her remembering that he asked for a man's name. After they had exchanged several propositions and innuendos, he brought the conversation gradually back to parties.

"I particularly remember the one in May."

She blinked. "I didn't hold one in May this year."

"*Last* May."

Her eyes went wide. "My, that must have been special. *I* can hardly remember any back that far."

"Do you remember who comes to which parties?"

She laughed. "Don't joke. Among all the people who come, and the friends who bring friends? I just worry about running out of alcohol and junk."

That meant he would have to work hard at jogging her memory about the man he wanted. He could not ask directly, then. He would have to do it roundabout.

"There was a couple I remember seeing at that party. I've seen them several times since, too. They look like twins: red-haired, blue-eyed, not terribly intellectual. They like to wear star body decals."

"That sounds like Michal and Michael Taber."

"Who?"

She spelled the names. "You aren't interested in them, are you? They're bi's. They like threesomes, especially with people who get a boost out of incest. They aren't really twins, though. They just pretend to be. Actually, they're married."

"I've never thought of them for sex. I just think they're interesting to watch. Are they from Lawrence?"

"No, from Topeka, like most of the people who

come to my parties. You know how it goes. The Topekaens come to Lawrence to orgy. Lawrence people go to Kansas City. I don't know where K.C.'s hedonists go."

He had what he needed. Without seeming too hasty, he closed the conversation and punched off. He turned to his computer keyboard and typed in a request for the phone directory, for the Taber number. It promptly appeared on the screen. He was starting to punch the number into the phone when he caught himself. He could always justify calling Colla. She was a friend. It might be harder to give investigators a reason for calling strangers.

He glanced at the chrono. It was almost noon. He punched the intercom. "I'm going out for lunch, Nina."

"Yes, sir," his secretary's reply came back.

He left the office casually, waving to the receptionist as he walked past the young Hispanic's desk. Robert smiled and waved back.

Jorge took the elevator down to the ground level. Outside the entrance of the Sunflower Federal Bank and near the elevators in the lobby was a bank of public phones. Jorge crossed to it and used one to call the Taber number.

The red-haired girl who answered was the one he had seen under the arm of the man he wanted. She gave Jorge a polite, vacuous smile. "Yes?"

Jorge introduced himself.

Her smile became more animated. "A friend of Colla? Well, welcome. What can I do for you?"

He wasted no time on social small talk. "Last year in May you were at one of Colla's mix-and-match parties. You and your . . . brother Michael were with a tall, brown-haired man in a peacock-blue velvet suit."

She thought a moment, then nodded. "Yes, I remember him. Nova body. A tongue that could send anyone into orbit."

"This will sound foolish, but I met him, too, and now I've forgotten his name. It's driving me off my tick trying to remember. Can you help?"

Her blue eyes went wide enough to swim in. "Oh, I wish I could, but I don't remember his name either."

Jorge scowled. "How can you not remember his name if he was such a memorable performer?"

She giggled. "Suns, who cares about *names* at a time like *that?* That is, he did say who he was, but, honestly, I don't remember it. I'm terrible about things like that. I've seen him at other parties, but we haven't put three with him since, so I've just never had another chance to hear what his name was."

Jorge wanted to reach into the phone and shake her. He dug his nails into the palms of his hands. "If he said his name once, maybe you can remember at least a part of it. This thing is annoying me to death."

"Suns, I know how you feel, but—" He would have thought it was impossible, but her eyes went wider yet. "I *do* remember something. I have a little trick I use sometimes, if I want to remember something particularly. I make an association and make a picture of it in my mind, you know? I remember I wanted to keep that jon's name because he was so good. The picture is a taxi floating on the ocean between Italy and Greece, an Adriatic taxi." She grinned.

He stifled a grimace. "Adriatic taxi?" What kind of name generated a picture like that?

"That's right." She beamed with pride at her cleverness. "And he owns a business in Topeka. He mentioned that. Does that help?"

Not a bit. Still, he had as much as he was going to learn from her. It was time to get off the line before the conversation became memorable. He made himself smile. "It helps a great deal. You've jogged my memory and made me remember the name. Thank you so very much."

He punched off before she could ask him what the name was. Adriatic taxi. Disappointment was bitterly sharp. An Adriatic taxi who owned a business in Topeka.

He thought about it while he ate a sandwich at a cafe down the street. He could not see that what she had told him could help at all. Going back to the office, he had to force himself to smile at Robert on the reception desk and at his secretary. Lunch's sandwich lay like lead in his stomach.

It was only when he was behind the closed door of his office that he relaxed his control of his face. He kicked the wastebasket and swore passionately. That man at the party could be the key to everything. Jorge felt it. Yet there seemed to be no way to reach him . . . no way. All because a bibi with an overactive libido and a featherweight brain could not remember names. Adriatic taxi! There must be something more useful than that. There had to be!

He sat down and chewed on the knuckle of a doubled fist. Perhaps something the man had said would help. Jorge went over the conversation as he remembered it, playing it back sentence by sentence. *Would you believe I'm in two places at once?* Nothing helpful there. *My wife, my very devout Bible cultist wife thinks I'm*—Jorge sat up straight—*in Omaha at a home furnishings show*. Home furnishings show! The man had told the Tabers he owned his own business. Now what business would send a man to a home furnishings show?

Jorge reached for the computer keyboard. He typed a request for the phone listings of all the furniture dealers in the city. Dutifully, the computer put the list on the screen and printed out a sheet. It was a long list.

Jorge went over it. Some could be eliminated right away. Used furniture dealers, for example. That still left quite a number. He sighed and started punching numbers into the phone.

He made up a speech while the first number was ringing. "Hello, this is the chamber of commerce. We're surveying for the new city directory. Who is the owner of your business?"

The gambit worked. The employee who answered the phone gave him the owner's name. It did not remotely resemble anything that would suggest the image of an Adriatic taxi. Jorge punched off and went on to the next number . . . and the next . . . and the next. As he progressed down the list, Jorge felt a knot growing in his stomach. Damn that bibi. This calling was going to be endless, and it might all be in vain. He contemplated giving up only briefly, though. The man was his key to saving himself from a Tescott prosecution. He had to find that man.

He reached the last name without having any luck. He wanted to cry. He punched the intercom. "Nina, bring me some caff."

She had a cup on his desk almost immediately. Setting it down, she noticed the list of furniture dealers. "Is that something I can help with?"

He shook his head. "I'm just trying to find a chair to match one in my study at home."

"And you're calling everywhere yourself? Why not do it the easy way?" she asked.

He looked up. "What easy way?"

"Call one of the decorating firms. Ask them to find the chair for you."

He stared at her. Decorating firms? Lord. He had completely overlooked decorators. They bought furniture, too.

"I'll call one if you like," Ms. Abram offered.

"No, that isn't necessary." He smiled to soften the refusal. He must not seem adamant about doing it himself. "Thank you for the suggestion, though."

She smiled back. "Anything I can do to help."

He punched the computer for a list of decorators. The computer printed it out.

He noticed Ms. Abram still hovering around the desk. "That's all, Nina."

She sighed. "Yes, sir." She left in a soft sway of hips and swish of ankle-length skirt. The door closed behind her.

He punched the first decorator's number. A young woman answered. He used the same speech on her that he had on the furniture dealers, and it worked just as well. He moved from American Interiors through Contemporary Homes down the list to The Kastle Keep. None of the faces answering was familiar. None of the names suggested an Adriatic Taxi. Many Mansions was next.

The woman who answered had a tempting pouty mouth and impossibly blue eyes, all framed by a magnificent mane of chestnut hair. "Many Mansions, Marca Laclede speaking."

Jorge smiled. "I'm from the chamber of commerce. We're surveying for the new city directory. May I ask the name of your firm's owner?"

"Mr. Adrian Cabot is chief decorator of Many Mansions," the woman replied.

The name jabbed him like a pin. "Adrian Cabot?" Adrian . . . Adriatic? That could be, but . . . taxi? Then it came to him . . . taxi on the water, a cab boat . . . Cabot.

His heart was pounding, but he tried not to let himself hope too much. "Excuse me, but I think Mr. Cabot and I may have met before. Is he a tall man with a brown lion's mane hair style, a very elegant-looking man?"

The pouty lips parted to show small white teeth. The mouth smiled invitingly. "That sounds like Mr. Cabot."

Jorge took a breath to clear his throat so he could breathe and talk. "This is really fortunate. I'm trying to locate a certain type of chair for my study. Do you suppose Mr. Cabot would have time this afternoon to talk about it?"

"Just a minute." She put him on hold. In a couple of minutes she was back. "He's free at the moment. I'll put him on the line."

That would never do. He could not talk about what he needed over the phone. "May I come over instead?" He checked the address. Many Mansions was in the Santa Fe Building. That was just a few blocks away. "I'm close. I can be there in fifteen minutes. I'll bring a photograph of the chair."

"I suppose that will be all right. What is your name, please?"

"Jorge Hazlett."

"We'll be expecting you, Mr. Hazlett."

He punched off and touched the intercom. "Nina, I found a decorator who can help me, but I have to take him a picture of the chair. I'm going over."

"Don't forget you have an appointment with Mr. Schlegel of the Citadel Company at two o'clock."

He checked the chrono. *Damn!* It was ten to two now. "Give my apologies to the gentleman and entertain him until I get back."

"Yes, sir."

She sounded astonished. He could not blame her. Clients were supposed to come first before everything else at Hazlett and Kellener. It must certainly seem strange to give a mere chair precedence. The incident might also seem suspicious looking back on it later.

He made himself chuckle. "It's brainbent to be so obsessed with a chair, I suppose, but I've been trying to find this match for some time. Don't tell Andy I put it before the client."

"No, I won't."

He could count on her loyalty, he felt sure. "You're priceless, Nina. I'll be back as soon as I can."

He walked the distance to the Santa Fe Building. It was faster than taking his car out of the Sunflower Federal Building's parking lot and trying to find another space near the Santa Fe Building, which was right across the street from the Statehouse. Parking spaces were hard to find there. According to the building directory, Many Mansions was on the third floor. He took the stairs and almost ran up in his eagerness.

The entrance to the suite was a wide glass door which slid open at his approach. The panel beside the door bore the legend: *Superior Interior Designs to Make Any Castle a Home.* Inside, the large reception room had a floor that looked like tile but gave with the soft resiliency of carpet. Around the room were scattered chairs in a dozen styles and materials: molded plastic, plastic foam, tip-overs, colloidal plastics, and the heavy fiber paper called hardboard. In the center of the floor was a piece of carpet. At least Jorge assumed it was carpet, but it was so dark in color, so black, it swallowed all the light and looked like a gaping hole.

Jorge tested it, cautiously, with a toe. It felt solid. Still, he could not quite bring himself to walk on it. He skirted the area.

"You're very prompt, Mr. Hazlett."

He looked up to see Marca Laclede in the doorway of an inner room. Her body was as desirable as her face, draped in what was, he discovered with interest, little more than half a dress. It had an ankle-length skirt, but above that it was difficult to tell what was fabric and what was merely painted on her skin. No wonder Cabot's wife was worried about her husband's counting coup on his assistant. Jorge would not have minded counting coup on her himself.

Marca Laclede looked back at him with equal interest, running the tip of a silver-nailed finger along her full lower lip. After a minute, she turned away, and made the most of the motion in swinging hips and swishing hair.

"Mr. Cabot is this way, Mr. Hazlett."

Jorge enjoyed the delicious motion of her back as she led the way. He was sorry when she stopped in the doorway of a room and made him go in alone.

Adrian Cabot stood up behind his desk, a massive structure of chrome and lucite. He extended a hand. "Sit down, Mr. Hazlett. What can I do for you?"

Cabot looked as elegant as Jorge remembered. His suit this time, though, was as black as the carpet in the reception area. It made his head and hands look disembodied. He sat down when Jorge did.

"What's this chair you need?"

Jorge cleared his throat. "Actually, there's no chair. It's a personal matter and I felt you would want discretion."

Cabot's brows rose a millimeter.

"I was at a party Colla Hayden gave in Lawrence a year ago May. I saw you there and—"

Cabot's face congealed into the immobility of a mannequin's. "You're mistaken. I don't ever recall

31

being at a party in Lawrence. In fact, the only time I left town that May was to go to—"

"Omaha, to a furniture show. You were telling that story to people at the party. You also said you were managing to be in two places at one time. I find I need to know that trick."

"I repeat," Cabot said, "you're mistaken. I don't know what you're talking about. I don't know any Colla Hayden. Now, I'm a busy man, Mr. Hazlett, so you must excuse me."

Jorge stood up. There were people whom pushing could break; others merely became more stubborn. Jorge judged Cabot to be the latter. The man was terrified. Damn him. Gambit denied. "Of course."

Jorge masked his anger in a smile and backed toward the door. Damn the man! So close, and still Jorge was being denied the knowledge he needed.

He almost ran over the assistant outside the door. "Look at me," she said. Before he understood what she was doing, she had taken his picture with a small camera. "I heard," she said.

Jorge waited. Anger began draining away, replaced by hope. "Do you make a habit of listening at doors?"

"Sometimes, when it seems like the thing to do." She regarded the silver perfection of her nails with intense concentration. "I have a friend who looks remarkably like Mr. Cabot. This friend and I went to Omaha with Mr. Cabot's Scib Card." She looked down at the picture extruding from the camera. "If my friend can find someone who looks like you, I can help you, Mr. Hazlett." She smiled up at him.

He felt like a bishop with a long, clear diagonal to his opponent's king. He refrained from cheering, though. "What will the price be?"

"Let's not talk about that until I know if I can help you. I'll call you when I know, Mr. Hazlett."

"It's important that I arrange this matter soon . . . this week, if possible."

"I'll try, Mr. Hazlett."

She saw him to the door of the suite and watched

32

him leave with great satisfaction. Another potential client. Colonial contractors made good credit. If Tarl could find a match, Mr. Jorge Hazlett should be able to pay well for a doppelgänger.

Marca put the camera back in her desk and dropped the 2-D photograph in her purse. She strapped the purse around her waist. She leaned in through the door of Adrian Cabot's office.

"I have some important errands to run, Adrian. May I leave early?"

Adrian looked gray. "That man saw me at a mix-and-match party. I had better quit going to parties so close to home."

Marca sighed. "I doubt he plans to publish what he knows. Your wife will never hear about it. Good night, Adrian."

He was so busy muttering and wringing his hands, he never saw her go.

The man was a fool, she thought. He either ought to confess his bi preference to his wife or accept the monogamous sacramental marriage he had made with her. That anyone in this permissive time would allow himself to be hagridden by guilt over sexual needs was to her ridiculous. When she found out what a toad Karel was, she had not sat around gnashing her teeth; she had dissolved the marriage contract at light-speed. She had taken only his name—Laclede was infinitely preferable to, immeasurably more elegant than, Dolitsky—and run. He could have been as rich as Adrian's wife was; she would have done the same.

She would have let Adrian stew in his own cowardice but it had been such a shame not to take advantage of that surprising likeness between him and her old cohab of college days. It was so profitable. She also loved the feeling of power it gave her to manipulate the supposedly foolproof bankcard system.

In the building garage, she unplugged her little bubble-shaped VW Moth from the charger and climbed in, switching on the motor and the fans. The Moth trembled, then lifted clear of the ground and floated toward the exit. On the street, she headed east.

33

Crossing the Sixth Street Bridge over Interstate-70, she could hear the hiss of the occasional passing cars below. A hundred years ago, there had been solid strings of traffic on cross-country highways, most of the traffic privately-owned road cars. That was before energy rationing, of course, and before metal started being saved for building ships to go to the Moon and Mars and the stars, to build cities on the Moon and Mars, instead of being wasted on earthbound vehicles.

Marca revved the fans to full speed. The Moth leaped ahead at its maximum of thirty kph. The speed limit was a crawling twenty-five. She checked her mirrors to make sure no prowling lions were around to catch her, then headed toward the area of town called Oakland.

Tarl worked at a market on Sardou Street. She pulled into the cracked, trashy parking area and set the Moth down on its parking rollers. While she climbed out of the runabout, she steeled herself to go into the market. If only there were a way to contact Tarl without coming down here to see him. This was the only part of their arrangement she hated. The decay in Oakland and especially this market disgusted her.

She pushed through the door. Grime was everywhere. The floor looked permanently gray. The cans and boxes on the shelves looked as if they had been sitting there for decades. The place smelled of dust, unwashed humanity, and overripe vegetables. Marca kept her arms at her sides, holding up her skirt, trying to keep from touching anything.

"Where's Tarl?" she asked the Hispanic girl at the checkout counter.

Even the girl looked grimy. Her dark eyes swept Marca. "I don' know any Tarl."

Marca sighed. Did they have to go through this every time? "Of course you do. He's the sligh who works in the back."

"Then why don' you try lookin' in the back?"

Marca twitched away from her. She was careful,

making her way back through the dirty aisles, to keep clear of the occasional shopper.

She found Tarl in the rear section of the store, opening cartons. He nodded as she pushed through the swinging doors. "I'll be finished in a few minutes."

She looked around for a place to sit but saw nowhere she felt she could tolerate. She remained standing. How could Tarl bear working here day after day? He had done the same kind of thing in college. She had thought that he would change when she brought him to Topeka to introduce him to Adrian and to help her in the business Adrian's likeness to him had inspired.

Not that they were *really* alike. They resembled each other only physically. Tarl had none of Adrian's polish, and Adrian had never felt the inner anger that leaked out in everything Tarl said and did. Tarl had a backbone, too.

She frowned. She wished she could understand slighs. Tarl was one of many she had met in college. Her group had considered it kicky to mix with the holdouts of society, to give them bed space and food, and help them drop in on classes. Marca went along, but she never understood why the slighs did what they did. She even shared her quarters with Tarl for over a year in an effort to understand, but this hatred of even the most innocuous government regulation or documentation was incomprehensible. How could anyone find identation such an abhorrent invasion of privacy that he would refuse to enroll in social care, that he would refuse to take out a Scib Card and lose all its benefits, just to remain unrecorded by the government? She had never minded the fingerprinting when she started school, nor the fingerprinting and photographs of her retinal patterns when she enrolled in social care.

Look what slighs missed by not having a card: medical care, unemployment benefits, food and housing coupons when there was no income for such things, old age care, bankcredit. They had to live by barter. Tarl would be given a few cans of food and some meat or produce when he left today, items the manager could mark off his inventory as "damaged" goods. He worked somewhere else to earn a bed.

"Is it really worth it?" she asked.

He glanced around. There was no need for him to ask what she meant. She had asked the same question for years.

"Yes!" he came back. "It's worth it because in spite of everything, it's freedom . . . complete personal freedom."

That was what made him incomprehensible. Marca never felt a lack of freedom. If anything, he had less freedom than she because he had no bankcard and no bankcredit.

Tarl finished unpacking the carton and came over to her, wiping his hands on an already filthy apron. "Does Cabot want to slip his leash again, or is it one of the others, this time?"

"I have a new one."

He frowned. "Don't you have enough clients already?"

She sighed in exasperation. "Tarl, there can be very big credit in this if we let ourselves grow."

He shook his head, sharply, emphatically. "There can be very big trouble. The half dozen pairs we have now are good. They use us regularly and keep their mouths shut. Get too many and we'll end up with one-timers who won't be so careful. Either a sligh or a citizen will talk and eventually the lions will hear about it. We have a nice little thing here; don't spoil it with ambition." He took a breath. "Do you have a picture?"

She brought it out of her purse. "He wants it arranged this week if possible."

Tarl studied the photograph, frowning. "He's in a hurry? I don't like that."

"It's probably a business deal. Tarl, he's a colonial contractor. He can afford to pay *well*, and I'll check him out before I commit us to anything."

"All right." He put the photograph in a sleeve pocket. "I'll start looking for a match this evening."

CHAPTER THREE

Janna hardly recognized Wim. In two days the man she knew as well as the face she saw in her mirror every day had become a stranger in a hospital bed, his head helmeted in bandages. Not much more than his mouth and the end of his nose were visible, and she had never seen that thin, grim set of his lips before. He lay with unnatural stillness, hands folded across his stomach. It gave the box created around him by the wood-grain ends and raised side panels of the bed a disturbing likeness to a coffin. There was only the rise and fall of his chest and the green LED readings of the vitals signs indicators in the side of the bed to reassure her he was still alive. She recognized him mostly because beside the bed, sitting in a molded foam chair reading a pamphlet on organic gardening, was Vada Kiest.

Vada looked up as the door closed behind Janna. She adored her husband. She was one of the few women Janna knew who had adopted her husband's name even though they had just the standard marriage contract. Vada was suffering for Wim, Janna could see. The Dresden perfection of her face looked ready to crack and shatter. When she saw Janna, it did crack. She rose up out of the chair and buried her face against Janna's chest.

In the bed, Wim rolled his bandaged head toward them. "You don't have to be quiet; I'm not asleep. That you, Jan?"

Janna held on to Vada. Silent sobs wracked the body of the smaller woman as if tearing it apart. "It's me. How are you feeling?"

He paused before answering. "The doctors decided about my eyes this morning."

She held Vada tighter. "I heard."

The SCPD director's office checked every day on officers wounded in the line of duty. This morning Director Thomas Paget himself had called Lieutenant Vradel to report to Wim. Pass-the-Word Morello, the squad clerk, whose name was nothing if not well-earned, had overheard. By midmorning it had been common knowledge throughout the Capitol division that there was irreparable damage to Wim Kiest's eyes due to the lacerations. The scar tissue was going to leave him blind.

"Can't they give you transplants?" she asked.

With the genoadaptive vaccines solving the rejection problem, the medicos claimed they could rebuild anyone.

"We asked about transplants." Vada pulled away from Janna. Her voice was bitter. "They can't replace eyes."

"The problem is in the optic nerve and ciliary muscles, they tell me." Wim spoke with the careful precision he used in court. "Nerves are hard to connect." He paused. "I'm going to a new world but I'll never be able to see it."

Janna felt totally helpless. What could she say? She reached out to touch him on the shoulder. "Luck is a bitch."

His fingers came up and locked around her wrist. "I was careless. I was running a straight chase, never thinking about lion traps."

"We weren't in Oakland, after all, and even there we made mistakes. Remember that time I fell into the ankle snare?"

Oakland was the lion trap capitol of the county, the war zone. Any leo careless enough to leave a watchcar without a helmet was asking for someone on a rooftop to trephine his skull with a brick or bottle. The vacant lots were full of pits to break legs and snares to trap the unwary. The snare Janna tripped had been made of monofilament wire. The jerk of hitting it had cut clean through her boot. They found a shallow laceration on her skin when they worked her foot free of the boot. If she had happened to jerk at the snare, the wire would have gone to the bone. She might have lost her foot.

"It was just luck I didn't cripple myself then."

She saw Vada develop the wistful frown she so often did when Janna and Wim started referring to some common experience she could never really understand because she had not shared it with them.

Wim sighed. "Deeks are deeks everywhere. As soon as I lost sight of him I should have started watching for him over my shoulder. I forgot to, and now I'm paying hard card for it."

"It's a rotten, terrible job," Vada said. "I should have listened to Grandma and made you quit years ago."

Wim's head rolled toward her. "Your grandfather belonged to another generation of police work."

"Did he? So they call you law enforcement officers now instead of cops and you have to have college degrees to make rank, and you have to visit the department psychiatrist every month to remain stable. What else has changed? Grandma warned me I'd sit home worried sick wondering whether you were going to come home after your watch. She said there are people out there who hate you and will kill you if you let them. She said your supervisors know that and still send you out into the street. You can't even carry guns to protect yourselves now."

"We carry guns," Janna said. "We just don't carry shooters, except for the shotguns in the cars."

"You can't protect yourselves. I think the tick tech is braintraining you on those visits, to keep you on the job even when it makes you risk your lives." Vada stared up at Janna with an intensity that startled the taller woman. "Quit, Jan. Wim told me he invited you to come out to Champaign with us. Please do it. You're like a sister to me. Quit before some madman kills or maims you, too." She reached out for Janna's hands.

Janna evaded her. "Vada, I can't—Wim . . . ?"

"You'll like it on Champaign," he said. "People out there don't wait for someone else to do everything for them. They know they have to depend on themselves. I've met most of the others who will be on our ship and they're all fine people. We'll be building something new and clean. Come out and be a part of it."

Janna felt as if she were being backed into a corner. "How am I going to raise that kind of credit? A share costs fifty thousand, you told me. I can't find that much in time to join the ship leaving next year."

"I have a pension coming to me, but since I won't be here, I won't need it. I'll have the department make a lump settlement and I'll give it to you. That should buy you a share."

"I—" She could not take it. How could she? "I'll thing about it," she said.

She started for the door. "I'd better go. I'm just on my lunch break. Vradel expects me to keep working for my bankcredit. I'll drop by this evening."

"All the pictures sent back by the probe show Champaign is a lovely world," Vada said.

Janna nodded.

Leaving the hospital, she looked up toward the heat-bleached sky. She had no desire to leave Earth. Still, what might it be like living under a different sky, she wondered idly. Did Champaign have cooler summers? Climbing into Indian Thirty to drive back down to the station, she wondered whether she ought to think about Wim's offer, and if not, how was she going to tell him no?

About the time Janna was returning to work, Marca Laclede had Tarl on the phone. "I have a match," he advised her.

Satisfaction warmed her. "A good one?"

"He's a bit thinner, otherwise they look like twins. His name is—"

Marca cut him off. "I don't care who he is. Does he understand what we want him to do?"

"He understands."

"And he's agreed?"

"Absolutely. He grew up as a sligh, going to illegal schools with one eye on the teacher and the other watching for Juvenile leos coming through the door on a raid. He's never had a chance like this and he wants it."

"Can he be trusted not to talk?"

There was a pause on the other end of the line. Marca frowned at her blank screen. She wished she had an image, to see Tarl's expression. He was calling from an Oakland public phone, though, so the screen at that end was probably broken.

"I don't know him personally," Tarl said at last. "I do know slighs, though, and I don't believe this one is a Mouth. He's waiting for me to tell him when and where to meet your client."

"I'll have to talk to the man first. Meet me at the Lion's Den at five o'clock. I'll bring everything our doppelgänger will need."

The pause at the other end was longer this time, followed by an audible hiss. "Woman, you're off your tick. That bar is two blocks from the police station. It's a lion watering hole. At five o'clock it'll be filled with lions. Forget whatever boost putting your head in the lion's mouth gives you; choose another place."

"Now, Tarl." She made her voice a persuasive purr. "They'll be busy talking shop and drinking. They'll never notice us."

He laughed, a short, sharp bark without amusement. "I can't believe you expect me to accept that. Everyone notices you. You'd be furious if they didn't. We'll be lucky if one of them doesn't take you for a girl from the Doll's House and try arguing you into a free trip upstairs."

"Everything will be all right, Tarl. The Lion's Den, at five. Be there."

She punched off the phone. After the connection was broken, Marca sat contemplating the mirror finish of her nails and thinking about Mr. Jorge Hazlett, wealthy and successful colonial contractor. She had spent most of Thursday and some of this morning

41

checking on him. She had told Adrian she was hunting some paintings for a client, then driven her Moth to Hazlett's house. He had a luxury sunken townhouse on Brentwood, out near the governor's mansion. She had stopped and struck up a conversation with a man doing yardwork. According to the yardman, Hazlett had let his last marriage contract lapse years ago. Now a succession of houseguests the yardman described as "flash bibis" rotated through the master bedroom. Hazlett owned a car, not a runabout or pedal car but a real road car, a Mercedes Vulcan sportster that he drove to work every day. The yardman was obviously impressed.

Marca was impressed, too. She rubbed at a tiny flaw in the finish of her left thumbnail. Mr. Jorge Hazlett could well afford any price she might care to ask for her services. It was best not to be too greedy, of course; she wanted him to come back for more. Steady clients were the real creditmakers.

She punched the phone on and punched in Hazlett and Kellener's number. "Mr. Hazlett, please," she told the beautiful Hispanic young man who answered. "This is Marca Laclede of Many Mansions."

Jorge had clients in his office, four members of the board of a forming colonial company. He was explaining to them why they did not want to have Lockheed build their ramjet—why, when two other builders were right here in Kansas—and why they did not want Beech-Cessna's custom-built ship.

"It's true the B-C Pilgrim will be tailored specifically to meet your needs, but that kind of special service is expensive. You can buy one of the standard Boeing Starmaster models for less money and have some extra space in case you find people who want to buy shares at the last minute."

The colonials looked over the literature he spread before them. They frowned thoughtfully.

The intercom chimed. "A Marca Laclede of Many Mansions for you, Mr. Hazlett."

Jorge's pulse leaped. So soon! This was wonderful. "Just a moment," he told the clients. He punched on the phone. "Hello, Ms. Laclede. I have clients here so I have only a minute or two." He did not want her saying anything incriminating when someone could hear.

Laclede's impossibly blue eyes smiled back at him from the phone's screen. "I've found that duplicate you wanted. Can you come over soon and discuss placement and price?"

He glanced at the clients and at the chrono readout on his computer outlet. "I'll be right there."

Punching off, he turned back to his clients. He handed them the ramjet specifications literature. "Here. Take these and look them over. Talk about them with your company if you have a meeting before your next appointment here. We'll make a decision on the ship the next time." He eased them toward the door, talking all the way. "I certainly don't want to force you into anything, nor make you feel your arm is being twisted." He accompanied them through the reception room. "Our objective is to get you to your destination planet as inexpensively and yet as safely as possible. You are the future of the human race." He looked at the receptionist. "I'm walking our clients to the elevator, Robert. I'll be right back."

He walked them to the elevator. They looked pleased with all the attention he was giving them. He had no trouble getting on the elevator and riding down. At street level, he shook hands with them, letting the doors close behind him. He walked them through the lobby to the front door. Instead of returning upstairs when they were gone, he lingered a moment or two, then left the building and ducked across the street at the first pedestrian crossing. He headed for the Santa Fe Building and Many Mansions.

When he came back he would tell Robert and Nina that the colonial company had kept him in the lobby talking. He might even embellish the story with some invented bits of conversation. That should account for the length of his absence.

Hazlett was certainly eager, Marca reflected. She

welcomed him to her office and made him comfortable in a colloid plastic chair. Its hard surface softened at contact and molded itself to his hips and back. Every movement he made was accompanied by a slight shift of the chair, so that the chair always fitted perfectly. Marca sat informally on the transparent top of her desk.

She went straight to business.

"As I said on the phone, Mr. Hazlett, we have a doppelgänger for you. All I need to know now is when you want to use him and if you're willing to pay for the service."

"How much are you asking and exactly what kind of service do I get for my credit?" He could be as blunt as she.

She smiled. She crossed legs sheathed in skintight hip boots. What there was of her romper had a waistline that pushed her breasts high, almost out over the neckline. She leaned forward, threatening the neckline still more. "What you get, Mr. Hazlett, is freedom for as long as you desire. You can't purchase anything, of course, but you can move around unrecorded. Meanwhile, your doppelgänger will be busy elsewhere, making purchases in your name and establishing your location as there, rather than where you actually are. The charge depends on how long you use the doppelgänger, and on how risky his impersonation is. If he has to fool someone who knows you, for instance, that takes time and education and is, naturally, more expensive."

"He can go anywhere he wants as long as it isn't anywhere I'm known. I'll give you a list of places for him to avoid. I need him for just one evening, three or four hours at most."

Marca uncrossed her legs and recrossed them the other direction. "Five thousand, then."

Jorge rubbed his nose. Five thousand. Not cheap. Still, for what he needed, it was a bargain. "How do I pay you without giving myself away?"

"The doppelgänger makes purchases worth five thousand on your card. Most of it will be jewelry. You can always explain the purchases away, if you need to, as gifts for your various houseguests."

He nodded. Gems, gold, and silver were the few portable credit equivalents. Nothing could be bought directly with them, unfortunately, but they could be sold at any time for bankcredit.

Marca took a card and pen off the desk and handed them to him. "I need your signature, and that list of places to avoid." She picked up what looked like a powder compact but when she opened it, Jorge saw that the bottom was filled with a jellylike substance. "You have to press your thumb against this," she said, passing the compact to him. "How soon do you want to use the doppelgänger?"

Jorge lifted his brows. "This evening?"

She shook her head. "That's too soon. He'll need time to practice your signature. How about tomorrow night? The stores are open late on Saturday; he'll have time to make the necessary purchases."

"Tomorrow, then." Still much sooner than he had dared hope. "How do we do it?"

"You'll meet the doppelgänger at a time and in a place no one is likely to notice you. You'll turn over your card to him. He can't drive, I'm sure, so you'll have to find an excuse for not using your car."

That was easy enough. Jorge felt excitement rise in him. It was the opening of the game. Pawn to King three.

"You should also have a reason for your signature not being quite the same. People don't become expert forgers in one day. I suggest a slight sprain of the wrist. Wear a bandage Sunday and Monday. It may be needless preparation, but . . ."

But one should always plan ahead, should be covered in case the need arose. Jorge understood that very well. He could have taught this young thing a lesson or two about planning ahead. "How do I get my card back?"

"You'll meet again at the end of the evening. He'll return your card and give you the purchase receipts, then you both go home." Marca smiled. "Any more questions?"

"How does he counterfeit my thumbprint?"

"I'd rather not explain that. It can be done, though."

"One more. I don't know anything about this person you've found to double for me, but he'll know me. What's to prevent him from blackmailing me later?"

Her eyes widened. She considered the question for a moment. It was a possibility she had not thought of before. Blackmail was unthinkable with a steady customer, of course, but there might be a time when it could be used on a one-timer. She blinked, a bit shocked at herself. What was she thinking about? Blackmail was dishonest. "This is a sligh, an Undocumented. The last thing he wants is for the government to identify and document him. I don't think he'll try to make trouble, but if he does, call me. I know how to reach him and I'll see he's dealt with. Where and when do you want to meet him?"

They spent several more minutes setting up a time and location for him to meet his doppelgänger. He signed the card and listed the places the doppelgänger must not visit. Then Jorge headed back for his office.

Marca opened a desk drawer and took out two small bottles of clear fluid. She poured a little from each into a watch glass. She swirled them together, then poured the liquid over the jelly in the compact. She swirled it once there, too, and poured the excess into her wastebasket.

In a few minutes the liquid had become an elastic film. She peeled what was left from the watch glass and threw it away. Glass and bottles went back in her desk drawer. With more care, she lifted the sheet in the compact clear of the jelly. She held it to the light and squinted through it. Using small scissors, she carefully trimmed the plastic down to the edge of the thumbprint.

She regarded the result with satisfaction. In her palm lay a copy of Hazlett's thumbprint in a clear, porous plastic that could be glued to the doppelgänger's thumb. It would let the natural oils through so the whorls would print naturally on the register.

The plastic was the invention of another college friend of hers. He had developed it to be painted on the body to cover and protect the wearer so he or she could appear nude and yet be warm even in cold weather. Its porous nature was designed to keep the wearer from cooking to death inside.

Marca thought she was one of the few people to know of the plastic's existence. Luke was still trying to find a manufacturer to produce it. What she had was hand-mixed batches she had persuaded Luke to make up for her, claiming she needed it for personal use.

At times she pondered the coincidence of finding herself with a boss who looked like one friend and having another friend who invented the plastic that made forging thumbprints possible. Amazing. Without Luke's invention, she could never have made the doppelgängers work. Sometimes Marca thought it had to be more than coincidence. She was no Bible cultist, but she did wonder about fate, wondered if something very big and special was intended for her.

She slipped the thumbprint cast and Hazlett's signature card into an envelope and dropped it in her purse.

The Lion's Den was located on the ground floor of the building officially designated on city maps as the "New Hotel Jayhawk." That was for the benefit of strangers and the active—and vocal—local Bible cultists; everyone in Topeka knew the building was really the Doll's House. The bar was owned and operated by an ex-leo named Vernon Tuckwiller, who encouraged officers from the Capitol division to use his place for informal tick talks and to defuse any stress left over from the official debriefings at the station. He kept expendable glasses and chairs and tables of hardboard—cheap to replace, nonlethal when used as bludgeons. He tolerated almost any disorder short of a full riot, leaving the leos to referee themselves. There were just two unbreakable rules in Tuck's place; no uniforms and no rank—he treated Director Paget himself no better than the rawest rookie—and any damage had to be paid for before the officers involved left. As a result Tuck's had become one of the city's favorite lion bars, and around watch change experienced citizens found somewhere else to drink.

The Den started filling up about a quarter to five, as debriefing ended. The leos drifted up from the station in twos and threes. The lion buffs came out of the woodwork, women and a few men who loved the company of anything wearing a badge. The noise level increased exponentially with every new arrival. By the time Lieutenant Hari Vradel and Janna Brill came in just before five, anyone without a good set of lungs might as well have been content just to sit and watch.

During the walk up from the station Janna kept wondering why Vradel had asked her to join him. She had been to the Den often before, but not usually with Vradel, except as part of a group celebrating something. Vradel liked to mother his squad, though, and he had not really spoken to her since Wim was hurt. He must have brought her here to comfort her.

In the Den, Tuck himself was behind the bar. Janna could well believe he had worked Vice. He was built for kicking down the doors of unlicensed and after-hours bars and gambling parlors. In fact, she thought he looked as if he could take out a door just by casually leaning against it. She was amazed that a man his size could turn around behind the bar without wiping out the entire stock of glasses.

"What'll it be?" Without any visible strain, Tuck managed to make his voice clearly audible.

Janna could not hear Vradel order. Tuck, though, either had excellent hearing or was a lip reader. He set up a glass of iced tea and a noxious blue drink the Ares I crew had invented those first bleak months on Mars, known now as a Martian Cow. Janna was pleased that the lieutenant remembered her intolerance of alcohol. Vradel went even farther. He turned over his card to pay for both drinks. He made his thumbprint and signature on the register screen, then they picked up their drinks. As they started to leave the bar, Tuck handed Vradel a grease pencil. "Use this, will you? Ink doesn't come out of the tabletops."

Vradel grinned sheepishly.

He pointed toward the back of the room and plunged into the crowd. Janna followed, staying close, holding her glass above the arms that gesticulated with abandon while their owners talked shop or sex or argued whether a Jewish President would be able to get tough enough with Israel and if mining the asteroids, as the people in the Mars colony proposed, could really break the stranglehold Africa had on the mineral market.

At the back was a row of booths. Several of them were still unoccupied. Vradel slid in one side of the end booth. Janna sat down across from him. The colloid plastic of the bench molded to her hips.

Vradel took a sip of his Martian Cow and set it down. He started toying with the grease pencil. Above the roar of voices around them he bellowed, "I want you to know I'm sorry about Kiest. He was a fine investigator. It's a damned shame that had to happen so close to his resignation."

Janna nodded. She watched her knuckles whiten around her glass.

The grease pencil dipped inevitably toward the tabletop. Janna wondered if it were true the edges of the citations Vradel issued as a traffic officer had been adorned with caricatures of the cited individual, doodled there while Vradel talked to the citizen. She was inclined to believe it, accepting for fact the story that in one case where the identity of the citee was in question, it had been settled by comparing the individual who presented himself in court with the sketches on the citation.

Wim's face emerged from the tangle of lines Vradel made on the tabletop. "Times like these I regret not being able to be personal friends with every officer in my squad. Then maybe I'd know better things to say. Sometimes partners aren't friends. Sometimes they don't even like each other. Morello tells me you and

Kiest were close, though. Is there anything I can do?"

"He isn't dead, lieutenant."

Vradel looked up. His mustache twitched. "Blind, though—" He bent his head over his sketch. After a minute, he looked up again. "What are you doing with yourself these days, Brill? Taking any classes at Washburn? Still cohabiting with that assistant medical examiner?"

It felt strange to be holding casual conversation at the top of her lungs, but Janna answered, "I'm not taking any classes but yes, I'm still cohabs with Sid Chesney."

"Thinking of making a marriage contract with him?"

"With Sid?" She grinned and shook her head. "I'm the wrong sex for Sid. I don't believe in marriage for leos anyway. The job is a hellish anxiety for a spouse. Sid, now, doesn't get frantic if I'm late and we can talk to each other about our days without being shocked. He doesn't compete with me for dates the way a female roommate would. We're comfortable together. How many police marriages can make the same claim?"

Now it was Vradel, who was smiling. "Oh, there are a few." He drew another face. It was a woman's, round and gentle. Janna had seen him draw that face often and with great affection. "Hilly and I have been renewing for twenty years." He smiled at the sketch, then looked up at Janna. "I ought to find you another partner. Is there anyone you—"

He broke off as a disturbance rippled through the bar. At first Janna thought it might be a fight, but the source became evident in a moment. Out of the jam of leos came a man and a woman. The woman was pure flash . . . rich mahogany-red hair, silver hip boots, shreds of a romper that matched her improbably blue eyes. A path opened for her like Moses passing through the Red Sea. The sound of falling jaws and dripping saliva marked her wake.

"A new girl of Risa's, do you suppose, or a lion buff?" Vradel said.

Janna eyed the couple. They were taking a booth at the far end of the line. "A kind of buff. She flirts, and always wears something to raise the blood pressure. The sligh with her is new, though."

Vradel looked past Janna at them. "He is a sligh, isn't he? I wonder what he's doing in here."

Exactly what marked the sligh, Janna could not say. There was nothing unusual about his hair or clothing, but then, slighs were usually careful to blend in. Probably it was the studied indifference of his walk, as if he wanted to be invisible, but lacking that, was fighting the urge to bolt or dive under the nearest table. She, too, wondered what a sligh was doing walking into a bar full of lions.

Vradel began sketching the man. "I'm curious. How do you feel about Undocumenteds?"

"They're brainbent, but there's nothing illegal in being unidented. I say let them live the way they want to. In Oakland I had a number of sligh friends. I always hated raiding schools."

Vradel grunted. "Anyone except a rock jock hates strapping schools."

The slithyschools were illegal because they were uninspected and unlicensed. Licensing, after all, required identation of all students. It was only a misdemeanor to run a school, though, or to send children to one. That made it dirty work holding a bunch of kids just to force their parents to come in and plead guilty to a misdemeanor. In Janna's opinion, raiding schools was an underhanded ruse to ident sligh kids and their parents.

"What?" She realized belatedly that Vradel was talking to her again.

"Is there anyone you'd like to team with? Anyone you'd rather *not?*"

She gave his question some thought, then shook her head. Most of the squad were good leos. The toads and timesliders were all paired off already.

"Any objection to taking a new man? I have one coming in Monday from the Soldier Creek division."

Janna smiled. "I'll bet he's glad to be joining civilization."

Vradel put down his pencil and took a long swallow of his drink. After a moment of thought, he took another. "He's been other places besides Soldier Creek. He's been everywhere, one time or another, including Capitol."

Janna had a sudden feeling she was going to be sorry she had not named someone she wanted to team with. "What's this leo's name?"

"Sergeant Mahlon Maxwell."

Janna clutched her tea. "Oh, god."

Vradel looked unhappy. "You've met him?"

"I've run into his reputation. He left Oakland just a few months before I transferred in. Mama Maxwell has been with the department for twelve years. He has a law degree, but he's still a sergeant. In Oakland he's infamous for the Night of the Caged Lion."

Vradel chewed on the end of his mustache. "His jacket doesn't list offenses by title, I'm afraid. What's the Night of the Caged Lion?"

Janna leaned back. The colloid of the bench flowed with her. "Once upon a very quiet and boring morning watch, Mama Maxwell and his partner decided that since nothing else was happening, they would count a little coup to pass the time. They climbed into the back of their watchcar, being very careful to wedge the door open, and started in. Along came one of the local citizens on the way home after the bars had closed. The citizen evidently saw what was happening in the car and kicked out the wedge."

"Christ." Vradel reached for his Martian Cow.

"Wait. The best is yet to come. They were parked in their favorite hole and since they didn't want the squad sergeant to learn where the hole was, they disconnected the car's transponder and their button transponders. So when they didn't roger their next call, the dispatcher couldn't find them on the map. She notified their sergeant, and every car in the division was put to work looking for them. The hunt lasted over two hours and eventually included not only the alpha and beta squad sergeants but also the watch supervisor."

Vradel finished his drink. "And the rest is recorded in the disciplinary action in his jacket. He was suspended for six months, then sent to Cullen Village division. His partner resigned."

"How did you happen to get stuck with him?" asked Janna.

"He's been doing good work in Soldier Creek, apparently. His present supervisors recommended promotion to Investigator I." Vradel chewed on his mustache. "He's collected a number of commendations over the years and he's been using his law degree to defend officers against charges brought by Internal Affairs. He's won more cases than he's lost. Brill, he can't be too bad; will you team with him?"

She grimaced. "Why me?"

"You need a partner. Besides, maybe you'll be a good influence on him."

Her lip curled.

"Take him at least until you find someone else you want to work with. I'd make it an order but this is Tuck's place. No rank. I'll just say please."

Today was her day for being pushed into corners, it seemed. She sighed. "All right." She paused, shaking her head. "Mama Maxwell? Lord." She sighed again. "I can hardly wait until Monday."

Maybe it was time to give Wim's offer serious thought.

CHAPTER FOUR

Jorge spent Saturday vacillating between excitement and depression, between the high he felt in a game when his opponent was making all the moves Jorge wanted, and the cold, sweaty certainty that the Laclede woman was wrong, that the sligh could never successfully pass for him. The sligh would be caught, and start the entire domino row going down. He was tempted to call the woman and cancel everything. Perhaps there would be no trouble convincing Andy to help falsify the records. About the time he thought that, though, Jorge also started thinking what would happen if Andy would not help. That brought on the cold sweat again.

By evening, he had decided that no matter how risky the gambit, he had to use it. The doppelgänger was insurance, just in case.

Jorge dressed for the evening with care, a simple gold and blue jumpsuit and dark blue ankle boots. He wrapped his right wrist in a support bandage. He could claim he sprained it in a fall or during calisthenics. He glanced at the chrono on his dresser top. Six-thirty. Half an hour until he was to meet the doppelgänger.

He went to his study. After a momentary hesitation, he pulled open the top drawer of his desk. A .22 revolver lay inside. He regarded the weapon for a moment, licking his lips, then shook his head and closed the drawer. A gun was not only noisy, but this particular one could be traced to him. As part of maintaining a license on it, he had to leave a new test bullet with the police department every fifty firings or every six months. The image of any bullet removed from a body was routinely run through the ballistics computer, he knew, and compared to the images of the test bullets stored in its memory. No, he could not use the gun.

Then he turned around to the Moses landscape on the wall behind his desk, swung it aside and spun the three concentric rings on the lock of the safe concealed behind the painting. When the three rings were in their proper relationship, the lock clicked. He pulled open the door, reached in and took out a small amber plastic pill bottle.

The lid twisted open hard. Jorge struggled with it for a minute before it gave. The bottle was about half full of a talcum-fine, herbal-scented brown powder —trichlorlysergic something-or-other. Trick. Jorge shook the bottle. It made colors that tasted and sounds that had scent. It was the ultimate trip, some said, and it could be a one-way ticket.

He recapped the bottle and pushed it into a thigh pocket. He had taken this particular sample away from a weekend guest, who brought it hoping to make sex a new experience. Jorge preferred the old variety to a *new* that could become a *last*. He understood his reasons for taking the stuff from Serena, but until now he had sometimes wondered why he had kept it. He should have thrown it away. Perhaps he had been subconsciously thinking even then that the day might come when he would need something deadly that would be untraceable to him.

Jorge glanced at the study chrono. Six thirty-five.

He crossed to the phone and punched in Andy's number. It buzzed twice and then the elegant face of Liann Seaton, Andy's wife, appeared on the screen.

She smiled. "Hello. Jorge."

He smiled back. "Hi, you gorgeous creature. Let's run away together."

"I'm busy tonight. How about next week? Do you want Andy?"

"As long as you're busy, yes."

The screen went white as she put him on hold.

Jorge waited, and found himself drumming his fingers in nervous anticipation. He forced himself to stop as soon as he realized what he was doing. Surely there was no need to be nervous. He could manipulate Andy. The trick was getting Andy to leave the house without Liann's learning where he was going.

Andy's face appeared on the screen. "What is it, Jorge?"

"Are you alone there?"

Andy's brows rose. "You mean here at the phone? Yes. Why?"

"I was going over the Laheli records late this afternoon and—" He broke off.

Andy's raised brows pulled toward each other in a concerned frown. "And?" he prompted.

Jorge pretended to debate. After a moment he said, "I don't think I better talk about it over the phone. I'd better show you. Are you free this evening?"

His partner's frown deepened. "I promised Liann and the kids we'd go to the cinaround."

"We really ought to go over this matter before Monday. We don't know when the government will start its inquiry. What I've found could make or break the firm."

Now it was Andy's turn to debate. He did it with obvious effort.

"It won't take long," Jorge added persuasively. "You'll be back in time to take them to a late showing."

Andy gave in. "All right. Shall I come to the office?"

"Yes." Now came the hard part. "And would you mind not telling Liann that I'm the one who is dragging you away? I don't want her mad at me for spoiling your evening."

"She won't be. You know she has the disposition of a saint."

"I don't want to spoil that disposition, either. Please."

Andy nodded. "All right, I'll make up some excuse

that has nothing to do with you. See you at the office in half an hour."

Jorge punched off the line. He headed for the door smiling in satisfaction. Now if the sligh could only carry off *his* part, the gambit just might work.

Owan Desfosses spent Saturday sick with fear. This scheme would never work. He could not hope to pass as this Jorge Hazlett, no matter what Tarl said. He was an Undocumented, a social truant. He had lived his life avoiding those places and activities a citizen accepted as everyday normals. Who was this Tarl anyway? Owan did not know him. Maybe Tarl was a leo, setting a slithytove trap.

But even while he sweated and his stomach churned, Owan sat in his room preparing for the job. First, he cut his hair to shoulder length and curled it to match the lion's mane of the man in the 2-D photograph Tarl had given him. Then he practiced copying the signature on the card and memorized the list of places he must not visit. Owan wrote the name over and over, laboriously at first, then with increasing ease as the day progressed. He covered both sides of sheet after sheet of paper. After he filled each sheet, he destroyed it, tearing it into pieces so small no one would ever be able to tell what he had written.

Watching the signature come closer and closer to matching the one on the card, Owan's fear quieted. He even began to feel a touch of excitement. This just might work. If it did—if it did work, he could enjoy the life of a citizen for an entire evening.

Owan had envied citizens as long as he could remember. They could go anywhere, live anywhere. They never had to cross the street to avoid a leo or take abuse from a store owner who made them work long hours for little compensation. He was not quite sure why he remained a sligh, except that it was the only life he knew. His parents had raised him as a sligh.

Combing his hair, he thought about the times he had considered applying for a Scib Card. He had even tried. Once he had gotten as far as asking for the application at a Social Care office, but he had never been able to make himself fill out the form. Something in him curdled at the idea of committing facts about himself to paper.

He looked at the clock on his dresser. It was an old thing the apartment manager had given him so he would not be late for work, an antique with a round face and hands. It read twenty minutes to seven.

He took one last look at himself in the mirror and compared the image to the photograph. It was a strange sensation to see a stranger looking up at him with his own face.

Owan opened the envelope lying beside the picture. He shook it. A small tube of glue and an oval of transparent plastic fell out into his hand.

His hands started to sweat. He put everything down while he dried them, then opened the tube and dropped some of the liquid onto the center of his left thumb, spreading it around to the edges of the ridged area. Carefully, he picked up the piece of plastic. He held it obliquely to the light to make sure which was the smooth side and that he had the correct end toward his thumbnail, then he pressed the plastic onto his thumb. He smoothed it down, smoothed the edges.

He waited a minute to make sure the plastic had set, and while it finished drying, he tossed envelope, glue, and picture into the top drawer of his dresser. Then he looked at the thumb. He could hardly tell the plastic was on it.

Owan took a deep breath. Time to begin.

He left his room and climbed the stairs to the ground floor. Outside, he unlocked his bicycle and backed it out of the rack. He was proud of the bike. He had built it himself of parts he acquired one way or another while he worked at a bike shop. He felt the result was a bike every bit as good as a commercially built machine. At the very least it freed him from having to find ways of earning transport tokens for buses. Except in bad weather, he could travel almost as fast by bike as he could have in a runabout or pedal car.

He swung onto the bike and headed it toward the downtown area. The evening was unbearably hot and humid. How many days had the temperature been over thirty-five now? It seemed like weeks. It had to be nearly forty degrees tonight. In no time his forehead was running sweat and his pioneer-style shirt sticking to his back. He did not slow down, though. The time had to be close to seven o'clock and he did not want to be late.

Every red light was an irritant, a demoniacal plot to delay him. What was the actual time? If he were late would this Hazlett wait?

Just over the Interstate, he hit a yellow light. It would be a long red, he knew. He pedaled hard and raced through.

Behind him, a siren burped once. Owan froze.

The black-and-white bullet-on-a-plate shape of a watchcar drifted up beside him and slowed to hover. A she-lion leaned out, folded arms on the edge of the window.

"You can get hurt racing yellows," she said.

Owan could feel the air kicked out by the car's fans. It was hot against his ankles. The rest of him, sweat or not, felt wrapped in ice. His stomach knotted. He swallowed. "Yes, officer."

"A bicycle will lose a contest with a car or runabout every time."

She did not necessarily recognize him as a sligh, he told himself. She was probably not trophy hunting. He gripped the handlebars tighter to keep his hands from shaking. "I know, officer."

She looked him over with narrowed eyes. "Something wrong, jon?"

His stomach lurched. When they started calling someone "jon" they were smelling lion meat.

He made himself smile. "Nothing wrong except I'm late for work."

He thought he said it smoothly but she sat up. Her voice sharpened. "What's your name, jon?"

Traffic was swinging around them. People in the

runabouts and cars stared. Owan wanted to run. "Tris." Never, ever give a real name to a lion.

"No last name? Let's see your card, jon."

"I—" His smile widened. "I don't have one."

The she-lion's brows went up. She grinned. "Hey, Cade," she said to her partner at the wheel, "we have a sligh. How'd you get your bike licensed, jon? Do you suppose he stole it, Cade? We better take him in and check on it."

A trophy hunter. Owan could have wept. They could not take him in, not now, of all times . . . not *now*. "It's registered to a friend," he said desperately. "Clio de Garza."

"Well, we'll just see." She touched the radio. "Alpha Cap Eleven to control, stolen property check. Hey, Cade, do you suppose he'll resist arrest?"

"Let him go," the lion at the wheel said. He sounded tired. "It's too hot for games."

The she-lion frowned, then pulled back into the car. "Alpha Cap Eleven to control, cancel the call." Her eyes bored holes in Owan. "Watch yourself in traffic after this, jon."

The watchcar's fans revved and it pulled away from him.

Owan did not have time to be relieved. He leaned on the pedals and raced for downtown.

At the Sunco parking lot on Jackson Street Owan lifted the bike over the entrance gate and hurriedly parked and locked it in the bicycle section. The lot served workers in the office buildings nearby. At this time of evening it was almost deserted. Owan looked around. He did not see anyone who seemed to be waiting. Could Hazlett have left already?

Then he heard a voice coming from the direction of the public phones. ". . . and the fans started to sound strange. I'll leave the car parked here. Have someone look at it as soon as possible, please. The address again is the Sunco parking lot. Thirteenth and Jackson."

Owan headed for the voice.

The man punched the phone off and turned around.

Owan felt as if he had been kicked in the stomach. A chill crawled up his spine. Even the photograph had not prepared him for the shock of meeting himself face to face.

Jorge Hazlett stared back. His eyes were coldly appraising. "You're late."

Under that withering stare, no excuse seemed justified enough to give. "I'm sorry." His voice sounded thin in his ears.

"You understand exactly what you're supposed to do?"

Owan nodded.

The man reached into the breast pocket of his jumpsuit and took out a card case. He handed over the Scib Card in it. "Five thousand bankcredits worth of merchandise, no more. Try to spend more and I'll hang both you and the woman."

Owan wondered what woman. He had met no one but Tarl.

"Be back here no later than ten o'clock, and don't forget the purchase receipts. Don't go near the places on that list I wrote out." His tone said that Owan could not hope to fool anyone who knew Jorge Hazlett at all.

"Ten o'clock. I'll bring the receipts. I won't go to any of those places." He would not have had the nerve in any case. Clubs and game parlors like those were places slighs saw only from the kitchen.

Owan left the lot as quickly as he could without seeming to be running away. He was glad to escape from Hazlett. The man made him nervous. He was glad the likeness between them was only physical.

He wished he could use his bike, but Tarl had told him he must act as Hazlett would and Hazlett had no bicycle. Owan stood at the bus stop for several minutes before he realized he had no transport tokens. There was a token machine in the lobby of the building behind the bus stop. Owan stared at it, licking his lips. His palms started to sweat. Well, there was no time like now to find out if this crazy switch would work.

To his amazement, it worked. The machine accepted the thumbprint and signature and coughed out half a dozen tokens. Owan climbed on the next bus feeling giddy. Two of the tokens clattered into the bus's hopper. He could fool a machine at least.

He was aboard the bus for five minutes before he happened to wonder where it was going. He checked the next street marker it passed. Twenty-third and Kansas Avenue. The bus was going to south Topeka.

For a moment he was jubilant—he could visit Clio and Tesha—but his pleasure faded almost immediately. He was supposed to be Jorge Hazlett. Hazlett would have no reason to visit Clio and Tesha. Owan had things Tarl had ordered him to buy, too. He would have to visit a shopping mall instead.

What he could and did do was to buy some vending tokens at the mall and use a public phone to call Clio.

He had cohabited with Clio de Garza for nearly three years some eight years before. There was no marriage contract because contracts required registration and identification. The arrangement might have lasted indefinitely except Clio became pregnant. Understandably, she wanted to raise the child with all the benefits of full citizenship. Clio herself was a citizen. When Owan could not bring himself to be idented so they could marry, Clio finally moved out. Owan did not hold that against her. He found it miraculous that a woman as beautiful as she and some twenty years his junior could have found him worth living with for even three years. They were still friends.

Clio's face appeared on the screen, Hispanic, darkly beautiful. She looked surprised but pleased to see him. "You're in south Topeka? Are you coming to visit?"

He shook his head, sighing. "I can't. That's why I called. Is Tesha still up?"

"She was on her way to bed, but I'll go get her."

Moments later he saw the olive face of his daughter on the screen. Tesha was the real miracle of the time with Clio. Every time Owan saw her he marveled that he could have been part of producing this exquisite creature. Watching her grow up was the joy of his life. He lived every week for the Sunday afternoon visit with her.

"How are you, *chiquita?*" he asked.

She launched into an enthusiastic description of what she had learned at school that week. It was a real school. No illegal schools for Tesha, no fearful waiting for police raids.

Clio interrupted finally. "That's enough for tonight. You can tell him the rest tomorrow. You will be here tomorrow, won't you?"

"Of course. And I'll have a surprise for you, *chiquita.*"

Tesha's eyes widened. "What kind of surprise?"

"If I told you, it wouldn't be a surprise, would it? Good night."

She blew him a kiss.

Clio did, too. "Collect the real one, and more, tomorrow."

After he punched off he wandered through the three levels of the mall, trying to decide what to buy first. Five hundred of the five thousand bankcredits were his to spend on whatever he wanted. What did he want? There was so much to choose from.

He saw a toy shop. Tesha's surprise ought to be the first order of business.

As he entered the toy shop, he wondered if it were wise when he saw the polished perfection of the clerk. He knew enough about places like this to know clerks like that sold merchandise that cost dearly. Still, he had five hundred to play with.

"I'm looking for something for a very bright seven-year-old girl."

The clerk smiled. "This way, sir."

Sir. As if he were a citizen. Owan felt a meter taller.

The selection of toys she showed him was dazzling. He had never dreamed such things existed. They had certainly never been part of the world of a sligh child. The toys crowded the shelves around him: dolls, educational put-togethers, toys to develop learning skills, toys to exercise the imagination, toys to develop physical dexterity, toys to cuddle, role-practice toys.

It took him twenty minutes, but out of them all he finally chose two: a small computer which the clerk assured him would be an invaluable school aid, and a Dyan Pennock doll. Owan had never heard the name before. It was the dark beauty of the doll that attracted him. Until he read the biographical booklet that came with the doll, he had not known that the most famous shuttlejocky in the world was a black woman.

The computer was the largest of the two packages and awkward to carry. He had to set it down several times to get a better hold on it. The clerk had offered to have it delivered, but he could not risk that.

While he was struggling with the package, he found himself standing in front of a clothing shop. The two jumpsuits on display almost made him forget Tesha's computer. The colors were soft but glowing. They shifted subtly as the light on them changed. He reached out to touch one, drawn almost magnetically. He had never felt anything in his life that soft and light. What a rich feeling it would be to own and wear a suit like that.

Owan picked up his package and walked into the shop.

Even with the doppelgänger late to the meeting, Jorge still reached the office before Andy. He left the lights off and sat in the reception room letting the air-conditioning cool him off.

He had been disappointed by the doppelgänger. Did the Laclede woman really think that rabbit looked like him? A poor expression of judgment, if so. Still, if the fool stayed away from the places on the list, the substitution might work. Card photos were always so bad that the doppelgänger came close enough to matching the one on Jorge's card.

The office door hummed. Jorge sat up. Someone was pressing a palm to the capacitant plate of the lock. In a few moments the information on the size, shape, and salt content of the hand on the plate was relayed through the computer and the computer satisfied itself that the hand belonged to someone who had access rights. The lock opened with a click.

Andy came in, wiping his forehead. "Terrible heat outside, isn't it? Murderous. I wonder how many people it will drive into assaults this weekend." He plucked at his jumpsuit, pulling it away from his body. "The air-conditioning was out on my bus, too. Now, what is it you need to show me?"

"Let's go to your office."

If someone came by, such as the building security guard, Jorge wanted lights nowhere in the suite but Andy's office.

Andy pressed his hand to the plate of his office door. The door hummed, consulting the computer again, and clicked open. The room was still bright with light coming through the window strips. Andy did not bother turning on any lamps.

Like Jorge's office, Andy's was dominated by his big L-shaped desk. The chairs in the room were arranged facing it, except for several grouped around a low table near the door. Whereas Jorge had covered his walls with pictures of ramjets and photographs of distant worlds taken from orbit by tachyon bioprobes, Andy's were decorated with matted and framed cartoons of lawyers, part of his legal humor collection. Behind Andy's desk hung a large brush-and-ink drawing of Justice peeping, winking, from under her blindfold.

"Now what did you need me to see?" Andy asked. He sat in his desk chair and leaned back, raising expectant brows at Jorge.

Jorge came around the desk to the computer outlet. He punched it on. "I finally found the code for retrieving the Laheli records."

He punched in the request for the records.

The computer screen said: WHAT'S THE PASSWORD?
Jorge punched: RUY LOPEZ . . . RUN . . . PRINTOUT.

The computer hummed. Facsimile pages began dropping one after the other into the tray.

"I need help, Andy." Jorge made it a plea.

"You said this could ruin the firm?"

"It can. Read that."

Andy picked up the pages and began reading. At first his eyes raced down the sheet quickly, then with an almost audible roar of reversing fans, he stopped. He went back and began rereading, this time with slow care. After several pages, he looked up at Jorge in horror.

"Good god, Jorge. Why?"

Jorge shrugged. "I don't know. I have the house and those flash girlfriends who like expensive presents. I—I didn't think anyone would be hurt."

"Not *hurt?* Jorge, those letters from Boeing say it all. Where is it?"

He flipped back through the printout sheets. "Here. 'We cannot guarantee the continued function of these systems without constant, expert maintenance.' *Constant, expert* maintenance, Jorge. You surely couldn't have thought the colonists were going to be able to become expert in life-support systems maintenance with the crash course they take." He stared at Jorge in disbelief. "You had to know how dangerous it was. I can't believe any of this. Those people's lives were dependent on those systems. There's no walking home from a ramjet. Yet you let them—" He broke off and dropped the sheets on his desk as if they were burning his hands. "Lord. You know what this means, don't you? If a government investigator sees this, he'll invoke the Tescott Act. You willfully and deceitfully jeopardized those people's lives."

"Not willfully, I swear." Jorge leaned toward Andy. "That's why you have to help me alter the records."

Andy stiffened. "Alter the records?"

"We're partners, remember. We're both liable. You wouldn't want Liann or the kids dragged into anything as nasty as a Tescott prosecution."

The worry frown cleared off Andy's face. His mouth thinned. "We're partners, yes. That makes the partnership liable in a civil suit; but the Tescott Act is a criminal prosecution. I'm *not* liable in a criminal action. I won't make myself a party by becoming an accessory.

Jorge—" Andy ran both hands through his hair. He sighed. "I don't understand what in god's name you thought you were doing. We're dedicated to helping colonists build new worlds and new lives. To send them off in what's essentially a leaky rowboat is a total contradiction of our goals."

Andy's goals, maybe. Irritation was rising in Jorge. He tried to keep it under control and look frantic instead. "We certainly can't help colonists if we're out of business. Help me staighten this Laheli thing out."

Jorge still hoped Andy would cooperate. They had been friends and partners a long time. They had shared an apartment during their senior year at law school, sweated out their exams and then the bar exams together, counted coup on the same girls. They had comforted each other in their starvation those early years trying to develop a law practice. He hoped Andy would not be a fool and force him into a corner.

Andy's eyes dropped to the computer pages. "We can't cover this up. I ought to let you face it alone. After all, you got into it alone. You ought to be responsible for your own actions."

Jorge almost hissed. Lord, a sermon. If this turned into a recitation of Libertarian cant, he was going to strangle Andy.

"But we're friends," Andy said.

Jorge felt a wash of relief.

"Maybe we can avoid the Tescott Act." Andy picked up the printout again. "I wish your answers to Boeing had been less arrogant. 'I have explained the situation to my clients. They say they understand perfectly and are prepared to cope with any possible problem. They would not have ordered this particular ship if it was not what they wanted.' " He looked up, frowning. "But you hadn't talked to them, had you? You never warned them at all. You let them think crewing the ship would be just a matter of following the computer's orders and feeding in new programs when required."

"I didn't think there was any need to warn them."

Andy shook his head as if something were biting at it that he wanted to shake off. "You, the chess player, the master of alternatives and planner of seven moves ahead—you didn't consider what might happen to them? I can't believe that." He flipped through the sheets.

Jorge waited, very still. He had a sudden fear what Andy was about to do. He hoped he was wrong.

Andy regarded him thoughtfully. His mouth thinned. "I think you did know they ought to be warned. I think you knew very well what might happen. You always have a good idea how everything you do will turn out. You just didn't *care* what happened to those people."

His voice was so calmly unemotional Jorge felt panic grab him. A calm Andy was a thinking Andy. A thinking Andy was a dangerous man. Jorge met the accusation with an unwavering gaze. "I would never consciously do anything to harm a client."

Andy threw down the printout. "Crap. When you're playing games, other people are just pawns. You treat them all as expendable. You were that way in the moot court in law school. You were that way with the clients we had in law practice." He stopped. His face grayed.

Jorge wondered if Andy were considering that the Laheli Company was not the first client Jorge had defrauded.

"Jorge, I need to know something. Be honest with me. Is this the first time you've put clients aboard a ship that's too small and too crowded?"

Jorge was ready for him. He let his jaw drop as though in dismay. "Andy, what do you think I am? Of course this is the first time it's happened. I swear."

Andy smiled, but there was steel under it. "Then you won't mind going over the records of all our past clients, will you?"

Silently, Jorge cursed his partner. The fool. He had to back Jorge into a corner. He had given Andy a chance to help, but Andy would not take it. God only knew what Andy would do when he saw the other records. At the least he would denounce Jorge to the Colonial Agency and the U.S. District Attorney. It was a check, and the easiest counter this time was to remove the attacking piece.

Jorge smiled back. "Of course I don't mind. That's going to take a while, though. I think I'd like some caff to drink while we work. How about you?"

Andy nodded. "Good idea."

"I'll have it ready in a minute."

Jorge knew where the office staff kept the cups and caff and tea mixes. He took the ingredients out of their cabinet and mixed two cups of caff with hot water from the suite washroom. He dropped a tablet of sweetener and a cube of lightened powder into his drink. Two sweetener tabs and no lightener went into Andy's. Jorge glanced toward Andy's office door to make sure he was not being observed, then reached into his pocket for the tube of trick. He had tried everything to avoid this. He had given Andy every opportunity to cooperate. The consequences were Andy's fault.

He poured a third of the powder into Andy's caff. A swirl with a stirrer dissolved it. He carried the steaming cups back to Andy's office.

His partner was watching the computer print out a list of their clients. Andy accepted the mug with a murmur of thanks and sipped it. After the first swallow, he drew back and frowned at the cup.

"Something wrong?" Jorge asked.

"It tastes a little different. Did you put in two sweetener tabs."

"Yes."

Andy took another swallow.

The list finished printing out. Each client had a code number ending in either *K* or *H,* indicating which of the partners handled them. Andy started down the list with a red pen and, between sips of caff, circled all the H numbers.

He paused over one. "Strange."

Jorge lifted a brow. "What is?"

"I don't remember handling an Outreach Company, but it has a K number."

He would be doubly shocked, and perhaps realize what was happening, when he saw the Laheli Company had a K number, too. Jorge hoped the trick would work before then.

"Curiouser and curiouser," Ander murmured. He circled another number. "When I move the pen, I hear a chiming sound." He looked up and around him with surprise. "And when I talk, the air is filled with a minty scent." He sniffed the caff. "It isn't the caff. That smells rich purple." He took a large swallow. "It tastes green, though. It—"

Andy stared into the cup in horror. Suddenly he whipped around and threw it across the room. Caff splashed on the wall. "You put something in it, Jorge. What are gray and greeb iffing snoways for?" The horror overwhelmed his eyes. He put both hands over his mouth. "I didn't creech the say and yoder meaning."

Jorge finished his own caff. He went to pick up Andy's cup. "I don't suppose you did, Andy, but you can't help yourself. Your brain's working on new directions. Enjoy them while you can."

Andy lunged for him, but the trick's cross-wiring effect was so strong now, different sets of muscles reacted to the orders of the brain. He jerked backward and fell flat. Then the convulsions started.

Jorge turned his back. He wiped the wall clean. He set Andy's cup on the desk. He picked up all the printout sheets and cleared the computer. He recoded access to the Laheli records with a new password: WRITE ME A VERBAL CONTRACT.

He heard Andy gasp, looked around. His partner's mouth and throat were working as he struggled to breathe, but his diaphragm had forgotten how to work. Andy was turning blue.

Jorge carried his own cup to the washroom and cleaned it. After drying it carefully, he put it away. Finally, he closed the door of Andy's office. It locked with a soft click.

Jorge looked at the closed door for a moment. He sighed. Why did Andy have to be so difficult? Jorge hoped this would not be too hard on Liann and the kids.

He left the suite, letting the outer door lock behind him, and walked down the firestairs into the hot street.

70

Monday morning no unfamiliar faces appeared at roll-call, but Pass-the-Word Morello read the crimes list in Vradel's place. Janna noticed her colleagues eyeing her with expressions ranging from amused through sympathetic to pitying. That was not very encouraging, particularly after what Wim had told her over the weekend.

Though she had had to work both Saturday and Sunday, she had managed to spend the evenings at the hospital. Watching Wim start the painful process of learning to live with blindness, she had wondered how he was ever going to be able to cope with an entirely alien world. Even while Wim struggled with the problem of feeding himself, however, his voiced worries had all been for her.

"You ought to come along with us. It would be much better than putting up with Mama Maxwell." He shook his bandaged head. "You should have refused to team with him. He's a lunatic. He'll pull you into things you'd never do on your own."

"Like counting coup in the back seat of a watchcar?"

"Yes, like counting coup in the back seat of a watch-car." He chased peas around his plate with his fork. "I think dieticians are sadists." He captured a single pea. "He had me lying to two sergeants, a lieutenant, the division captain, and an I.A. peep, to keep them from learning he carried a shooter walking his beat one night."

Janna stared. "He carried a *shooter?*" She could just bet the man did not want his superiors to know about that. "Why were you in on it?"

71

"I was driving his mobile back-up. The shooter was a beautiful weapon, an old Colt .38 revolver he'd taken off some suspect and never turned in. He must have had it in his runabout and switched it for his Starke after rollcall inspection. I never asked him and he never volunteered that information. What I know for certain is that I got a call from him about three o'clock one morning to pick up a breaker he'd caught going into the back of one of the stores on Stuart Street. I found him in the alley behind the store. The place reeked of gunpowder. The prisoner was a greaser turned albino with fear. He kept screeching that Maxwell had tried to kill him. That fool Maxwell had not only carried the shooter, he'd fired a warning shot at the breaker with it. The ammunition in that shooter was hot-loaded. It must have sounded like a cannon going off. No wonder the breaker was scared shitless."

Janna felt chill. Shooters and warning shots were both against regulations. "Did he tell the booking officer about being shot at?"

Wim snorted. "He told everyone in the station about it. The booking officer had to report it to the sergeant and lieutenant, of course. It went up the line clear to Internal Affairs. Maxwell and I swore there'd never been a shooter. We said the breaker was just trying to make trouble because after his prior list of convictions, he was in big trouble. I'd switched weapons with Maxwell driving in so when the breaker started wailing and weeping about having been put in fear of his life, Maxwell had an innocent Starke to show. Let me tell you, I sweated blood until the furor died. Facing the peeps I was sorry I'd ever agreed to help Maxwell."

"Why did you?"

"Hell, I don't know. I guess because being mobile back-up is almost like being partners. Damn!" The peas kept evading him. With a hiss, he gave up formality and started trapping them against his fork with his fingers. "If the man isn't off his tick, he's at least brain-bent, running on a bugged program."

Janna sucked her lower lip. "Vradel says he has commendations."

72

"He never earned one while I was working with him. I think they promoted him from a walker to car patrol because he talked Irin Vadose into asking for him. That ruined her career." He quit eating and turned his head toward her. His voice was intense. "Jan, he can get you in trouble. Worse, he can get you killed. Shed him as fast as you can."

It was not a good thought to be taking to work with her. Now the squad was looking at her as if she were a sacrificial lamb. Pass-the-Word Morello had been talking, of course. The question in Janna's mind was what had he been telling everyone? After rollcall she caught the squad clerk's eye and crooked a finger at him. "Morello, I'd like to talk to you."

"Your new partner's waiting for you in Vradel's office. The lieutenant said to send you right in after rollcall."

Janna took a deep breath and turned toward Vradel's door, pausing a moment to gather courage before knocking. She felt the eyes of the entire squad on her. She squared her shoulders. She would be senior partner. Surely she could keep control of him. She knocked.

"Come in."

Vradel sat behind his desk, sketching on his memo pad. He looked up. "Morning, Brill." His voice was brisk. He pointed his pencil from Janna to the man across the desk from him. "Brill, Mahlon Maxwell. Maxwell, Janna Brill."

Janna hardly heard the introduction. She was staring in dismay at the man who unfolded from the chair, pushing at heavy-rimmed glasses that were sliding down his nose. Now she understood the pitying looks outside. Mahlon Maxwell was a freak! He was even taller and thinner than she, a fact emphasized by the narrow cut of his green and purple jumpsuit. His head was bald as an egg—a Dutch-chocolate egg. He looked grotesque, like some child's drawing of a black stickman.

"Just call me Mama," he said in a deep, resonant voice. He held out his hand.

She shook it gingerly. She could already hear the

wisecracks the other squadmembers would make, comments on the partnership's being like night and day, or salt and pepper. There were other black/white partners, of course, but none where the partners were so well matched in height and build they could be considered almost a positive and negative of each other. Christ. She wanted to get sick and go home. "Good morning, Sergeant Maxwell."

How did he get away with that head? The hair regs forbid lengths and styles that could obscure vision, but the rules had never been intended to encourage officers to go skinhead, like trippers. Maxwell had to realize how unprofessional it looked. If his baldness were natural, he ought to have a hair transplant.

The glasses puzzled her, too. The only people she knew who wore window frames in preference to contact lenses were those like Sid Chesney, who hoped glasses would add maturity to his babyish face. Why did Maxwell wear his?

"I now pronounce you partners." Vradel picked up a stack of papers. "Put him to work, Brill."

Janna stood looking at him but Vradel kept his head bent over the papers. Janna sighed and led the way out into the squadroom. "Have you ever done investigative work before?"

"I've been Investigator I twice." He pushed his glasses up his nose.

"And was demoted back to patrol both times?" The words were out before she realized it, and with an acid edge she never intended.

He followed her to her table without responding. Pass-the-Word Morello had left a pile of complaint sheets in the middle. Maxwell picked them up and began tapping the edges even. "I take it you don't much like the idea of teaming with me."

"No." Her squadmates were still covertly watching her. She kept her voice down so only Maxwell could hear. "I agreed because I lost my partner and I'm a sucker when the lieutenant says please."

He replaced the complaint sheets in the exact center of the table, squared with the edges. "Lost your partner. Oh." He looked up. The sharpness of the move sent his glasses down his nose. He pushed them back up. "Wim Kiest was your partner? Hell of a thing." He took the pencils and pens out of the cup she used as a holder and began replacing them writing tip down, pencils leaning to her right, pens to her left. "I once worked with Kiest myself."

"He told me."

His eyebrows lifted. She did not need to be a telepath to know what he was thinking. He had to be remembering the shooter incident, and maybe others when Wim had covered for him. He must be wondering how much Wim had told her. Let him wonder.

The newscanner murmured that employee shortages were increasing. The number of unfilled jobs in the U.S. had reached four-point-two percent.

"Maxwell, I'm not hard to live with. I have a good record as Investigator II, and I intend to make Investigator III. Just remember that. If you follow the rules and don't try any of your lightwit stunts with me, we'll get along fine." She sorted through the complaint sheets. "Now, we have six assaults, including one ADW and three batteries, to investigate. If you're done housecleaning, let's get started."

She was turning away when the phone buzzed. She looked around the squadroom. Everyone was buried in papers or away from their tables.

The phone sounded like an angry insect.

"Someone get that," Morello said.

No one moved.

"Brill," Morello said.

She glared at him. "No, damn it." She waved the complaint sheets. "I have a day's work already."

Vradel's head came out of his office. "That better not ring a fourth time."

Janna stabbed the phone on. "Crimes Against Persons, Sergeant Brill."

It was the basset-faced civil servant on the 911 desk. "We have a report of a body in the Sunflower Federal Bank Building. Suite ten-oh-three. They don't know if it's homicide, suicide, or accident."

Janna grimaced. A deader. A fine start for the week. "Send a forensic team and notify the medical examiner. Someone from here will be on the way in a minute." She punched the phone off. "You want me to take it, lieutenant?"

"Go ahead." His head disappeared back into his office. Morello went back to paper shuffling.

Janna looked at Mama Maxwell. "Let's sail."

A watchcar was parked at the curb outside the Sunflower Federal Bank Building's main door. Janna stopped Indian Thirty just behind it and let the Monitor settle to its parking rollers. The guard on duty at the bank door watched them curiously and waved as they came into the lobby.

"Have you seen the team from that watch unit?" Janna asked the guard.

"They went upstairs."

She and Mama took the elevator up to the tenth floor. She found the mobile team waiting by the door of Suite 1003. She knew them by sight though not by name.

"Morning," she said.

They nodded to her. "Morning, sergeant."

Janna read the lettering on the door. *Hazlett and Kellener, Colonial Contractors.* "What do we have?"

"The body of a Mr. Andrew Hamilton Kellener, according to the people inside," one of the watchcar team said. "Maggie—that's Margaret Pfeiffer, the local walker—is inside with them."

Janna went in, Mama Maxwell following. The expensive simplicity of the reception room made Officer Pfeiffer's uniform look as out of place as a cannon at a flower show, but the two men and one woman with her were clustered around the walker's sturdy form.

Janna showed them her identification. "I'm Sergeant Brill from Crimes Against Persons. This is Sergeant Maxwell."

Their eyes regarded him skeptically. The walker looked as if she were straining to keep a straight face. This is a lion? their expressions said.

Janna returned her ID to a sleeve pocket. As she did, she tapped on the flat little microcorder she kept there. "Will someone please tell me who all of you are and what's happened?"

A wispy-haired man with a face like two profiles glued together said in a shaky voice, "I'm Nels Peddicord."

"He's Mr. Kellener's secretary," Officer Pfeiffer replied. She pointed to a beautiful Hispanic man and a plump girl whose hand he was holding. "This is Robert Sandoz, the receptionist, and Lilla Zontine, the files librarian. The body is in that office. Mr. Peddicord found it."

The secretary ran nervous hands through what remained of his hair. "It? That's Mr. Kellener, not an it. I wish he were an it. I hardly recognized him."

Janna and Mama crossed to the indicated door.

"Christ," Mama muttered. "Poor devil."

His had not been an easy death. Andrew Kellener's body lay on its side on the floor beside a big desk. His face was pulled awry and colored dark blue around the lips. His arms and legs were twisted directions human limbs were never designed to bend. He looked as if some giant had practiced knot-tieing with him. Making the situation all the more bizarre were the cartoons on the walls all around and the big drawing of Justice winking from under her blindfold at him.

Janna did not go in. She looked around the office from the doorway, briefly studied the door itself, then came back to Pfeiffer and the office staff.

"How did you happen to find him?"

Peddicord rubbed his hands together. The fingers twined together, came apart, retwined. "I went in to get some papers I knew were on Mr. Kellener's desk."

Janna lifted her brows. "That's a biolock on the door. Was it programmed for you or was it unlocked?"

The secretary's eyes widened. "Neither. When it appeared Mr. Kellener was going to be late, I had Lilla override the lock."

"Override?"

The plump girl spoke. "As files librarian all functions of the computer are my responsibility. Since the lock is programmed through the computer, too, Mr. Kellener had an override command put in, for use in emergencies. We never thought the emergency would be something like—" She clutched the hand of the receptionist. "I'm the only one who knows the command, aside from Mr. Kellener and Mr. Hazlett."

Close to Janna's ear, Mama murmured, "I hadn't noticed it was a biolock."

Janna felt a flash of satisfaction. She saved it to enjoy later. Right now she checked the reception room chrono. "It's eight thirty-five. If Mr. Kellener were late at—" She paused.

Peddicord filled in the time. "Eight fifteen."

"Thank you. If he were late at eight fifteen, what time did he normally come in?"

"A bit before eight."

"You open that early?"

Peddicord nodded. "Many of our clients are working hard to pay for their ships. We open early and close late so they can see us without losing work time. Mr. Kellener worked from eight until about three, or later. Mr. Hazlett and his secretary Ms. Abram work from eleven until six."

Janna heard footsteps in the hall. The team from Forensics arrived towing an equipment case on a leash. The case moved with near floating silence on its glide bearings.

"In there." Janna pointed.

The team opened the case and began removing holo cameras. They carried them into Kellener's office.

"When did you last see Mr. Kellener alive?"

"Saturday afternoon when I left work." Peddicord's eyes followed the forensic team. "When I opened that door and saw him there this morning—what could do that to a man?"

"We'll try to find out. Do you keep any poisons in the office?"

"Not unless you count the chemicals for the duplicator and telescriber," Lilla Zontine said.

"Do you know who his enemies were?" Mama asked.

Peddicord looked shocked. The receptionist and librarian looked startled. too. Janna wished she had a gag to use on Mama. He could have started with genler questions.

"I can't believe anyone hated Mr. Kellener," Peddicord said. "He was a loved and respected man."

As long as they were covering all possibilities, Janna brought up one they would probably like even less than murder. "What had his mood been like lately?"

Now Peddicord was outraged. "You can't mean you think he killed himself? Impossible. Mr. Kellener wasn't that kind of person. His mood had been fine."

"I thought he was worried about something." It was the first thing the receptionist had said. His accent was just enough to be charming.

Peddicord glared at him.

Janna smiled encouragement. "How long had he acted worried?"

"Since Wednesday."

Janna reflected that it must have been a bad day all 'round. First the message came in from the *Invictus,* then Wim was assaulted, and finally something happened to upset Mr. Andrew Hamilton Kellener.

"When you found Mr. Kellener, did you touch anything?"

"Just Mr. Kellener." The secretary swallowed. "I felt for a pulse. When I realized he was cold, I came right back out and called the nine-eleven emergency number from Robert's phone."

That ought to take care of the preliminaries. Janna tapped her sleeve pocket to shut off the microcorder. She headed back for the door of Kellener's office. The forensic team was holotaping the body.

One of them looked around from banging the cup on the desk. "IR scan didn't show anything, not even the body. He's room temperature. You can take a look at him now. Don't touch anything. We're starting to dust for prints."

"Be sure to check the floor and wastebasket. Look for anything that seems out of place and may relate to poison." Where was the medical examiner?

79

As if summoned by her thought, Dr. Sid Chesney walked into the reception room, followed by two aides and a gliding stretcher. Janna smiled at the sight of his earnest, boyish face with its wire-rimmed glasses and struggling attempt at a mustache. His insistence on looking mature always amused her. What did his patients care about how old and wise he looked?

"Did you draw us, Sid, or volunteer?"

"I volunteered when I heard you were the investigating officer." He sent a glance toward Mama Maxwell. "Is that your new—"

Janna nodded. "The body is in here."

Passing her, Sid whispered, "Doesn't look much like a lion, does he? He's beautiful. Invite him dancing with us some night."

"Treece would scratch my eyes out, love." Mama Maxwell beautiful? Janna squinted at the black man, trying to see something she might have missed before. She shook her head; she did not see it.

Inside the office, Sid became totally professional. He knelt beside the body and opened his case. "Shut the door, will you?" The next events were not for the eyes of civilians.

Sid opened a pack and took out half a dozen sensor probes. He pushed the sharp needles into the body to the hub, into thorax, abdomen, neck, and extremities. He clipped leads from the medicorder to the probe hubs and began fiddling with the dials. "Temperature twenty-one degrees, same as the air temperature." He switched modes and flexed the limbs where the probes were located. "No rigor." He pulled out the probes and cleaned them off. "Dead probably between thirty and forty hours, by my rough estimation." He fiddled with the medicorder. "My little black box here narrows it down to thirty-six hours, give an hour or so each way. The post-mortem exam of stomach contents may help narrow the time some more."

Sid straightened the body, palpating each limb as he moved it. "Crepitation in the left radius and ulna, and in the right femur. He has some broken bones, it would seem." He sniffed the dead man's mouth. He

80

eeled back the half-closed lids to check the eyes.
[e looked at the arms, turning them this way and that
a the light. His hands probed the skull. With the aides'
elp he rolled the body onto its side and stripped down
ie jumpsuit. He saw dark marks, bruises, on the
1oulder, ribs, and hip. "Homeostasis indicates he died
a the position he was found. Cyanosis of the lips and
ngers. No bruises, no contusions, no blood. No ex-
ernal signs of trauma."

Mama pushed his glasses up his nose. "You can't
1ean he just lay there and let someone do that to him.
)r do you mean you think he did it to himself?"

Sid looked up with raised brows. "It depends on what
ou mean by doing it to himself. If you find a cow
ead in a field after a storm and she has both femurs
roken, what killed her?"

Mama stared at him. "What does that have to do with
1is?"

"Think about it. What actually killed this citizen
vas suffocation. The cyanosis is definite indication of
noxia. What caused the anoxia, however . . ." He
hrugged.

"Come on, Sid. You must have some idea."

Sid smoothed the hair on his upper lip. "Well, when
ou see his spouse, spouses, or cohab, you might ask if
e ever tripped, particularly on hallucinogens."

Janna blinked. "Hallucinogens?" She stared at the
ody. "Trick?"

"Sure," Mama said. "It must be."

Sid frowned. "He shows anoxia and convulsions. It
ould be. Let me do my post before jumping to con-
lusions, please, sergeant. Okay," he said to the aides.
Package him."

They lifted the body onto the stretcher and zipped
1e cover over it. Mama opened the door for them.
'hey were gliding the stretcher across the reception
oom when Janna noticed a new addition to the group,
woman as quietly elegant as the room itself. She
'as looking at the stretcher with an expression so con-
'olled Janna wondered what storms lay beneath.

81

She lifted her eyes and looked at Janna. "I'm Liann Seaton, Andrew Kellener's wife."

Peddicord said, "I called her after I called you."

"May I see him?"

The aides looked at Janna. She nodded. The body would have to be formally identified and if not here, at the morgue. It was better done here. They unzipped the cover just enough to expose the face.

The woman flinched once, then looked hard at the face. "Yes, that's Andy." She sat down abruptly in the nearest chair.

Sid motioned his people out. They disappeared with the stretcher. Janna reached for her pocket to tap on the microcorder again.

"When did you last see your husband, Ms. Seaton?"

She did not answer immediately. Her mouth was pressed in a trembling line. Her breathing was quick and ragged. Janna waited. After several minutes, Liann Seaton said with careful deliberation, "He's been missing since Saturday evening at fifteen minutes to seven. He said he had an errand here at the office and would be back in time to take the children and me to the late showing of a cinaround show. Yesterday I reported him missing to the Gage division police."

"What kind of errand, did he say?"

"No."

"Had anything happened immediately prior to the time he left that might suggest what the errand was?"

"He had a call from his partner Jorge Hazlett."

Janna exchanged glances with Mama and Officer Pfeiffer. "Do you think he was meeting Hazlett here?"

"I asked him that. But he said Jorge was not involved in his coming down here. He was emphatic about it, said the call had been about something else and talking to Jorge just happened to remind him of something he'd forgotten to do."

The phone chimed. The volume was low. Janna could not hear the party on the other end. The receptionist listened, then said, "I'll tell him." He looked up at the leos. "That was Mr. Hazlett's garage service. I'm supposed to tell him they checked out his car and can't find anything wrong."

"You say Mr. Hazlett comes in about eleven?" Janna asked Peddicord.

"And his secretary."

"Call him for me now, will you, please?"

The receptionist picked a card out of a file and fed it into the phone. Janna moved over by the screen.

The image that came on the screen was that of a modish-looking man approaching middle age. "Mr. Jorge Hazlett, I'm Sergeant Janna Brill of the Shawnee County Police. There's been an accident at your office. Will you come down right away, please?"

Jorge allowed himself some surprise, some concern, nothing more. He met the eyes of the bony, smoky-haired she-lion with what he hoped looked like candidness. "Accident? What kind? Is my partner there?"

"He isn't at the moment."

Jorge admired her smooth lie. It was a much more honorable game when played against people who were also playing. "I'll be down as soon as I catch a bus."

He punched off feeling hot and cold simultaneously. The game was truly on now. Did the she-lion want to break the news to him gently, or with a shock, to see how he would react? Was he already a suspect? He would not know until he reached the office.

While they waited for Hazlett, Janna watched the forensic team finish and pack. Every so often her eyes returned to the winking Justice.

"What's that for?" she finally asked.

Liann Seaton came to the office door. "Judicial humor is my—*was* my husband's hobby. He collected books and poems and cartoons that involved lawyers and the law. I had that Justice drawn for him as a birthday present last year."

Janna toured the office, reading the captions on the cartoons. They were yellowed, ancient things, now sealed in plastic to preserve them from further deterioration. She thought one of the truest ones was the lawyer saying to his client, "You have a pretty good case, Mr. Pitkin; how much justice can you afford?"

Without warning, Mama Maxwell said, "Did your husband trip?"

The woman stiffened. "Never. Andy believed a person should be responsible for his actions. He never took more than one mildly alcoholic drink in an evening and he never used any drugs except dreamtime."

"Never used hallucinogens?" Janna asked.

"Especially not hallucinogens." She was emphatic.

"Did you hear any of the conversation between your husband and his partner Saturday night?"

She shook her head. "Andy took the call in his study."

"Had your husband been worried about anything lately?"

"You don't have to answer that, Ms. Seaton," Peddicord advised her.

She raised her brows at him. "Why shouldn't I? He had some problem, yes. He'd been preoccupied since Wednesday. I asked him about it but he said it was nothing serious yet, and he wasn't ready to talk about it. I left it at that. He has always talked to me when he needed to." She frowned. "You're thinking about suicide? I assure you, whatever the problem, it was nowhere near that serious."

Janna went over the situation with the office staff, but they seemed to feel the same way—even Peddicord, once he finally admitted he had also noticed Kellener worrying. Whatever had been bothering Kellener had been affecting him no more than problems with clients' accounts usually did.

When Jorge Hazlett arrived, nattily dressed in a pioneer gingham jumpsuit, she felt like a recording loop as she prepared to go over everything again. Hazlett was shocked by the news. He held out his arms to Liann Seaton. "Liann, I can't believe. I talked to him just Saturday evening. I'm so sorry. Is there anything I can do?"

She took his hands and squeezed them. "You're a dear, Jorge. I'll let you know. Thank you for asking."

Mama took the offensive. "For openers, you can tell

us about your phone call to Kellener and what went on when you met him later."

Janna bit her lip. The query could have been made with more diplomacy.

Hazlett blinked. "We didn't meet later. There was just the call. That didn't amount to much, either." He dropped Liann Seaton's hands. "There was a client's account I needed to go over with him. I asked him to have the records printed out first thing this morning so we could review it when I came in."

"Sergeant," Liann Seaton turned to Janna, "there will be an inquest, of course. Do you know when?"

Janna shook her head. "As soon as the medical examiner can schedule it—two or three days. You'll be contacted."

"I don't suppose I can have my husband's body until after that."

"The morgue will release it once the autopsy findings are complete. That could be as early as tomorrow."

The widow looked relieved. "Thank you. Is there anything else you need me for?"

"You may go."

"If anything does come up, I'll be at home."

She left.

Mama looked after her with admiration. "That is one nova bibi. Past pluto."

Peddicord bristled. "That is a *lady,* sergeant."

Mama turned and looked down at Hazlett. "You say you went out for the evening. Where?"

Hazlett frowned at the blunt, accusing tone. "Shopping in Whitelakes Mall. I bought a few things, had dinner at Peron's there, and caught a bus home."

"You ride the bus?" Mama sounded skeptical.

"When something is wrong with my car, yes. Saturday the fans sounded strange. I parked the car in a lot and rode the bus."

Janna remembered the call from his service garage. "Your garage says they didn't find anything wrong."

Hazlett looked pleased. "That's good. I'll drive it home tonight, then. I really prefer the Vulcan to a bus."

A Mercedes Vulcan? Janna was impressed.

"What happened to your wrist?" Mama asked.

Hazlett's mouth thinned. "I sprained it pushing the car into a parking slot. I don't think I like your tone, officer. Do you suspect me of something? Check my bank records if you don't believe where I was."

Mama pushed his glasses up his nose. "We will, jon."

Janna interrupted. "Thank you for answering our questions, Mr. Hazlett." She edged toward the door. "We may have more questions later. If not, we'll see you at the inquest."

She sent Pfeiffer back to her beat and the watchcar leos on their way. Mama she backed into a corner of the lobby. "Just what the hell are you trying to do, Maxwell?"

"He killed his partner."

"What?" She stared at him. "Where in the wild blue yonder did you find that idea? There's nothing yet to suggest anyone *killed* Kellener at all."

Mama shrugged. "Not yet, but there will be. Bibi, I've never seen a man who was such walking lion meat. Hazlett reeked of killing the moment he walked into the office."

"Smelled like a killer?" Janna snorted.

"Yes. I've had twelve years on the force. I get these feelings about people. I'm not usually wrong. You know investigative work is an art, not a science. Intuition is a valid and valuable tool."

"Which has to be backed up by scientific method to gather evidence." She spoke carefully, as if to a retarded child. "You have a law degree. You ought to know the rules of evidence. Right now anything we take or hope to take to court has to be impeccable. This is an election year. John Dias wants to be D.A. for another term before he moves on to higher government office. He isn't prosecuting any cases these days that don't guarantee him a conviction. If we could take him something like the San Francisco Terrorist prosecutions that put Dannel Lippe on the road to the White House, he'd love us. You take him a *feeling,* though, a gut reaction, and your next transfer won't be to Cullen Village; it'll be to Silver Lake or Pauline."

"You were recording the interviews, of course. At least we can check Hazlett's voice for stress and take a look at his bank records to see just how good his alibi is."

"Take a look at—christ." Janna grimaced in disgust. "What do you intend to list as probable cause? Forget it; the authorization request will never pass Lieutenant Vradel. We'll check the stress indicators in the voices, if you want, but first we're going to look for the security guards on duty in this building Saturday and Sunday and find out what they know, if anything."

The light from the bright street outside was reflecting off his scalp. A skinhead leo. He was starting to show his peculiarities of thinking already. With a chill, she remembered Wim's words. *He can get you in trouble. Worse, he can get you killed.* Now she believed it. She suddenly felt as if she were strapped to a time bomb. She crossed her fingers, hoping she would be able to get loose before it went off.

CHAPTER SIX

Jorge Hazlett had no thoughts of time bombs. He was exuberant. It was a struggle to keep a solemn face. Thanks to Andy's philanthropies, he and Andy were well known in the city. Within an hour after the police left, newscanner station reporters were calling. They came by to see the death scene and to interview him. They taped him in Andy's office. The incongruity of the winking Justice fascinated them.

"No, we don't know how it happened yet," he told them. "It's a great shock. Andy and I have been like

87

brothers since law school. His death leaves a hole in my life that won't soon be filled."

"No, I'm not closing the office. We have people who are depending on us. Andy was vitally concerned about the hopes and aspirations of our clients. He considered colonial contracting almost a holy mission, a service to people in whom the pioneer spirit still burns. I think remaining open is a more fitting tribute and memorial than closing in mourning."

By afternoon, he had the pleasure of seeing himself on the newscanner channels. He watched the broadcasts with satisfaction. He had photographed well. The views shown were all flattering. He thought his words sounded elegant.

Marca Laclede felt satisfaction, too. She and Tarl met in the back of the store where he worked to divide the jewelry Tarl collected from the doppelgänger Sunday morning. She let herself be talked out of the Lion's Den for the meeting. Even she had to concede that any lions hanging around the Den this time of day were likely to be curious about a pile of jewelry.

She tried on a sapphire bracelet and held it up to the light. "I must say the sligh followed instructions well enough. He bought what we ordered him to and wasn't distracted by the flash baubles. What did he buy for himself, do you know? Food and clothes, as usual?"

"He said he had dinner at Peron's and bought two novalon suits."

Her brows went up. "He treated himself better than most."

"He bought some toys for his kid, too."

"Toys?" She laughed. "I wonder what Mr. Jorge Hazlett will think of finding purchase receipts for toys. I'd like to hear his explanation for them."

Tarl smiled dryly. "He's going with younger girls these days?"

Marca shrieked in delight. "Tarl, that's beautifully wicked. I wish you'd joke more often, the way you used to when I was in college."

"Things have changed since college." His head bent over the jewelry.

She looked around at the filthy storeroom, thinking of the places he had worked then. "Not all that much. Why do you still work this way? With what we've made off the doppelgängers, you could afford not to work for a while at all."

"Restaurants don't take barter, and even if they did, how would they make change?"

"What *do* you do with your share?"

He held up a pearl pendant. "I'm saving to buy a colonial share."

She stared at him. "Share? You can't really want to leave Earth. There's no way of knowing what's out there."

"Freedom is out there." He dropped the pendant in his pocket.

"Freedom?" She sniffed.

He shrugged. "I don't expect you to understand. Just let me know when you need another doppelgänger."

Owan wore one of his new suits to work. Since he ran the dishcleaning machine for the Pioneer's Pleasure, his finery came in for some kidding. The other club employees raised brows.

"Now we know; you aren't a sligh at all. You're a rich eccentric. No sligh can afford novalon."

Owan answered the kidding with a smile. Some days the sarcasm of the legitimate employees stung, but today it was as if the blue of the suit were a force field insulating him from their slings and arrows.

"Where did you get it? Did you steal it?" The bartender was curious.

After the question had been asked several times, in different ways, Owan said, "I have a friend who gave it to me."

With a glow of pleasure, he remembered the previous afternoon. Tesha had been ecstatic about the computer and the doll, particularly the doll.

"It's just what I've wanted, Daddy!"

A faint line had appeared between Clio's brows.

"Where did you get those, Owan? No store owner ever gives away merchandise like that."

Her suspicions had almost spoiled the afternoon. He had been hoping she would not ask that question. He had never lied to Clio. They were proud their relationship was an honest one. There were so few people a sligh could trust completely and be completely honest with. He tried to find an answer that was not a lie.

"I did a favor for someone. He let me put a few items on his card in return."

"A few items? Owan these things have to be worth several hundred bankcredits. What kind of favor was it?"

He bit his lip in anguish. "I can't tell you that."

Her eyes widened in horror. "It was illegal, wasn't it? Oh, Owan . . . you earned toys for Tesha by doing something illegal?"

"It wasn't very illegal. I wouldn't get involved in something really serious."

"If it isn't serious, why can't you tell me about it?"

He sighed. "Because I promised I wouldn't say anything to anyone. Clio, I won't get in trouble. Please let Tesha keep the toys."

He had suffered agonies while she debated, but finally she gave in. After that, she had not pressed him about how he had earned the toys, either. The rest of the afternoon had been a delight. He had not even minded the heat. He had worn the yellow suit and felt as if it were made of gold. When they went out to dinner, which Clio paid for, he felt almost like the head of a real family with a marriage contract and everything. He had sat with his head up. It was even better than dinner at Peron's had been, where the waiters had bowed and *sir'd* him until he felt like a real citizen. The yellow novalon suit had impressed them, too.

The bartender of the Pioneer's Pleasure interrupted Owan's daydreaming. He called into the kitchen, "Hey, sligh, you're on the newscanner."

All pleasure disappeared. Owan's heart and stomach turned to ice. On the newscanner? How? His body wanted to bolt out the door, but he fought to resist the urge. Pushing his reluctant feet, he forced himself to leave the kitchen and go watch the newscanner.

"It isn't really you," the bartender said when he appeared. "But it's some jon who looks enough like you to be your twin. Weird, isn't it? Just think, you could probably go change places with him, like in *The Prince and the Pauper*. How would you like that?"

Owan's tongue was frozen solid in his mouth. The novalon suit felt as if it were constricting around him, suffocating him. His hands sweated. "No, thank you." His voice was a ragged squeak.

He lifted his eyes to the newscanner set above the bar. The man on the tape was Jorge Hazlett. Owan did not listen to the story at first. He was too busy wondering how many people would see it and think how much alike this man and a sligh named Owan were. Would Clio see it?

". . . a more fitting tribute and memorial than closing in mourning," Hazlett said.

Mourning? Owan started listening.

The voice-over announcer continued. "Post-mortem examination is expected to be performed this afternoon but until it is finished, officials in the medical examiner's office refuse to speculate on the cause of death."

"Whose death?" Owan asked.

"A jon named Andrew Kellener. He and that fellow who looks like you were partners—colonial contractors. I met that dead one once. He contracted for the ship my sister emigrated in."

Owan reached up and tapped the replay button. The story started again. He watched it through, ice creeping out from his heart to his hands and feet. He had trouble breathing. He used a citizen's card and that same night the citizen's partner died mysteriously. Maybe it was just a coincidence, but—Owan swallowed—what if it were not?

He crept back to the kitchen on legs that shook. His stomach churned. He wanted to throw up. Could he have helped murder a man?

The autopsy on Andrew Kellener was over by three o'clock. Sid called up to the squadroom to tell Janna.

"Thanks, Sid. We'll be right down."

She tapped Mama on the shoulder. He was watching Jorge Hazlett on the newscanner. "Sanctimonious bastard. Look at him, bibi. Grief-stricken, indeed."

"Come on." She tugged at him.

He came, still grumbling. "He kills his partner and now he's parading all over the newscanner channels shedding crocodile tears. Makes me sick."

Janna tried to ignore him. "Did you read the report on the analysis of the contents of that cup found on Kellener's desk?"

That distracted him momentarily. "No. What did it say?"

They passed the medical examiner himself, Dr. Sandor Kolb, who was shuffling along the hall muttering to himself. As he had every time Janna had ever seen him, he wore an aged gray jumpsuit that draped around him in great wrinkles.

"Does he really spend his nights here, like they say, sleeping in the cooler drawers?" Mama whispered.

"I always heard it was the autopsy tables." He certainly looked as if he did.

"I don't understand how he keeps his job. He looks senile."

"Not always," Janna said.

They found Sid fiddling with gas chromatographs and electron microscopes in the laboratory. He peered over the tops of his glasses at them. "It was trick, all right. Massive overdose. Ingested, probably."

"Put in his food?" Mama asked.

Sid shook his head. "He'd eaten about an hour before he died but he couldn't have gotten the trick that way. The stuff is absorbed too fast. At most he would have had to have taken it within five or ten minutes of the time he died. A dose that big would have hit him hard and fast. The convulsions were so severe they broke his bones."

Mama pushed his glasses up his nose. *"Oh!* Like the

cow. She was hit by lightning and the muscle contractions broke her legs."

Sid arched his brows. "Right. Very good." He stacked up several graphs. "Other findings are what I expected. There were hemorrhages in the mucous membrane of the trachea and on the pericardium. It confirms that what actually killed him was anoxia, like all trick OD's. Now all you have to find out is how he got the trick."

"Easy," Janna said. "Forensics says there were traces of trick in the cup we found on the desk."

Sid considered that. "So the next question—answering a question just changes the question, doesn't it—is who put it in the caff?"

"Hazlett did," Mama said.

Sid peered over his glasses at Mama. He looked at Janna, lifting a brow.

She shook her head. "The reasoning process by which he arrived at that conclusion is called fantasizing."

"I'm not fantasizing." Mama's voice climbed toward falsetto. "The man reeks of murder. If we check his bank records, I'm betting we'll find they don't support his alibi."

Janna rolled her eyes. Christ. He certainly was persistent.

"Well . . ."

The long syllable was Sid's. Janna looked sharply at him.

Sid smiled a cringing dog smile. "Why would a man take that much by himself? If he wanted to trip, he would have to be stupid to use a dose that size. Even if he were trying to kill himself, he wouldn't have had to take anywhere near that amount, not if he understood the drug. Becoming a pretzel is a painful way to go, and most suicides don't like pain. He was probably dosed by someone else."

"Thanks, Judas."

Sid winced at the acid in her voice. "But maybe he took it by accident," he added.

Mama sniffed. "Of course. There was a big jar of it

93

in the cabinet with the caff supplies and he thought it was brown sugar."

Janna made a try at introducing scientific method into the conversation. "None of the security guards saw Hazlett in the building Saturday."

"What does that prove? None of them saw Kellener either. We need to look at Hazlett's bank records, I tell you."

Janna gritted her teeth. "Maxwell, what we need to do is clear six assaults. Let's not look for more work. Thanks, Sid. I'll see you this evening . . . if I get caught up here."

It was too late to visit the complainants in person, so she called each by phone. That cleared a couple in a hurry. One of the simple assaults decided he did not want to press charges. One of the batteries punched off in fury when Janna explained that rape was no longer a criminal charge. Sexual assaults were all prosecuted as batteries.

She tried to talk the ADW out of prosecuting. The case was very poor.

The complainant insisted. "He had a knife. I want that son of a bitch put away."

"Yes, ma'am." Janna punched off with a sigh. "We'll follow it up, collect our points for the squad, then Dias or one of his assistants will refuse to take it to court."

She could not reach the other simple assault. She did reach the other batteries, however, and both men wanted to prosecute.

Punching off after the last call, Janna totaled it up. "Two cleared. That leaves us one simple, the ADW, and two batteries to work on tomorrow, plus your obsession with Hazlett, and whatever new complaints Morello gives us. After that, all we have is half a kilo of paperwork—my very favorite part of police work. Did you ever stop to think how many billions of words police departments turn out each year?"

Mama shuddered.

Janna started on the day's paperwork. She would go

visit Wim, she decided, and cry on his shoulder a bit. Did colonists have miserable days or did they find endless satisfaction in digging their toes and fingers in the soil and making things grow?

She slid a side glance at Mama Maxwell. He was fussing with the pens and pencils again, and shaking papers into perfect stacks. She rolled her eyes. Maybe she should ask for a special appointment with the tick tech. She did not know if her sanity would last the two weeks until her regular visit.

Owan tried to rationalize away the fear the news story started. As he washed glasses, he used every argument he could think of. The death of the man's partner was a coincidence—no concern of his. No one knew who he was, except Tarl. Not even Tarl knew where to find him. If anything should come of it, he was safe. No matter how nearly he convinced himself of his own safety, however, he could not avoid the thought that he might have helped kill a man. If nothing else mattered, that fact would continue to gnaw at him. Along with a fear of identation, his parents had instilled in him a fervent belief in the sacredness of life.

He was not sure quite when he first considered asking Jorge Hazlett about it. He did not like the idea—memory of the citizen's cold eyes tied his stomach in knots—but he needed reassurance that the death had no connection to his using Hazlett's card. All else was secondary. Hazlett was the best person, the only person, to give him that reassurance.

Owan asked the bartender for a vending token.

"You have to call someone now?" The bartender waved at the customers starting to come into the club for after work drinks and early dinner. "We need you running the washer." He gave Owan the token. "Make it quick."

Owan looked up Hazlett's business number. On the newscanner Hazlett had said something about keeping the office open the usual hours because his partner would have wanted it that way. He implied that meant working much later than most people.

It suddenly occurred to Owan that it might be bad if anyone else saw how much he looked like Hazlett. He put his hand over the screen just as a willowy, dark-haired woman answered the phone. "Jorge Hazlett, please."

"Who may I say is calling?"

What could he say? Hazlett did not know his name. Owan could not very well announce himself as a doppelgänger. "I met Mr. Hazlett Saturday night. He'll remember me."

Jorge was clearing up his desk in preparation for closing the office when Nina Abram announced the call. "A very mysterious man," she said. "He says you met him Saturday night. He wants to talk to you."

A surge of fury rose up through Jorge. There was only one person it could be. So the sligh would be no trouble? Here it was only two days and the sligh was already after him. He would tell the Laclede woman to take care of him and take care of him fast. This was not supposed to happen. The Pawn was not supposed to move like this.

He might as well see what the creature wanted, though.

He stabbed on the phone. It was the sligh all right, looking overdressed in a novalon suit. "How dare you call me!"

The sligh quaked visibly on the screen. "I'm sorry." His voice was little more than a whisper. "I don't want to cause trouble, but—"

Here it came. "But—" Jorge prompted.

The sligh took a breath. "I saw the news story about your partner. That didn't have anything to do with—with you know, did it? I've been worrying about that. I don't want to be a party to—to—"

Well thank god he was not blurting out everything over the phone. "No, of course it didn't have anything to do with Andy. That was just coincidence."

The sligh chewed his lip. "You're sure."

What a miserable piece of humanity the creature was. "Of course I'm sure!"

The sligh flinched again. "Yes, of course."

Belatedly, Jorge started thinking. The rabbit was frightened. He wanted to be comforted. Without that comfort, there was no guessing what erratic behavior might result. The man was therefore dangerous to him. Another threatened check. Again, there were three ways to deal with it.

Jorge swallowed his anger and made himself smile. "I can see you're upset. Naturally. I'm upset myself. That's why I'm snapping at you. I tell you what I'll do. Just for your peace of mind, I'll meet you again, same place, ten o'clock. I'll show you what I was doing that evening. Will that help?"

The sligh grinned in relief. "It certainly would." His forehead creased in concern again. "It won't inconvenience you or ruin something for you to show me, will it?"

What a question. Jorge lied. "Quite the contrary. Now you just relax and I'll see you later."

He stabbed the phone off with a violence that scooted it halfway across the desk. He wanted to slam his fist through the desk top. That unmitigated fool! Jorge was going to tell Laclede just what he thought of her blithe promises about troubleless slighs. Before he touched the phone, however, he caught himself. No, he had better not tell her. All the rabbit wanted was a clean conscience. The woman would be the one to see the possibilities in blackmail. Jorge would deal with the sligh by himself.

He considered what method to use. There was no doppelgänger for an alibi this time, so he would have to make himself as invisible as possible. Transportation could be by his car. Vulcan sportsters were not common, though; he would have to disguise the car somehow.

Changing the color was impractical. So was trying to hide the fact it was a Vulcan. If only he could think of a way to change the license number.

He studied the plates on vehicles in the building garage as he walked through to his Vulcan. Some numbers were similar to others. Eights and threes had the same basic shape. He squinted at his own license. Perhaps the numbers could be altered.

On the way home he stopped and bought a roll of plastic tape the same color as the plate background.

At home he went through his closet. He found the oldest, most nondescript clothes he had and put them on. He hunted up a pocket flask and half filled it with his best whiskey. Then he went to his wall safe again. Half the remaining trick went into the flask. He capped the flask and shook it.

While Janna Brill sat in a hospital room across the city listening to Wim Kiest extoll the virtues of a planet named Champaign and Owan Desfosses ran tableware through the sonics of the dishcleaner and Marca Laclede hummed a jivaqueme tune while she painted lace on her arms and legs, preparing to go dancing, Jorge Hazlett paced his house, waiting for nine thirty.

The wait seemed eternal. The seconds flicked with the crawl of hours. He almost cheered when the chrono finally read half past the hour.

He took the steps to the garage two at a time and vaulted over the door into the cockpit of the Vulcan, just missing the center bar of the safety frame. He backed the car out across the lawn to the street. The fans purred like some great cat.

Jorge forced himself to drive slowly, obeying all traffic regulations. The car felt impatient under his hands. He was impatient, too. He wanted to wrap up the fans and sail, to meet the sligh and deal with him, to get it over with. Instead, he restrained himself. Tonight was no time to be cited for traffic violations.

He passed several police cars on the way. The reflective stripes on their sides flared brilliantly red as his lights caught them. He smiled and waved at the leos in them.

He swung into the Sunco lot a full ten minutes before the sligh was supposed to meet him. So far, all was well. He climbed out of the car and, picking up a hand light, squatted down on his heels behind the Vulcan. He tore pieces of tape from the roll, which he carefully pressed over part of the numbers on his license plate. A four became a one, and an eight, a three. He worked quickly, with an ear alert for any approaching footsteps. It would not do to be seen doing this.

No one came. He sat back to admire his handiwork. License SHH 41348 had become SHH 11313. The alteration would not fool anyone on close inspection. The tape was not even a perfect color match. He hoped it would pass casual observation, though.

He had just time enough to put tape and hand light back in the car when he saw someone stop at the entry gate and lift a bicycle over the barrier. The newcomer slid around the end of the barrier and picked up his bike.

"Mr. Hazlett?" It was the voice of the sligh.

"Yes." Jorge made his voice hearty. "Welcome."

The sligh chained the bicycle to a rack. "I'm really grateful to you for doing this."

"Think nothing of it. I might need to use your services again, so I want us to be friends. Get in the car. I'll show you where I spent my recess time."

Owan climbed over the airfoil skirt into the cockpit. He sank into the deep seat with a thrill of pleasure. He had never even dreamed of riding in a car like this. It looked designed for interstellar flight, not ground travel. "Beautiful."

"It is," Jorge agreed. "The solar batteries give the car an almost unlimited range. Instead of mirrors, it has a screen for a hundred and eighty view to the rear and sides, adjustable for normal or magnified viewing. Vibration is minimal."

Jorge switched on the fans. Owan felt the car tremble, then float upward, off its parking rollers. What a world of difference there was between a car like this and Clio's runabout.

Jorge guided the Vulcan toward the street. "I was as shocked as anyone to learn about my partner this morning. I even found myself feeling guilty about him. While I was out enjoying myself, Andy was dying. It was a terrible thought."

Owan ran his hand down the interior paneling of the

door and over the dash. He caressed the seats. They were real leather. "Do you know how your partner died?"

"A drug overdose, they think." Jorge shook his head. "I never thought Andy was a ulysses. I guess people never know about their friends. They have secret inner lives we never touch."

The night was close and hot, but the air rushing into the open cockpit of the sportster felt cool. Owan reveled in it.

Jorge headed the car across I-70 into east Topeka and down into the Oakland area. He pulled the flask from his pocket. "Care for a drink?"

Owan shook his head. "No, thank you."

Jorge would not let himself frown. "It's fine whiskey." He uncapped it with one hand and tilted it up, pretending to drink. Not one drop passed the tight seal of his mouth. He lowered the flask and passed it to Owan. "Try just a sip."

Owan took the flask. He looked at it. He never drank much; alcohol and drugs were luxuries for slighs. Here he was in a fine suit, though, riding in one of the best cars made, being offered a drink by a rich citizen. Why not enjoy the experience while it lasted?

"Thanks." He tilted up the flask.

The liquor was good. He hardly tasted it until it was halfway down his throat, then a low heat spread up and down his throat and out of his stomach through his body. He took a few more swallows and passed the flask back to his new good friend and twin Jorge Hazlett.

Jorge pretended to drink and passed the flask back. Owan had another drink.

"What did you do down here?" Owan asked.

"I'm helping some sligh friends set up a school." The lie came easily. "I come down and teach law every few weeks. Lately, though, I've been afraid the lions have heard about the school. I didn't want them tracking me, so I decided to seem to be somewhere else."

Owan began experiencing some of the strangest

sensations of his life. The night was filled with a riot of color, and his nose drank in smells of indescribable deliciousness. He tried to tell Jorge about them but the words would not come out right. He giggled. So this was what it was like to be drunk. No wonder citizens liked to drink.

Then without warning the night was filled with excruciating pain. His body wrenched.

As soon as the sligh started babbling nonsense, Jorge looked for a place to dump him. He turned the Vulcan up Jacquot Street.

What had possessed the city officials to give the name of that most elegant of Presidents to this derelict street, Jorge could not begin to imagine. The ghost of the man must shudder to see his memorial. Weeds grew up through cracked and tilted paving, so high they scraped the bottom of the car. On either side, twentieth-century wood frame houses moldered in tanglewood yards.

Jorge eyed the houses. An empty one would be a good dumping place. Most of them along here looked empty, but he had no way of telling in passing which were unoccupied and which merely without lights.

He bit his lip. The sligh's convulsions were becoming louder and more violent. He was starting to shout nonsense. Jorge had to find an empty place soon.

Ahead, he saw a boarded-up store on a corner. Jorge stopped the car and was out of the cockpit even before it finished settling to the ground in the trash-choked area that had once been the store's parking area. He dragged the sligh out and around the back of the building. He hoped there would be a back door he could force open.

There was. Even better, the door was already open. Jorge hauled the sligh inside.

The air assaulted him like a kick in the stomach. Jorge gagged. Neighborhood trippers and winos evidently used the building for a latrine. In the stifling hot interior, the stench of drugs and alcohol mixed thickly with the reek of urine, excrement, and vomit. Jorge dropped his burden on the floor and bolted back into the outside air.

He stood for several minutes waiting for his stomach to settle back in place before he made himself edge close enough to the door to pull it closed. He was careful to scrape his ankle boots thoroughly clean before climbing back in the car.

Going home he used the same care he had driving down to the Sunco lot. He checked each street to make sure there were no police cars on it before driving that way. He drove through to Sardou and headed west over the Kansas River into north Topeka. There he stopped at an all-night automatic car wash where he stripped off the tape over his license numbers and scrubbed the Oakland dust from the Vulcan. From there he went to a bar for a drink. It took three to clear the stench of the building from his memory. When he felt clean again, he drove home.

The flask was rinsed out and put away. His clothes went into the laundry. Only then did he let himself relax. With relaxation came exultation. The check had been successfully countered. A dangerous Pawn was captured. Now there was only the inquest and the government inquiry into the Laheli Company to face.

CHAPTER SEVEN

Lieutenant Vradel leaned out of his office and pointed at Janna. He crooked his finger. "Brill, in here."

Janna picked up the complaint sheets and wound her way between the tables toward his door. Mama was late. He had not been at rollcall. Maybe she had gotten lucky. Maybe he had resigned during the night.

She closed Vradel's door behind her. "Yes, sir?"

Vradel held up a sheet of paper. Above it, his eyes had the glitter of winter sun on ice. "What's this?"

She leaned forward and peered at it. Oh, god. It was a request to examine Jorge Hazlett's bank records. Mama must have submitted it after she left yesterday. She looked to see what he had given as "probable cause."

"Subject is under suspicion for murder. It is necessary to verify his whereabouts during the time period involving the commission of the crime."

She winced.

"Do you know what this is about?"

Janna grimaced. "Unfortunately, yes." She told him about Mama Maxwell's conviction Hazlett was a murderer.

Vradel listened in silence. He chewed on his mustache and doodled on his memo pad.

"Lieutenant, I'm sorry about that request. I didn't know he was going to submit it. It looks like I can't control him. Maybe you'd better team me with someone else."

Vradel raised a brow. "I know he must be frustrating after Kiest."

That was an understatement.

"But all new partnerships need time to shake down. One day is hardly a fair trial of a team. Maxwell has turned in some brilliant police work during his yo-yo career. That's why he hasn't been fired. The brass want us to encourage street officers to be innovative and imaginative."

"Maxwell is imaginative, all right."

Vradel's mustache twitched. "A bit more so than Paget ever intended, probably, but some of his best work has come out of intuitive leaps. What he needs to do is learn to follow up his inspirations with solid evidence. Now you turn in careful investigative work that follows procedure, spirit and letter. I'm hoping the two of you will mesh well."

Her stomach felt somewhere in the vicinity of her knees. "So I'm stuck with him?"

"For a while."

Even five minutes would be an eternity. She pointed at the request. "What about that?"

Vradel wrote across it. "Denied. Make him produce a good reason, a documentable reason, for suspecting Hazlett, then I'll okay a bank check. All right; that's all."

She went back into the squadroom feeling ill. So the lieutenant wanted to make a permanent team of them.

The newscanner was running a press conference held by President Lippe the day before. Smiling, he was fending off questions about his plans for dealing with Israeli aggression in the Middle East.

Mama Maxwell was still nowhere in sight.

"Have you seen that black rack who was with me yesterday?" Janna asked Maro Desch.

Desch's reply was a wordless snarl.

Janna backed off. "Sorry. I didn't know Maxwell had made such fierce enemies already."

"It isn't your partner," Desch said. "It's atropine. I have a suspect in there." He pointed at the interview room. "He knows his pupil response to questions about a certain armed robbery is going to convict him so he took atropine before coming down. His pupils look like this." He made a circle with his thumb and forefinger. "But I'll fix him." He chuckled. "The deek can just sit in there until the atropine wears off. Then I'll ask my questions."

Mama Maxwell banged through the squadroom door. Janna winced. His suit this morning was orange and green paisley. A strip of graph tape hung from his hand.

"Stress, bibi," he said triumphantly. He came between the tables like a broken-field runner to thrust the tape at her. "That's a stress recording of Hazlett's voice. This section is his answer about the phone call Saturday night. It's full of stress. He was lying through his teeth."

Janna glanced at the tape, then looked at a bulge in the breast pocket of his jumpsuit. "Did you have Forensics run the other voices, too?"

Mama frowned. "Yes, but—"

She held out her hand. "Give them to me."

His frown deepened, but he opened the pocket and handed over three cylinders of rolled paper.

Janna unrolled the one marked "Seaton." She looked at it. "Stress, Mama. Did Liann Seaton also murder her husband?"

Mama shrugged. "Well, she's grief stricken."

"But you know for an absolute fact that the stress in Hazlett's voice is from lying. Crap. The stress alone proves nothing."

"I was watching his pupil response while you were talking to him and—"

"You know as well as I do that what you saw is only helpful to you." She tossed the tapes on their table. "Pupil responses count only when we have Hazlett videotaped so the experts can read him."

"Then let's bring him down for an interview."

"Forget it!"

Every eye in the squadroom turned on her.

"Need a referee?" Desch asked.

"No, thanks." She lowered her voice to a hiss. "We have six assaults to work on today. Let's go."

"Just a minute. I have to see the lieutenant about—"

"He saw me," she interrupted. "Your request is denied. *Denied!*" It gave her pleasure to say it. She pointed to the door. "Sail."

Two hours later she wished they had stayed at the office and interviewed Jorge Hazlett. Two hours later she was crouching behind a watchcar in the furnace sun with sweat soaking her jumpsuit. Bullets kicked up dust beyond her. It was her fault, too. She should have known better than to let Mama drive the car. She should have anticipated that something like the "man with a firearm" report on the radio would prove too much for him to resist.

As he had revved the fans and slewed Indian Thirty around in the middle of the street, she protested. "We're not a watchcar or jane unit. It isn't our job to answer calls. Do you know how much more paperwork this will make for us?"

He had not been listening. The car shot ahead and she could only hold on, swearing. She was no Bible cultist, but she prayed a little, too. Mama was not so much driving as piloting the Monitor.

"Slow down, damn it," she yelled at him. "We don't have to go this fast. Are you so afraid of missing the excitement? *Maxwell.*"

He had to be deaf.

They plowed through traffic with runabouts and bicycles fleeing before their siren. One runabout cut aside too sharply. The blast of its fans caught a bicycle. The bike wavered and tipped, throwing the rider into the Monitor's path. There was no time to stop or swerve around him. Janna prayed he had the sense to stay flat.

The Monitor skimmed over him. When Janna looked back, he was scrambling for his bike. Janna started breathing again.

The car rocketed on.

The man with the firearm was in one of the new apartment complexes in the lower end of the Highland Park division. Three black-and-whites and two jane units had reached the scene ahead of them, pulled up in front of one building. Janna saw a flash in a third-floor window. Mama parked the Monitor out of range around the corner of the next building and they climbed out to join a jane team and uniformed team standing with two frightened-looking women.

One of the women was the apartment manager. The other was the cohab of the man with the shooter. "He isn't a criminal; he's just tripping," she said. She was obviously afraid for him. "He was having a good flight and all of a sudden it went bad. He started yelling that someone was after him. He grabbed a rifle and started shooting out the window, saying he'd never let himself be taken. I slipped out the door and called a doctor. Why did you come instead?"

"Tripping on what?" one of the uniformed leos asked.

The girl bit her lip. "Dust."

A jane sighed. "With everything that's legal, why do people still use the forbidden junk?"

"Where did he get the shooter?" Janna asked.

"Roy collects guns. He has all kinds of antiques clear from World War I."

"I suppose he keeps them all in working condition and has ammunition for them."

The girl nodded. She chewed her lower lip.

The leos looked at each other. "So much for sitting under cover until he runs out of bullets."

"Has anyone tried talking him down?" Mama asked. "Dusters are suggestible."

"We tried. We tried using his cohab here, and none—"

The uniformed officer was interrupted by a shot and a yell of pain. As one, the leos spun toward the sound. A uniformed leo collapsed behind one of the watchcars and huddled groaning, holding his shoulder. Beneath his fingers, the iron gray of his uniform turned rusty red.

His partner hit her ear button, yelling for an ambulance. Keeping down, she reached into their car for the shotgun racked there. In another minute everyone was bringing out shotguns and moving up behind the cover cars.

The girl screamed. "Don't kill him! He doesn't mean to hurt anyone!"

"Don't damage the building," the manager called.

"Shit," the partner of the wounded leo spat in disgust.

"Isn't it wonderful?" someone muttered. "The public demands aggressive law enforcement and then expects us to ask for a national referendum before we can shoot back at some deek who's trying his best to kill us."

A bullet whined off the street behind them.

"How about gas?"

No one had any pellets, only some canisters of K-12. They peered up at the window. It was one of the new building designs. Instead of one single expanse of

107

glass, the windows consisted of four vertical strips separated by sections of stone, perfect for firing out through, terrible for hitting from the outside.

"How about going in the back and kicking in his door?" Janna asked.

"No back door," came the answer.

And none of them was going to slide through those window slits.

"There's some cover under the balconies," Mama said. "I could get up on that first balcony and go in through the balcony door, then on up the stairs."

"Alone?"

"One leo is a smaller target than two. Give me one of the K-12 canisters and I'll take it with me."

Janna snapped, "You'll get yourself killed."

He ignored her. He settled his glasses, took a can of gas, and was off running toward the building on an erratic course. A bullet kicked up dust near his feet. Janna pumped a shell into the breech of her shotgun and fired at the window.

Masonry chips flew. Somewhere off to the side of them the manager called angrily and the girlfriend screamed, "Roy!"

"Is your partner a rock jock or trying to be a hero?"

"He's brainbent." She pumped in another shell and kept her sights on the window. "The old Wyatt Earp syndrome."

Mama flattened against the building. The balcony was between him and the tripper. He leaped for the railing. His fingers locked around the uprights. Grunting, he pulled himself up and over the edge.

The balcony door was locked. Janna saw him trying it without success. A bullet struck the metal railing near him. The shot was answered by four shotgun blasts and screams from the manager and girlfriend.

Mama put a booted foot through the glass. In another minute he had the door open and was inside.

The leos crouched behind the watchcars, waiting. More units were arriving. It was beginning to look like rollcall at the station. One of the arrivals was the beta squad sergeant. The uniformed leos in her squad filled her in on what was happening. The ambulance sailed in. With the rest of them covering him, the wounded officer was helped over to it.

Janna frowned at the building. What was Mama doing that took so long?

A shooter went off three times in rapid succession. Janna stiffened. No bullets were coming their way. They must all have been fired inside.

The sergeant slapped four leos on the shoulder. "Go."

They all raced for the door, shotguns in hand. Janna pounded right behind them. She could hear the girlfriend still pleading with them not to shoot her cohab and the manager shrilly forbidding them to cause any more damage. They scrambled up the stairs.

On the third floor the apartment door was open, its lock smashed. Mama Maxwell was on his hands and knees in the opening, gasping hoarsely. His glasses lay lenses down on the floor beside him. The sergeant hauled him backward by the seat of his jumpsuit. He landed rolling and stopped against the wall, clutching at his throat. She stepped over him into the apartment.

"Mama!" Janna was beside him. Was he hit? She saw no blood. What was wrong with him? "Are you hurt?"

He just lay with his eyes squeezed shut, gasping as though he was strangling. Janna tore at the collar of his suit. Had his larynx been crushed?

"Mama, what happened?"

The sergeant came back out of the apartment. "The gas got him. Bring him out."

Two leos moved in. They reappeared with a tightly curled, whimpering knot of humanity who was trying to pull away from their grip and crawl into himself. They carried him down the stairs.

"Good old K-12," the sergeant said. "Replaces fight with fright." She knelt beside Janna. "Here. I'll help you with him."

Janna picked up Mama's glasses. They pulled his arms around their necks and, between them, carried him down the stairs to the ambulance. The medic took

109

one look and slapped the oxygen mask over Mama's face.

The apartment manager rapped on the door of the ambulance. "I want to talk to someone in authority."

The sergeant swore under her breath, but she put on a smile and climbed down out of the ambulance. "Yes, ma'am. What can I do for you?"

Mama whispered something. Janna could not hear what it was, but the medic nodded and reached into a drawer for a hypo.

"Look at that building. The stonework around the window is ruined. I don't know how something like that can be repaired," the manager said. "The balcony door and the one up in the hall will be expensive to replace. I want to know who's going to pay for this damage. I have to answer to the owners of the complex, you know."

The hypo hissed against the skin of Mama's arm.

"What's that?" Janna asked.

"Antihistamine. Your partner will be fine now."

That was hard to believe. Mama was dying one minute and would be fine the next? Before long she saw the medic was right, though. Mama began breathing easier. In a few more minutes he took off the oxygen mask and grinned at her. His eyes were red and puffy but otherwise he seemed almost normal.

"May I have my glasses?"

She handed them to him. "What was wrong with you?"

He held out his right arm. Two long red lines crossed the wrist. "There were cats in the downstairs apartment. One of them scratched me when I was trying to put them in a bedroom so they wouldn't get out through the broken door to the balcony. I'm allergic to cats."

She did not know whether to laugh or be exasperated at the idea of taking time from stopping a dangerous tripper with a shooter to shoo cats into a bedroom. It was several seconds before the last sentence registered. She blinked. "Allergic to cats?"

His grin was rueful. "And milk and weeds and dust and half the rest of what makes up the world. That's why I don't wear contact lenses and can't take a hair transplant."

"All that choking was just an allergy?"

Suddenly she was furious. She had worried about him. She had been afraid the tripper hurt him. What a waste of time. It was only an allergic reaction.

Outside, the manager's voice was shrill. "Someone has to pay for the repairs. Your trigger-happy storm-troopers did it all. I think the city ought to be responsible."

Janna swung out of the ambulance and stalked to Indian Thirty. An *allergy*. She passed the sergeant, listening to the manager with a polite smile, her knuckles white around the shotgun she still carried. Janna slid under the wheel of the Monitor. In a few minutes Mama climbed in the other side. They watched the ambulance sail out with the wounded leo.

Janna looked from the ambulance to the sergeant and complaining manager, then to Mama. "What a bitch of a day."

It did not improve, either.

Mama regarded her with a thoughtful expression. "You're very tense, bibi. Do you realize that? It comes from trying so hard to stick to the book. You should let your imagination loose, work by gut feel for a while."

She kept her eyes on the street ahead. "I'll think about it." Would using the shotgun on him be excusable homicide?

When they got back to the office, she was going to throw herself at the lieutenant's feet and plead with him to take this albatross off her neck. She had a clean record. Was there something wrong in keeping it that way? Why did Wim have to be blinded and leave her at fate's mercy?

The radio murmured, "Indian Thirty, return to the station."

Janna tapped the broadcast button on the car speaker. "Indian Thirty, *roger*."

Pass-the-Word Morello greeted them as they came into the squadroom. He jerked a thumb toward Vradel's office. "The lieutenant wants to see you."

111

Vradel was not alone in his office. With him was a paunchy man who blinked as if he were wearing irritating contact lenses. "Brill, Maxwell," Vradel said, "this is Agent Milo Talous, Department of Justice."

Department of Justice? Janna and Mama glanced at each other with raised brows.

Agent Talous looked them over. He raised brows at Mama, then turned his attention to Janna. "I understand you're investigating the death of Mr. Andrew Kellener."

Janna nodded. "Why does that interest the Department of Justice?"

"Kellener's firm handled the colonial contracting for the Laheli Company."

Janna stared at him. "The one on the *Invictus?*"

"Exactly." The government agent looked like a bookkeeper but he sounded authoritative. "It's my job to find out why the *Invictus* broke down. I thought you might like to be along when I interview the surviving partner."

"I sure would," Janna said. Kellener had been upset since Wednesday, the day the news of the *Invictus* was broadcast. That shed a lot of brand new light on Kellener's death.

She made herself the last out the door. Before she left, she caught Vradel's sleeve. "When we come back, I have to talk to you. The partnership isn't shaking down; I'm being shaken up."

Morello came up behind her. "There's been a woman calling for you. A Grania Huston. She wants you to call her back. She says it's important."

Janna barely listened to him. Her eyes were on Vradel. "I'll call her, Morello. Lieutenant, give me some time, please."

Vradel patted her shoulder. It was no comfort at all to take with her to Hazlett's office.

Jorge examined Milo Talous' identification and extended a cordial hand. "Welcome to our hotbox city, Mr. Talous." His pulse hammered in his throat. The opening moves were behind him. The middle game had begun.

"Washington is worse, I assure you." Talous looked past Jorge at the chessboard on the desk. "You're a player?"

"Addict, actually. I was just playing the computer a game." He cleared away the board. "I've been expecting you, Mr. Talous."

"Then perhaps we can go straight to examining your records of the Laheli Company."

Jorge rubbed his nose. "Unfortunately, it isn't that easy. The account was my partner's and when I try to retrieve the records, this is what I find."

He punched a request for the records into the keyboard beside his desk.

The screen printed: WHAT'S THE PASSWORD?

"Andy and I were going to go over the records yesterday morning, but . . ." He sighed.

Talous frowned at the screen. "Did your partner always lock records in under a code?"

"Never before in my knowledge."

The smoky-haired she-lion behind Talous said, "Is this the matter you called your partner about Saturday night?"

"Yes."

The she-lion sucked her lower lip. "There's an override command on the door locks. Might there be one on record retrieval?"

Jorge frowned, pretending to think. "I don't know of one, but then, I never code in my records. Andy may have set one up with our librarian." He touched the intercom button on the phone. "Lilla, we need the records on the Laheli Company but Andy seems to have coded retrieval of them. Do you have an override command?"

The plump librarian shook her head. "I didn't know any of the records were coded in."

Jorge grimaced. "Maybe Andy left a note of the code in his desk somewhere. Thank you, Lilla."

He led the way to Andy's office.

Mama murmured in Janna's ear. "He's lying. He

knows how to get the records. Watch his pupil response."

She watched, but only so she would have evidence from her own observation to refute him. Watching Hazlett was hard. She kept being distracted by motions of his hands and by the surroundings—like the Justice winking down at them from the wall. She could see why the experts wanted interviews taped, so they could study them at leisure and without distractions.

"What kind of codes might your partner use?" Talous asked.

"I've no idea." Hazlett's pupils dilated.

Janna looked quickly at Mama. The black man smirked in satisfaction.

Hazlett bent over the desk and began searching through it. Talous and the leos helped, each taking a drawer. They combed through, paper by paper. Every list was scrutinized, and promising ones tried on the computer. What appeared to be a grocery list proved to be just that. The computer did not respond to it in any way. The maddening WHAT'S THE PASSWORD? remained on the screen.

Janna found the list. It was in the top drawer, pushed clear to the back beneath a tray of paperclips and rubber bands. The paper had two columns. One was names: Rondeau, Novaterra, Sans souci, De novo, and, about midway down, Laheli. Down the other side of the paper were typed cryptic phrases: Wiersma v. Long Beach, Bardell v. Pickwick, write me a verbal contract, the laughing fox.

"Do these references have any special meaning?" Talous asked.

Hazlett studied the list. "Some are obviously legal references, though they aren't cases I'm familiar with. Wait a minute." He looked up. "Laughing fox. That's the name Andy gave Pearson versus Post when we studied it in law school. It's a landmark case that always attracted Andy because of the comic aspects of it. Now I can remember some of these other cases, too. Wiersma versus Long Beach is a humorous case involving the question of whether wrestlers are humans or dangerous animals. Every one of these references is to legal humor of some kind."

"Legal humor was Mr. Kellener's hobby, wasn't it?" Janna said. She looked up at the winking Justice.

Hazlett nodded. He looked down the list and his finger crossed the page from Laheli to "write me a verbal contract." He turned to the computer and punched in the phrase, then: RUN . . . PRINTOUT.

The computer hummed. It began feeding out facsimile pages.

Talous picked them up and read them as they dropped out. For a long while his face remained expressionless, then he stiffened. His nostrils flared. Janna wanted to snatch the sheets away from him to see what they said.

"You say Mr. Kellener handled the account?" Talous said.

"That's right."

"Then why do all these papers have your signature?"

Janna watched Hazlett's pupils dilate, contract, dilate again. "*My* signature?" He took the sheet Talous offered him. He peered at it. "I don't understand. That's my name but I don't remember signing—" He looked up at Talous. "That isn't my signature. There's a strong similarity, but—see here." He took a pen from Kellener's desk and signed his name on a memo sheet. He took his card from his pocket and gave them both to Talous.

Janna and Mama edged over to where they too could see. The signature on the card and memo pad matched almost exactly but on close examination the letter formations looked larger and more ornate than those on the Laheli records. The records showed signatures with tighter loops and squarer corners.

Talous studied the three signatures with pursed lips. "Do you have anything signed by your partner?"

Jorge punched on the computer's keyboard. In a few moments it kicked out another facsimile sheet, this one signed by Andrew Kellener. The signature was different from the other three but even Janna could see that the loops were small and neat and the letters generally angular.

"Would you like our handwriting people to go over those?" Janna asked.

"Thank you, yes." Talous handed her the sheets and the memo with Hazlett's signature. He returned the card to Hazlett.

"I can't imagine why Andy should sign my name to the papers."

"Can't you?" Mama muttered so only Janna could hear.

"Read these letters from Boeing." Talous handed them to Hazlett.

Hazlett read them over. "So? Colonists can be remarkably pig-headed and foolhardy. They can ignore all common sense in trying to save credit."

"But the Laheli bank records show they paid not for a modified 800 but a Starmaster 1000."

Hazlett's jaw dropped. His pupils dilated.

"What do you think?" Mama whispered.

"My god." Hazlett leaned on the desk. He seemed stunned. "My *god*. I can't believe this."

Talous's mouth was a single slash of lip. "I'd like to see the records on these other clients, too."

They were all similar. The groups had ordered Starmasters smaller than the size they needed and had the ships modified to carry more. In each case Boeing had cautioned about the function of the life-support systems and in each case been reassured that the customer was ordering exactly what it wanted.

"This is incredible," Hazlett kept saying. "I can't believe Andy would do anything like this."

Once Mama straightened up and opened his mouth, whereupon Janna kicked him in the ankle. "Don't you dare," she muttered.

They called in Nels Peddicord. "Does Mr. Kellener have a newscanner here at the office?" Talous asked.

The secretary looked wary. "Yes." He slid open a wall panel. A set lay behind it. "He always watched daily briefs first thing in the morning and when he had time throughout the day."

"And he was depressed since Wednesday, according to the police reports."

Peddicord stiffened. "Mr. Kellener was not depressed, only preoccupied and concerned about something."

Without knowing why, Janna looked over to Jorge Hazlett, and suddenly she knew what Mama meant by someone smelling guilty. The eight years she had been on the force had taught her all the body English people used. She had learned to differentiate between the nervousness of guilt and that of merely having to talk to a police officer. She could tell when a casual saunter was *too* casual, when a citizen's tears were faked. Hazlett showed none of the signs she knew and could identify. He was doing nothing except watching Milo Talous with apparently genuine bewilderment and concern, yet Janna had the overwhelming urge to wind him up in her wrap strap.

She shuddered. Oh, god; Mama was infectious. She was catching his lunacy.

With Mama and Talous, Janna headed for the office determined to corner Vradel, determined to plead her case so convincingly he would free her from Mama. She turned the Monitor down the ramp to the station garage.

"Do you really think Kellener killed himself when he realized he could be charged under the Tescott Act?" Mama asked Milo Talous. "Why save the state the trouble of executing him?"

From the rear seat of the car, Talous said, "Perhaps he was thinking of the effect of the disgrace on his family. We'll see how the coroner's jury feels about suicide at the inquest Friday."

"Another thing—why should he kill himself when he went to all the trouble of signing Hazlett's name to everything so his partner would be blamed?"

Talous had no immediate answer for that.

Janna parked the car. It settled to the concrete in a dying whine of fans. She pushed her door forward and swung out over the airfoil skirt. Let Talous and Mama argue if they wanted; she was going upstairs. She pushed into the squadroom, aiming for Vradel's door.

Morello intercepted her. "Brill, that Huston woman has called three more times for you."

Janna tried to circle him. "Put the number on my table. I'll call her as soon as I've talked to the lieutenant."

"You might as well call her now. The lieutenant's busy."

Damn. Bloody damn it to hell. She scowled. "All right. I'll call the woman. What's her number?"

Mama came into the squadroom while she was punching the number into the phone. He sat down on the edge of the table. "That Talous is a mule. He's convinced Kellener committed suicide because of the *Invictus*."

Janna did not look up. "Strange how some people fix on an idea and can't see anything else, isn't it?"

A man appeared on the screen. "Hough's Department Store, Publicity Department."

"Ms. Grania Huston, please."

The screen flickered. A square-faced woman came on. Her expression became grave at Janna's introduction. "Thank you for calling. The newscanner said you were the officer in charge of investigating the death of that man in the Sunflower Federal Bank Building."

"Yes, ma'am."

"Do you know yet how he died?"

"Why do you ask, ma'am?"

Ms. Huston chewed her lip. "Well, I saw something Saturday night. I don't know whether it had anything to do with that or not, but at the risk of seeming like a fool, I thought I ought to tell you about it."

Janna could feel Mama breathing down her neck. She elbowed him back. "Please do tell me."

"I saw a man leaving that building in what I can only describe as a very furtive manner. He kept looking around, as if he were afraid someone was going to see him, and he walked very fast."

Over Janna's shoulder, Mama asked, "What time was this?"

"A quarter past eight. I made a point of looking at the time."

Mama's breath felt hot on Janna's neck. "Praise Mouths from whom great blessings flow," he murmured in her ear.

Janna pursed her lips. "How did you happen to see him?"

"I'm a window designer for Hough's. I was working late Saturday getting a window ready for Monday morning. I looked out every so often, just to see what might be going on, and on one look out, I saw the man leaving the bank building."

"Can you describe him?"

Ms. Huston frowned in thought. "I couldn't see him really well. The trees in the sidewalk planters were a little in the way, and it was night. I think he was about medium height, and weight. I don't remember anything special about his hair. I do remember the clothes he was wearing, though."

"Describe them, please."

"He had on tank pants with flared trouser legs and a low cut to the top so that a lot of his chest was exposed. He wasn't wearing a shirt under it. The color was dark, blue or green, I think, and it had a lighter stripe crossing the trouser legs diagonally from the hip to the inseam at the cuff."

"Sounds like the kind of thing Hazlett would wear," Mama murmured.

Janna said, "Ms. Huston, do you think you could identify him if you saw him again?"

"I don't know. I'd be willing to try."

"Thank you. If you'll arrange to be free about ten tomorrow morning, we'll bring you down and let you look at some people."

"I'll be ready. Good-bye, sergeant."

Janna punched off.

An incandescent grin split the darkness of Mama's face. "Jackpot. The description fits old Jorge."

Janna frowned. "And half the male population of Topeka. Don't count your ID's before they're made."

"You're just annoyed because it might very well be

119

Hazlett, and if we place him in that building, it might
mean he's guilty and I'm right."

She looked at him coldly. "I'm not looking forward
to having to admit that you're right, but that won't
stop me from following up the lead." She stood. "Excuse me. I have to see the lieutenant."

Vradel stepped out of his office and headed for the
door.

"Lieutenant . . ."

"Sorry, Brill." He kept moving. "I have an appointment with the deputy director and then I have to leave
right away. There's a Commander's Exchange this
evening."

The door slammed behind him, leaving Janna staring impotently. Commander's Exchange? If he had
stayed to listen a few minutes she could have given
him a beautiful problem to take and share with his
fellow commanders. He could have shared the further
escapades of Mahlon Maxwell.

She dropped back into her chair, swearing a string
of profanities that raised the brows of her colleagues
and reddened the face of the one civilian woman in
the room. When she saw everyone staring, Janna broke
off, muttering an apology. She reached for the report
forms and went over to feed them into the dictyper.

CHAPTER EIGHT

Liann Seaton descended on the Crimes Against Persons squadroom like a tornado. She was a controlled,
elegant tornado, but a devastating storm all the same.

"I'm sorry," she told Lieutenant Vradel, "but this
is impossible. It's ridiculous. My husband could not
possibly have had anything to do with the deaths of

those people on the *Invictus.*" Her voice was quiet, but very firm.

She sat across his desk from him, in his office's most comfortable chair, looking polished and sophisticated even in her gingham pioneer dress. She regarded Vradel with unwavering eyes. Occasionally she lifted her head to look at Janna Brill and Mama Maxwell standing behind Vradel, but her gaze always came back down to the lieutenant.

That she had shaken him was evident. He toyed with a pencil but had not made a single mark on his memo pad with it. He was not even chewing on his mustache.

"Ma'am, we're not accusing Andrew Kellener of any such thing."

"Mr. Peddicord made it quite clear when he called me yesterday afternoon. You believe the records prove my husband perpetrated a fraud on those poor colonists, that he deceived them into buying a ship that was inadequate, and that because he was about to be exposed, he killed himself. An Agent Milo Talous of the Department of Justice visited me last night. He believes Andy made a practice of underequipping colonists. He spoke of something called the Tescott Act which it appears he regrets not being able to invoke. Lieutenant, I totally reject all your claims and assumptions."

Vradel ran his fingers up and down his pencil. Janna could see the sketching itch tingling his fingers, but he could not look away from Liann Seaton long enough to draw. "Ma'am, we merely gather evidence. The cause of death will be determined by the coroner's jury Friday and any guilt regarding the colonists is up to the Department of Justice."

"But you and that Mr. Talous are gathering the evidence. If you're biased, the evidence could be, too."

"Ms. Seaton—"

"I want you to know something about my husband. I want to make it clear to you why he could not have committed suicide and why he could not have

121

been responsible for the harm done to those colonists."

Vradel still did not chew his mustache, but he smoothed it with the fingers of his left hand. "Very well. Do you mind if we record this?"

"To check my voice for stress? No, certainly not."

Vradel took a microcorder out of a desk drawer and set it on top. He tapped it on.

"My husband," Liann Seaton said, "was a Libertarian. You can check his record. He was very active in campaigning for Libertarian party candidates in local and national elections. He believed that every person should be in control of his own life and totally responsible for it. He didn't approve of the womb-to-tomb care our society gives people. He believed it robs people of individualism, of initiative, and of pride. I suppose he might have become a sligh except that since slighs don't vote, they can hardly help shape or change society.

"What Andy did approve of, heartily, was colonization. Colonists, he would tell me, are people who take responsibility for themselves. They're going where there is no one to look after them but themselves."

It was almost an exact echo of Wim's words, Janna thought.

"Andrew Kellener wanted to help send everyone possible to the stars. He worked slave hours and inconvenienced himself in order to be available to clients. He and Jorge Hazlett charged just six percent instead of the usual ten percent commission for their services, so colonists would have to spend less to leave. Lieutenant, he wanted every one of his clients to arrive on his chosen world with the very best possible chance of survival. He would have done nothing"— she leaned forward and an elegant doubled fist came down emphatically on the top of Vradel's desk— "*nothing* to have jeopardized the lives of his clients in *any* way." She took a breath. "He spent his own credit to insure that the supplies and ship of every client met better than minimum standards. I can show you records that prove it. Andy earned a great deal of credit as a colonial contractor, but he spent most of it on colonists and contributing toward shares when deserving people could not quite buy them on their own. We live in an apartment instead of a house. Andy rode the bus to work. Our one runabout is an economy model. If he cheated the colonists as Mr. Talous claims, he would have accumulated much more credit. Where is it, lieutenant?"

If Liann Seaton had been pleading a case in court, Janna would have found for her client.

The woman stood up, extending her hand to Vradel. "I've taken enough of your time. Thank you for hearing me out. If you're interested in Andy's funeral, it's at two o'clock this afternoon."

Vradel shook her hand. She turned and left, closing the door quietly behind her.

Vradel slumped back in his chair. "That is what in my youth would have been called a hot apple."

Janna and Mama came around to the front of the desk. Mama picked up a stack of papers on one corner and started tapping them into line. "She's a fine fine bibi, and bright; but I'm surprised she missed mentioning that Hazlett spreads a lot of credit around. I checked on him. He has a luxury townhouse in addition to the Vulcan, and lots of very flash friends who take frequent weekend party trips to distant cities."

A winter glint came into Vradel's eyes. "And that makes him a murderer? The governor has a nice house and several road cars. She also travels on weekends and attends expensive parties. Available evidence says Hazlett is a respectable member of the community. What do you have that refutes that?"

"How many murderers and thieves have you known who were *respectable* people?"

"Not one who didn't have evidence against him."

Janna silently cheered. Go, Hari.

Mama turned the stack to shake it down the other way. "We have evidence against Hazlett, skipper. Like I told Agent Talous, why should Kellener kill himself if he planned to have his partner blamed for the frauds? And how did he bring the trick to the office?"

Both Vradel and Janna blinked.

Mama set the papers down and picked up another group. "We didn't find any kind of container in his pocket or the trash, not a bottle or an envelope."

Vradel frowned. "We could have been careless and not searched every wastebasket in the office. Kellener may have disposed of a container out where he mixed up the caff."

Mama sniffed.

Janna said, "He may have brought it in a gelatin capsule."

Vradel nodded in satisfaction. "That's a distinct possibility."

Mama turned on Janna. "How about you, bibi? You were watching Hazlett when we went over there with Talous. You saw his reactions." He tapped the papers on the desk top. "You saw how guilty he was."

"I saw his reactions." She remembered her irrational urge to strap Hazlett. It sent a cold flush of guilt through her. "I saw nothing to suggest he's guilty of anything."

"Your pupils are dilating. You're lying to me."

Vradel suddenly stood and leaned across the desk to snatch the papers away from Mama. "Will you stop that? When I need you to keep house for me, I'll see that it's added to your job description. Now, I like to encourage intuitive thinking in my officers, but I want more than that. Morello put a stack of complaint sheets on your table twenty minutes ago. Go take care of them. Don't bother me about Jorge Hazlett again until you can bring me documented, court-admissible evidence against him."

"Sign the authorization to look at his bank records. I'll bring you documented proof."

"Give me just cause first. Maxwell, if you loiter in here one more minute, you're going to lose a day off. Now both of you get to work. *Sail!*"

They left. Mama was breathing hard down Janna's neck. "You know he's guilty, bibi. You just won't let

124

ourself admit it. By-the-book Brill." He sounded cathingly pitying. "You're so tied to procedure by all he braintraining the department's forced on you that you can't believe good intuition. Look at it, bibi. Admit to it and believe in it."

He was never going to let this thing alone. She ground her teeth. There was only one thing to do. She scooped the complaint sheets from their table and thrust them at him. "Take these and go down to the car, unless you want to be the second partner I've ever hit."

Leos nearby looked around sharply.

"I'll join you in a bit. Sit on the rider side. *I'll* drive today."

Janna waited for him to leave the squadroom. The newscanner reported that Bible cultists were picketing the Statehouse today, insisting on revocation of taxes on church property. Farmers were counter-protesting, claiming reducing taxes anywhere else would drive farm taxes up.

When Mama was gone, she went back to Vradel's office. "Sir, may I have another minute?"

He looked at her, sighing. "Brill, I know he's difficult, but he hasn't really done anything yet to justify bouncing him out of here."

"I wasn't going to ask for that."

His brows went up. His mustache twitched.

Janna took a breath. "If he were convinced Hazlett had an alibi, maybe he would lose this obsession and start being more productive. On the other hand, if this Huston woman identifies Hazlett as the man she saw leaving the Sunflower Federal Building, we'll need to check his bank records anyway. So, lieutenant, sir, as a favor to me, will you please okay the authorization for the check on Hazlett's bank records?"

Vradel frowned. His pencil stroked his memo pad. A woman's face emerged, smiling up at him. He contemplated the drawing for a minute, then looked up. "All right. Go try to clear a few of those complaints. See if your witness recognizes Hazlett. The authorization will be waiting here for you when you get back."

125

Janna blew him a kiss. "You're nova, skipper. Thank you, sir."

If the heat had been broken by a long, cool rain storm she could not have felt better. She felt so good she slapped Morello on the rump as she left and hummed a jivaqueme tune while driving Indian Thirty to their first call.

Mama eyed her with suspicion. "You've gone happy all of a sudden. Did you talk the lieutenant into demoting me to patrol again?"

"No."

"You just wish you could have."

She stopped humming and sighed. "I'd like to like you, Mama, but you make it hard. What are you? Where do you come from?"

He pushed his glasses up his nose. "Ulysses, Kansas."

"I've never heard of it."

"It's west of Dodge City, almost on the far side of the Moon. We were one of two black families in the town. They're so conservative out there they still vote Republican."

"How'd you end up here?"

"I used to spend my summers in Dodge with an aunt, working in Front Street. I played one of the bad guys in the shootout enactments. I learned how to fall off a running horse and off the top of a building. I thought that gave me a calling to be an actor, so after high school I went to Kansas City to study acting. I fell in love with a girl in the UMKC Criminal Justice Course and switched curriculums to be near her. The relationship didn't last but I found I liked being a leo."

"So why didn't you go to work for the KCPD?"

He rolled his eyes. "The year I graduated, they were sniping lions all over K.C. I didn't need that. I applied several other places. They finally accepted me here."

The radio murmured, "Alpha Highland Three, a naked man in the intersection of Thirty-first Terrace and Burlingame."

126

"What about you, bibi?"

"I grew up in Wichita. My father is a designer for Boeing."

"Seeing all those ships getting ready to go to the stars didn't make you want to be a colonist?"

She shrugged. "Off and on it did, but mostly I wanted to be a lawyer. I was a year through the Washburn course when I realized what I really wanted to do was police work. I switched curriculums, too. Here's our first complainant. Possible kidnapping, complaint filed by a Mr. Ross Borel."

Mr. Borel was a portly man in his fifties, well dressed, well housed. It was his business partner who had been kidnapped. "I think some government took him to steal his invention."

"What invention is that?" Mama asked.

"A new spacedrive that will make ramjets obsolete. Sol—that's Sol Thoday—left for Wichita last week to arrange for an experimental model to be built. He said he'd call me this week, but he hasn't. That's why I think something's happened to him."

"What's this spacedrive like?" Janna asked.

When Borel explained she could hardly keep from wincing. It was the Dean Drive. That old skin again.

"When you paid your share of the partnership I don't suppose you used bankcredit?"

Borel shook his head. "I bought jewelry and gave that to Sol. He was afraid if I used bankcredit, the wrong people would learn about his invention and steal it. Looks like they learned about it anyway."

Mama said, "I don't think he was kidnapped."

They told him what had really happened to his "partner." While he was still recovering from the shock, they took down the facts of his meetings with the skinner and a description of the skinner himself. They invited Borel down to the station at his convenience to look at pictures.

They climbed back into Indian Thirty and marked the complaint for referral to Crimes Against Property.

Janna checked the car's chrono. "It's nearly ten. Let's go pick up our Ms. Huston."

"How do you want to handle it?"

"By secret show-up, of course."

She could not see bringing Hazlett down to the station for a formal show-up, and if they just marched Hazlett in to her and asked if he wcre the man, every defense attorney in the world could demolish a positive identification in court. They had to present Hazlett in such a way he did not know what was happening and she was not being influenced.

Grania Huston was waiting for them at the entrance of Hough's. Instead of opening a rear door for her, however, Janna set the car on its parking rollers at the curb, illegally, and they climbed out.

"Before we take you down to the station we have to run across the street to the bank building," Janna said. "Come on along. We won't be a minute."

Ms. Huston's eyes brightened. "All right." She followed them willingly, even eagerly.

They took the elevator to the tenth floor and strolled into the Hazlett/Kellener suite. The receptionist looked up and smiled politely. "Good morning, sergeants."

"Buenos días," Janna said. "Is Mr. Hazlett in?"

"Yes, but he is with a client."

"We don't want to disturb him, then. Would you just ask him to come out for a moment?"

The receptionist considered. He punched a button and murmured into the intercom.

Moments later Jorge Hazlett came out into the reception area. He smiled at them. "Good morning. What can I do for you?" Inside he wondered what the hell they were up to. The leos had expressions so carefully polite they were almost alarming. And who was that avid-faced little woman with them?

The she-lion drew Jorge to one end of the reception room while her black partner remained by the door with the little woman. "Your partner's wife was in visiting us this morning." She repeated Liann Seaton's remarks to him. "Is what she says about Kellener true?"

Jorge relaxed. "I would have said so before Monday

128

morning. That's how he's always acted like he believed, but now . . ." He shrugged. "How could he
believe in the holiness of colonials and still cheat
them?"

"You think he did?"

"Someone did, and I know I wasn't the guilty
party."

Janna watched him as Hazlett answered. He
looked back without flinching. His eyes dilated
slightly, however. She noted it for future considera-
tion. "Well, I won't take more of your time. Thank
you, Mr. Hazlett."

They left. Riding down in the elevator, Janna asked
Ms. Huston, "Have you seen either of those men before?"

Ms. Huston's eyes went wide. "You mean one of
them might have been the man I saw?" She frowned.
"I don't think they were. The young man was more
slender than the one I saw and Mr. Hazlett didn't
walk the same way the man I saw did."

Above her head, Janna and Mama exchanged
glances. Mama was disappointed. Janna had to admit
to feeling that way too. An ID would have settled
something, at least. This settled nothing. It raised
questions, in fact. If Hazlett were not the man, who
was?

They stepped off the elevator. The bank guard
nodded to them. As one, Janna and Mama stopped
cold. They looked at each other. The guard's uniform
was dark green. The trousers were flared and decorated by a gold stripe crossing each pantleg diagonally from hip to inseam at the cuff.

"Was the man wearing something like that?" Janna
asked.

Ms. Huston looked at the guard. "The trousers look
right, but he didn't have that kind of jacket."

Mama strolled over to the guard. He reached out to
finger one sleeve of the jacket. "That's nice material
and a nice cut. It almost looks good enough for street
wear. What are the pants like under the jacket?"

"They have a tank top," the guard replied.

"Do you wear a shirt under it?"

"In this weather? No. You really like this?" He looked down at the uniform with surprise.

"The color is too conservative, though. Have a good day."

They ushered Ms. Huston out to the street. Janna smiled at her. "I don't think we'll need you to identify the man after all. Thank you for calling. If it turns out we need you again, we'll reach you."

"I'm always happy to help the police. How else are the streets going to be made safe?"

They watched her cross the street and disappear into Hough's. Janna asked, "Do you still have the names of the security people on duty Saturday night?"

He pulled a notebook out of a thigh pocket. "I have them."

First on the list was Mr. Klim Hightower. Guard Hightower was not happy to see them. "This is the second time you've waked me up. What is it, more questions about Saturday? I already told you all I know."

Mama pushed his glasses up his nose. "Except which of the guards left in the middle of the shift Saturday night."

The guard stared at them. "Left? None of us left during the shift."

Janna shook her head. "Wrong. He was seen leaving. He took off his jacket so he wouldn't seem to be wearing a uniform." She paused. "Was it you?"

"No!" His face set. "I don't know what anyone thought they saw, but it wasn't one of us leaving. We were all three there the entire shift. Maybe your witness saw someone disguised as a guard."

They could not move him from that. They headed for the next name on the list.

"He has a point," Mama said. "Maybe Hazlett thought he could fool a possible witness that way."

"You don't really believe that."

Mama looked wistful, then shook his head. "No. He would have worn the entire uniform. The guard's lying."

"They all may, and stick to it."

"We'll shake them."

She looked at him. "The peeps couldn't make you and Wim change your minds about denying you carried a shooter on duty."

His eyes slid toward her. "So he told you about that."

"He wanted to warn me what your partners can find themselves involved in."

Mama opened his mouth as though to start a protest, then closed it again and sat back, shrugging. "I didn't ask him to lie for me. Wim was a good back-up."

The second guard also denied that anyone had left duty, but as he did, his pupils dilated. They smelled fear in him.

"Well, that's too bad," Janna said with a sigh. "We didn't want to bring your employers at the bank into this, but—"

"We'll have to," Mama interrupted. "It'll probably mean all three of you will be fired." He turned as though to leave.

The guard went gray. "Wait."

Mama stopped.

"There's no point getting the others in trouble. They're just covering for me. I'm the one who left."

"Why?"

"It was nothing to do with that business upstairs. There was trouble here at home, a fight between my wives. I had to stop it." He was sweating. "Don't tell the bank. I wasn't gone more than an hour."

"When did you leave?"

"A little after eight."

The two leos exchanged looks.

"All right," Janna said. "We won't mention it to the bank, but if you have to come to court, don't perjure yourself."

They headed back for the car.

"So much for our eyewitness, Mama, and so much for Hazlett being in the building. If he were there, Ms. Huston would probably have seen him leave."

"She couldn't have been looking out the window

every minute." He pushed his glasses up his nose. "We need to see his bank records."

Bank records. "So you say. Let's go back to the office."

His brows went up. "We haven't finished clearing these complaints yet."

"Let's go anyway."

Morello was waiting for them in the squadroom. "The lieutenant said to give you this."

It was the authorization, as promised. Mama stared at it incredulously for a long minute, then whooped and threw both arms around Janna. He would have danced her across the squadroom except that she broke his hold and dumped him flat on his back on the floor, much to the amusement of the entire squad.

Mama seemed undisturbed at being dropped. He got up grinning. "Bibi, I knew you could feel Hazlett's guilt, too. Count him lion meat as of now."

Janna did not like being her colleagues' entertainment. She towed Mama after her out of the squadroom. "I *don't* believe he's guilty," she snapped. "I'm just hoping this will prove his noninvolvement to you."

Mama's grin never wavered. He grinned all the way to the National Bank Central. As they parked and went into the bank, she said, "You're certainly stubborn."

"It makes me a good leo, bibi."

She rolled her eyes.

They presented the authorization to a teller. She took them to the manager. He handed them over to the computer librarian. She punched in Jorge Hazlett's number. In five minutes they were sitting studying Hazlett's purchase record for Saturday, July 30.

The first glance through the printout, Janna held her breath. All the while they were being shuffled through the bank, the fear had grown that the record would prove nothing. What she saw on reading relieved her. Purchases were recorded for the evening, from transport tokens at seven fifteen from a vending machine on Kansas Avenue to dinner at Peron's in the Whitelakes Mall, which had been paid for at nine forty. The records included a number of purchases from shops, all in the Whitelakes Mall.

Janna tried not to sound smug but some of it leaked into her voice anyway. "It looks like Hazlett was at the other end of town all evening."

Mama was disappointed for only a minute. "He could have killed Kellener before."

Janna closed her eyes. Give her strength. She opened them again. "Not possible. Kellener left home at a quarter to seven. The bus trip downtown had to take at least twenty minutes. I don't think that gives Hazlett time to meet him at the office, kill him, and run down the street to the vending machine by seven fifteen."

Mama pushed his glasses up his nose. "Then he faked the record, somehow."

"Faked the record?" She kept her voice down so the librarian would not hear, but it was a shrill whisper. "Maxwell, you are afflicted with the tightest tunnel vision I've ever seen. Fake a bank record? You've lost all your chips."

Mama shrugged. "I know it's supposed to be impossible, but I also know this deek killed his partner. I feel it in my bones. So the record has to be wrong."

She felt like pounding her head into a wall. "Christ."

"There's one way to find out. We'll check to see if his car was really in the parking lot, and we'll talk to his neighbors to see when he came home. We can also ask him to produce those things he bought." Mama frowned at the printout. "Buying this much jewelry suggests he was making a quiet payment to someone for something."

"The child's computer and doll don't fall into that category. And what about the meal and suits?"

"He was bound to buy some personal items. Or maybe we need to learn who was helping him. Someone had to help him, I'm sure. Maybe by finding who helped him, we can strap Hazlett."

Janna sighed. "You have the philosophy of investigation wrong, Mama. We're supposed to look at all the evidence, form a hypothesis based on what we've found, then prove or disprove the hypothesis. We don't randomly pick someone to be 'it' and look for evidence against him."

Mama took off his glasses and polished the lenses on his trouser leg. "My hypothesis is Hazlett did it, so let's prove it. Now, he said his car broke down and that's why he took the bus. Let's see if that's true." He put his glasses back on.

Janna considered. It would be good to have all the corroboration possible of Hazlett's alibi. It might even discourage Mama. "We'll check the parking lot records, but if we don't find anything there to suggest he's guilty, we're going to drop it and follow up these other complaints. Understood?"

"We'll find something."

Janna rolled her eyes.

They ate a quick sandwich for lunch, then drove to the central office of the Sunco Corporation.

Sunco's gates issued tickets to all incoming vehicles and required the return of that ticket plus enough tokens to pay for the parking time before the exit gate would open. Unknown to most people, the company taped all entries and exits from its lots. The visual record was what interested Janna and Mama.

"We do it because the bicycles cheat," the tape librarian said as she hunted up the tape reels they needed. "The riders lift the bikes over the gate. By taping, we can see them and have warrants issued on the license numbers."

"We're just interested in cars."

She ran the Saturday night tape for them. According to DMV, Hazlett's car was a tan Mercedes Vulcan (official color name of sundust), license number SHH 41348. The tape recorded the rear end of a vehicle with the number SHH 41348 entering the lot at Thirteenth and Jackson at seven o'clock in the evening. The entire rear end of the vehicle could not be seen in the frame but enough was visible to determine the approximate size and color of the car. It was a sportster's rear end colored that muted gold color that looked tan.

They had the librarian run the tape forward until the computer recognized the number again and froze the image. According to the time indicator on the tape, SHH 41348 had left the Sunco lot at six-twenty Monday evening.

"It looks like he didn't drive anywhere Saturday night," Mama conceded.

"So let's forget it and follow up complaints."

"Just one more stop, bibi. I want to check with Hazlett's neighbors."

"Maxwell, this is enough!"

He widened his eyes. "But we haven't found anything yet that either proves or disproves my hypothesis."

She must be brainbent, she decided, for continuing to go along with this madness, but . . . "We'll see the neighbors, then, but that's absolutely the last call we make on this case today. Absolutely."

"Unless we find evidence against Hazlett."

They knocked on the doors of the townhouses around Hazlett's. At most, there was no answer and among the few people they did find home, questioning established that people in the area either went to bed early or were immovably planted in front of the holo-v until they retired. However, across the street from Hazlett's townhouse, they found a woman who had seen him come home.

"It was a little after ten thirty. He was walking up from the bus stop. I called to him and asked him where his car was because I'd seen him drive out earlier. He told me one of the fans went bad and that he'd had to leave the car parked downtown. He said he couldn't understand how people managed to shop and ride the bus. He found it awkward riding and carrying packages."

"He was carrying packages?" Janna sent Mama a triumphant look. If Hazlett brought purchases home, there was a good chance he had bought them in the first place. Her relief vanished at the neighbor's next words.

"He wasn't when I saw him, no. He said after he'd

ridden halfway back from south Topeka with them, he decided to leave what he'd bought locked in his car and bring them home later."

He could very well have done that. The child's computer would have been a particularly awkward thing to handle on a bus. It also occurred to her that if he had never bought the items, he might still give the neighbor that story to explain why he had no packages.

But of course he *had* bought the items. The bank records said so. No matter what wild blue yonder notion had stuck in the glue that served Mahlon Maxwell for a brain, bank records could not be faked. The computer checked the signature on the register plate against that on the card. It checked the thumbprints. Prints were certainly impossible to forge.

She led the way back to the car. "That's it, Mama. Now we start clearing other cases. Nothing we've learned out here suggests Hazlett is guilty of either tampering with a bank record or with his partner's life."

"Nothing suggests he didn't, either."

"You forget, *guilt* has to be proven. Lacking that, a party is assumed innocent." She climbed over the airfoil skirt into the Monitor and started the engine.

Mama swung in, too. "How do you think Kellener got that trick?"

"I'll leave that for the coroner's jury to decide."

"For god's *sake,* Brill!"

His exclamation was almost a scream. It startled Janna so much she jumped almost clear of the seat. She whirled on him.

He was staring at her, eyes passionate behind the glasses. "There are times to say to *hell* with the book! Bibi, this deek is guilty as *sin.* I *know* it. Somewhere there's evidence, and if I don't have a try at finding it, I'm going to be wondering the rest of my life if there's a murderer free because I didn't try hard enough to strap him."

She stared at him. That sounded like some idealistic rookie just out of college. He must know, as she did, that there were thousands of guilty deeks walking around who had caused police officers to lose sleep and gain ulcers looking for admissible evidence against them. It was a harsh and hated fact no one wanted to accept, but somewhere around the third or fourth year on the force, leos interested in keeping their stomachs and sanity gave up torturing themselves over hopeless chases.

Having survived twelve years on the force, Mama must have learned that lesson, too, yet here he was in full cry after what looked like a wild goose. It disturbed her. Was it indicative of a pathologic process, or was his conviction really that strong?

Even more disturbing, however, was that part of her wanted to run with him. She distrusted intuition on principle, as emotional and therefore unreliable. Still, she had felt that one urge to strap Hazlett and even now something about the case bothered her enough that she could not quite bring herself to choke Mama down.

She considered what they had. If she were to ignore the evidence of the bank records, everything else was equivocal. It did not suggest guilt nor confirm innocence. It all left loose ends. She sucked her lower lip. She hated loose ends.

"All right, we'll give it an honest try . . . at least until the inquest. After that, the decision will be official and the case will be out of our hands."

"But that gives us just the rest of today and tomorrow," he protested.

"That's right. If you'll agree to that limit, we'll go on. If you can't, I'll insist we drop it right now. I can go to Lieutenant Vradel for back-up enforcement if I have to."

He sighed, a gusty hiss of disgust and surrender. "Okay. After the inquest, it's closed. I'll forget about Hazlett."

She switched on the fans. "Then let's get busy cracking him."

CHAPTER NINE

"Do you mind telling me who we're looking for, Mama? It's almost the end of the watch." They were cruising all the streets around the Statehouse. Mama called the turns at each corner.

"That trick had to come from somewhere. I'm looking for an Ear who can give us names of street dealers who might have sold the junk to Hazlett."

Janna looked away from her driving long enough to glance at him. "You amaze me. You've just come in from Soldier Creek. How can you have any contacts in Capitol division?"

"I've been in Capitol twice before. I still remember people from then."

Oh, yes . . . the two other times he was an Investigator I. She had forgotten.

"What does this Ear look like?"

"Very female. She always works the streets around the Statehouse, catering to the legislators and their staffs."

Janna clucked in disapproval. "I don't understand why the boys and girls work the street when they have perfectly legal houses to work out of. If they're caught, the fines are worse than the house fees they're avoiding, not to mention the working time lost in jail."

"Why does a sligh give up social care? I don't know. People are perverse."

Janna swung the car onto Jackson and started gliding along the east side of the Statehouse grounds. "Speaking of perversity, why were you broken back to uniform from Investigator those other times?"

"One was a crock. I called a supervisor an asshole.

n debriefing and he wouldn't forget it. He gave me a poor rating the next time I was evaluated."

There were commanders like that, despite the fact debriefing was supposed to have free speech with no penalties attached.

"What about the other time?"

He shrugged. "I pushed a suspect a little and some citizens happened to see him bleeding. There she is." He pointed ahead.

They were coming up on a girl in a scarlet romper and matching hip boots, sauntering along the pavement. Her round posterior swayed invitingly. Mama leaned out the window of the Monitor.

"Sit on it or give it away, bibi, but move it off the street before you try selling it."

The prostitute turned. Her face betrayed the fact that she was older than she had looked from the rear. She stopped with her hands on her hips. "Well, well, look who's back."

Janna eased the Monitor to the curb and set it down.

Mama grinned at the prostitute. "Come tell Mama what you've been doing with yourself."

"Working with my back to the wall as usual." She waltzed over to the car, swinging her hips. "Are you working in the neighborhood again or just passing through?"

"Working, and about to offer you a chance to earn credit without adding to the calluses on your gluteus."

"You want me to play Ear for you? What do I get in return?"

"The usual: reasonable credit, my help keeping you out of jail, and a bonus if you want it." He leered. "I'm older and better this time 'round, bibi."

She sniffed. "That's what they all say. I've yet to tell the difference between you with my eyes closed. What do you need to know?"

He pushed his glasses up his nose. "The names of street dealers a local businessman might buy illegal drugs from."

"I can think of five to start with. I saw one of them in a bar down the street not five minutes ago."

Mama pushed the car door forward. "Show m where." He looked back at Janna. "If that jewelry i part of a payment, the payee will be wanting to turn into credit. Why don't you go on back to the statio and have the jewelry descriptions sent out to all the lo cal gem people? I'll talk to this dealer."

He swung out and headed back up Jackson with th prostitute. Janna revved the fans and sent the Monito coasting toward the station.

Getting descriptions of the jewelry took some twenty five minutes longer than she anticipated, in phone cal to the jewelers in Whitelakes who sold the pieces an in waiting for them to look up descriptions in their rec ords. It was after four thirty before she could fill ou the description forms in Communications. Mama wa still not back when she finished. She wondere whether he was talking to the dealer or had convince the prostitute to let him give her a bonus.

She punched on the intradepartment phone an put in the number of the stolen property computer.

"Wait, please," came the throaty voice of the com puter.

No one knew whose voice had been recorded fo the computer but Janna had heard a number of he male leos and some ho she-lions say they would giv anything to find out. Throughout the SCPD it wa fondly called The Voice. She knew one investigato who claimed he had transferred to Crimes Agains Property just so he would have an excuse to call Th Voice several times a day and arouse himself listenin to it.

"Go ahead," purred The Voice.

"Sergeant Janna Brill, Capitol division, badge num ber four-five-five, requesting a watchdog program.

There was a heartbeat before The Voice came bac breathily, "State length of program and items to be i cluded, please."

"Program begins now, retroactive to nine o'cloc A.M., Monday, August first. Program to end twelv o'clock noon, Friday, August fifth. Items are: numbers one and two, novalon suits made by Stellar Fashions; number three, Dyan Pennock action doll made by Mattel; number four, Eduvac Junior computer made by Battershell Electronics; number five . . ." One by one, she described each item of jewelry.

When she finished The Voice said, "Thank you. Wait, please, for a memory check."

While the computer reviewed its activity back to Monday, Janna reached for a pencil and note pad, in case the computer found anything. She just had time to get ready to write when The Voice came back on the line.

"There have been three incidents of activity involving items described in program. Number one: seven novalon suits made by Stellar Fashions were among twenty recovered in a raid at 917 West Seventeenth Street at eight-oh-five P.M., Monday, August first. Number two: one novalon suit made by Stellar Fashions, one Dyan Pennock action doll made by Mattel, one Eduvac Junior computer made by Battershell Electronics were listed in a stolen property query made at nine forty-three A.M., Tuesday, August second. Number three: two novalon suits made by Stellar Fashions were included in a stolen property query on items found in the car of Mr. Frederick Weltmann at two ten A.M., Wednesday, August third."

Janna wrote fast. "Who made the stolen property query in activity number two?"

"The stolen property query number two was made by Officer Niall Cushman, Highland Park division."

"Thank you." She knew the computer did not need any expression of gratitude, but she always thanked it anyway. She could not bring herself simply to punch off, not even with a computer—certainly not with one that sounded so human.

She leaned against the Communications counter, her finger traveling down the list. Number two looked very promising, but there was no point in trying to follow up on it now. Officer Cushman was probably on his way home, as she should be. He was not

likely to welcome being called tonight. The matter wa
not that urgent anyway. Tomorrow would be soo
enough.

She considered whether or not to go down and se
if debriefing were still going. Missing was likely t
bring Schnauzer Venn around asking why, twitchin
the heavy brows and mustache that had earned th
tick tech his nickname. The doc was a personabl
man, easy to talk to, but he could be a troublesom
mother hen if an officer showed signs of changing a be
havior pattern.

Mama stuck his head into the room. "There yo
are. Come on, bibi."

"Where?"

"We have dealers to visit." He caught her arm an
pulled her down the hall.

She freed herself with one deft twist. "Tonight?"

"If I have just until Friday to strap Hazlett, I inten
to use every possible minute. You didn't have any
thing better to do, did you?"

"As a matter of fact, I was going to a concert at th
university with Sid and Treece. An air-conditione
concert," she added, "where I won't feel in imminen
danger of heat stroke."

"I'll treat you to dinner at the coldest club in tow
when Hazlett is locked up."

"How can I refuse an offer like that?"

If he heard the irony in her voice, he chose to ig
nore it. He put a hand between her shoulders an
propelled her toward the garage.

"Indian Thirty is checked in. What car are we goin
to use, or are we going to double on my bicycle?
she asked.

"We'll use my runabout."

There was one thing to be said for a runabout, sh
reflected as she climbed into the passenger side of hi
D-F Firefly; it could not be driven over a safe spee
and was virtually impossible to tip over. "Where first?

"Kay says we can find Roan Kinnis at or around th
Carousel Club. Let me go in first and try to intersec

then you come along. If I haven't found him, we'll see who wants to bolt when you come in.''

The Carousel was on Quincy, near Seventh. Mama went in with the head-bobbing, sliding walk affected by trippers, as if he were moving in time to jiva-queme music. Janna sat in the Firefly and counted off five minutes, then she followed him.

Mama was seated in a rear booth, talking to a small man in a pink and purple jumpsuit. She walked up to the bar. The Carousel's clientele were business people. A number of them, male and female, looked her over as she came in, some with casual interest, some with speculation. The man with Mama, however, suddenly became very relaxed. He pretended not to notice her at all.

She moved to his table. "Am I spoiling a transaction, Kinnis?" She sat down beside him, trapping him between Mama and her.

The street dealer raked her with his eyes. "I don't know what you're talking about, leo."

"She's talking about the trick you were going to sell me," Mama said.

Kinnis tried to look innocent but the attempt did not quite succeed. He looked from one to the other and clutched at the edge of the table as if considering trying to leap over it. "So you're a lion, too. When did they start pinning badges on skinheads?" His contempt could not conceal the nervous quiver in his voice. "He's lying about me selling trick. He can't prove anything I said," he told Janna.

"Want to hear the playback on my microcorder, jon?"

Kinnis looked gray even in the Carousel's dusky rose lighting. "Bastard!"

"Peace," Janna said. "We aren't Vice. We won't strap you . . . not this time." She was for damn sure going to pass his name on to Vice, though. "We just want to ask you a few questions. If we like the answers, then we'll just stand up and walk away, and you can go back to peddling your cut-rate happiness pills to these sterling citizens.''

Kinnis chewed his lip. "What do you want to know?"

Janna pushed down the contempt that wanted to curl her lip. He was an amateur. It must be soft working downtown with middle and upper class citizens. One of the dealers from Oakland or a similar area would never have surrendered so fast.

"Have you ever sold any trick to this man?" Mama pulled a picture of Hazlett out of a hip pocket.

Kinnis looked it over. "No, I don't think so."

"You aren't sure?"

He shrugged. "I transact my business in places like this. The light's never bright. People's faces look strange. I don't think I've dealt with him, but I can't be sure."

"Does the name Hazlett sound familiar?"

"They don't tell me their names."

"But you learn them anyway, don't you?" Janna said. "You check on them?"

He chewed his lip. "I never checked on anyone whose name turned out to be Hazlett."

"How about Kellener?"

Mama's eyes widened for one surprised moment.

Janna lifted a brow at him. "Let's not be too one-track, Mama."

"I don't know that name either," Kinnis said.

Janna described Kellener. Kinnis kept shaking his head. "That could be any one of a hundred jons I've met, but none of them was named Kellener."

Janna caught Mama's eye and looked toward the door. They had all they were going to get out of this toad. In unison, they stood.

"The answers could have been better, jon, but we'll accept them for now. Don't take any bad card."

They left him shaking and pale.

Theresa Olivera was next. Olivera was more streetwise than Kinnis. She was harder to find and harder to corner. The effort of making her talk proved equally unrewarding. She had nothing more useful to say than Kinnis had. They could not find Joe Luther at all, nor Fran DiMartin.

Janna was hoping Mama would quit and take her home. She was tired. Her jumpsuit was wringing wet with sweat and had plastered itself to her chest and back.

"This isn't my favorite way to spend my free time, you know, Mama."

"I just want to talk to one more jon."

The jon was a bear of a man with hands large enough to sit in. They found him in a computer games arcade, toxy on narcotics.

Janna eyed him. "Another of your contacts?"

"Let me talk to him alone."

Janna shrugged and went back to the Firefly. She leaned against the side of it, spreading herself to catch the slightest breeze.

Mama came out of the arcade in a few minutes, jubilant. "He gave me the names of some dealers operating in Hazlett's neighborhood. He even gave the name of one in Kellener's apartment area. You can't accuse me of having tunnel vision now."

Janna sighed. "I suppose you want to talk to them tonight?"

"Of course. It won't take long."

They found just one of the three dealers supposedly operating in the Brentwood area. The one they found swore he had never heard of either Hazlett or Kellener, nor sold either of them trick.

"I've never sold anyone trick."

Janna felt he was lying about that. However, his denials about selling to Hazlett and Kellener had the ring of truth. They dropped him off on a corner of his choosing.

Watching the dealer disappear up the street, Mama sighed. "I give up for the night. Let's hunt the rest tomorrow."

Some perverse impulse spurred Janna. "Just one more."

He stared at her. "I thought you wanted to quit."

"I did, until you stopped short of looking up the Kellener neighborhood dealer. Now I want to find her, too."

He frowned. "Bibi, I never thought you'd be that kind of woman."

"I'm just asking for equality for all the suspects."

He shook his head but lifted the Firefly off its parking rollers and turned it toward west Tenth.

The address they had been given was a very ordinary house in a quiet residential neighborhood. The woman who looked out through the door's security peep could have been anyone's mother or wife.

Mama checked the address again. "Bez Hilos?" he asked.

She nodded, smiling. "May I help you?"

Janna showed her ID and badge. "May we come in?"

Ms. Hilos led them to a comfortable living room. Janna watched her closely. The woman seemed completely at ease. Too much so? Most people were a little disturbed by the appearance of police officers on their doorsteps.

"What can I do for you, officers?"

Janna watched the woman's eyes. "Does the name Kellener mean anything to you?"

"Why, no. Should it?" Her pupils dilated as she said it.

"You've never sold drugs to anyone by that name?"

"Drugs?" Her eyes widened in astonishment. "I don't know anything about drugs. I've never sold any to anyone."

"According to our sources you do a bonanza business among housewives and adolescents," Mama said.

Her eyes were innocent. "I don't know who your sources are, but they aren't reliable. I ask you, do I look like a street dealer?"

"Do I look like a leo?"

She stared at him a moment, then laughed. "All right, appearances don't count. I'm no dealer, but if I were, what would you want with me?"

"Just some information," Janna said.

"Are you Vice?"

"No, Crimes Against Persons."

Janna watched the circuits hum in the woman's head. In her way, Hilos was as tough and street-wise as any dealer. Being a housewife working out of her home did not mean she was an amateur. The woman was in control of herself and appeared to suffer from no pangs of guilt.

She said, "Why are you interested in this Kellener?"

"We need to know if you've ever sold him drugs."

"Him?"

The exclamation slipped out before Hilos stopped herself. Janna and Mama exchanged quick glances.

"You mean it's Kellener's wife Liann Seaton who's been your customer?" Janna asked.

Hilos considered for a long minute, then nodded.

"What do you sell her?" Mama asked.

"A few hallucinogens and some boosts and tranks . . . the usual housewives' medley."

"Have you ever sold her any trick?"

Hilos snapped around to glare up at Janna. "Certainly not," she snapped. "I like my customers in condition to remain my customers. I wouldn't sell trick to my biggest competitor, or even to a lion."

"Has Seaton ever asked where she might buy trick?"

The dealer's mouth set in a thin slash of lip. "No, and I wouldn't have told her if she had. If I knew anyone selling illegals, I'd have made a call to Vice long ago. Someone who sells trick or dust is as good as an executioner and ought to be locked away for life, or better yet, given their own junk."

Janna bit her lip to hide a smile. The dealer's outrage tickled her. Criminals could be so self-righteous about other criminals and other crimes.

Mama grinned outright. "Very civic-spirited of you."

His sarcasm did not endear them to her. Hilos pointed at the door. "I think that's enough. I'll bid you good night, leos. I don't want you here when my husband brings the kids back from the park."

They let her throw them out.

Climbing into the runabout, Janna said, "Well, what do you think?"

"You can't be thinking she killed him?"

"Why not? She's a tripper. She knows drugs and has access to them. You know how many spouses murder each other every year?"

He frowned. "I suppose you want to talk to her."

"Of course."

He started the Firefly's fans and sailed the runabout the few short blocks to the Kellener apartment.

Liann Seaton's smile was puzzled as she opened the door to let them in. "What brings you out at this time of night?"

Janna listened to every nuance of the question. There was curiosity in it, and hesitant hope, but not a single note of fear that Janna could detect.

"May I bring you anything? Caff? Tea? Liquor?"

"No, thank you."

Janna was tempted to sit in a deep chair that reminded her of one her grandfather used to have. In it, one felt surrounded, almost hidden. She turned away from it to choose one that was straight and hard.

"We've just been talking to Bez Hilos, Ms. Seaton."

The lovely face froze. "Bez." Her voice sounded strangled.

"How long have you been a tripper?"

"Since—since college. I've never seen any harm in it if done in moderation," she said defensively.

Mama regarded her keenly. "Your husband didn't approve of drugs, though."

She looked away. "No."

"Is that why you went to a street dealer, so you wouldn't have narcotics purchases on your bank record?"

"What business is it of yours, may I ask?"

"Your husband died of a trick overdose."

She snapped around to stare at him, then at Janna. "Trick?" Her breath caught and her face bleached. "No. You can't think that I— I adored him."

"You never fought over your use of drugs?" Janna asked.

"He never knew. I was very careful never to boost around him. Sergeant." Her voice was intense. "I've

148

never used illegals. *Never.* I don't have the slightest idea where to buy them."

Janna had to admire her. She was obviously terrified, but she was not giving in to panic. She was as controlled as she had been the day her husband was found. Too controlled, maybe?

"Still," Mama said, "it's interesting that he should be an OD when you're the tripper."

"I was here with my children the entire evening."

Mama's shrug dismissed her children as witnesses. Liann Seaton looked from him to Janna. Tension twitched muscles in her jaw. "Did you come here to arrest me?"

"No, we're just investigating all possibilities, Ms. Seaton."

"If you're looking for someone who trips, you won't have any shortage of suspects." She paused. "Does this mean you don't think he committed suicide, or that he had anything to do with those poor people on the *Invictus?*"

Even when she seemed to be a suspect for murder, she wanted her husband's name clean. Extraordinary woman. Janna said, "As I said, we're investigating all possibilities."

"What did you mean, we won't have any shortage of suspects if we're looking for a tripper?"

She shrugged at Mama. "Doesn't almost everyone use some drugs?"

"Does Jorge Hazlett?"

She thought. "I don't know. Sometimes when we've seen him socially he's seemed a bit toxy, but whether from drugs or alcohol, I'm sure I couldn't say. I hope you don't suspect Jorge of anything. He can't be responsible. He's been a real rock for me these past few days and he and Andy were always like brothers."

"Siblings kill each other as often as spouses do."

"If Jorge has any aggressions, he takes them out on a chessboard. Have you considered that perhaps Andy died by accident? Maybe one of his office staff left some trick and Andy took it by mistake."

"We've considered that," Janna said.

"And rejected it?"

"We're taking everything to the coroner's jury on Friday."

She became very still. "Including the possibility that I killed him? Why would I have wanted him dead?"

"He made a great deal of credit and gave it away. Without him you could be a rich widow. Or perhaps he caught you boosting and was planning to dissolve the marriage contract. There could be a dozen reasons." Janna grimaced. "I've seen wives attack to kill because the husband wouldn't carry the trash cans to the street on collection day."

The widow laced her hands together in her lap. They were clenched so tight the fingers were white. "You have a very unpleasant job, but I suppose it has to be done. I swear to you, I didn't buy any trick, nor did I give any to my husband. I was here all Saturday evening. I can bring in my children to tell you that if necessary. If you won't believe them, arrest me and let me contact my attorney."

Janna felt dirty and sweaty. She wanted to go home and take a bath. If she went to Champaign with Wim, she would not have to spend her life harassing widows with accusations and innuendos.

She stood up. "It won't be necessary to call your children. Just answer one more question. Could your husband possibly have bought the trick himself, for any reason at all, even an outrageous one?"

Seaton shook her head. "Absolutely not. Andy would have sooner cut off his hands than contaminate them with any kind of narcotics. Andy would never *ever* have bought that trick."

"I think that's all we need for now. I'm sorry to have bothered you so late. Good night."

Janna made Mama take her back to the station to pick up her bicycle. She pedaled hard for home, trying to outrun the feeling of being unclean. The woman was right. It could be a very unpleasant job. She considered Wim's offer some more.

Not until she was stripping for a bath and heard the

crackle of paper in her hip pocket did she remember the computer's response to the watchdog program. She took the list of computer activity out of the pocket and smoothed it on the bathroom countertop. Her finger traced the items listed under number two. They might find who sold someone near Kellener some trick, but the odds were long. This track looked much more promising. In the morning she would have to call Officer Niall Cushman in Highland Park and ask him why he was interested in a novalon suit, a doll, and a child's computer.

CHAPTER TEN

Mama strolled into the squadroom looking ready to sail. He shifted impatiently in his chair during rollcall and raced through dictyping the reports on yesterday's work. He pushed at Janna. "Come on, bibi. We have those dealers to find."

She brought out the list the watchdog had produced. "We have these to check out, too."

He grimaced in indecision. "You just haven't given me enough time. How about another day?"

She shook her head. "The inquest stops it."

"Then we'll have to split up. I'll hunt down the dealers. I can probably pose as a tripper and find them faster anyway. You check out these."

Janna frowned. One of the cardinal rules pounded into them in the Criminal Justice Course and as rookies was: don't work alone. She could still hear the instructor, a veteran officer, pounding his fist on the desk as he strove to make his point emphatic enough. "Isolation is the police officer's biggest enemy. It is the primary factor in mental illness, accident, and death. Don't work alone. No matter how tempting a lead, remember you're part of a team. Safety is in unity."

Mama seemed to read her mind. "We aren't really working alone. You know what I'm doing. I know what you're doing. You have your ear button to keep in touch with the dispatcher."

She considered. "All right. Be careful. Don't push any of them too hard."

"Yes, Mother." He blew her a kiss and hurried out the door of the squadroom.

Janna punched the Highland Park division number into the phone. "Niall Cushman, please," she told the officer who answered. "Sergeant Janna Brill of Crimes Against Persons calling."

"Just a minute."

She waited more than a minute. It was more like ten, and when the screen went off hold, the face on the screen was the answering officer's. "Cushman's left the station already. I'll have the dispatcher tell him to call you."

She gave him her number and extension and punched off.

A shadow fell across her. She looked up at Morello. He was holding a stack of complaints. "Happy unbirthday. It's gift time."

She grimaced. "Take those away. I still have all these." She pointed to a stack on her table.

"You haven't cleared very many cases the past couple of days, have you?"

"This Kellener case is time-consuming."

His brows went up. "I thought it was pretty clearly a suicide."

She shuffled through some reports. "There's nothing very clear about it."

Morello regarded her speculatively. "You sure you're not letting Maxwell run away with the investigation?"

She was not at all sure, but she would sooner cut out her tongue than admit that to Morello. "I'm sure. I'm senior partner; I'm running it."

The phone buzzed. She stabbed the on button. "Crimes Against Persons, Sergeant Brill."

The screen brightened into the image of a stocky, freckle-faced man in civilian clothes but with the unmistakable look of leo about him. Jane, she thought.

"I'm Niall Cushman. The dispatcher said you wanted me to call you."

"Yes. Tuesday you made a stolen property query on a novalon suit, a Dyan Pennock doll, and an Eduvac Junior computer. Those items, or ones like them, are part of an investigation. May I ask why you made the query?"

"One of my neighbors asked me to." His forehead creased in concern. "What investigation?"

"The Kellener death. The items in your query turned up on a bank record. Tell me about this neighbor of yours."

"Her name is Clio de Garza." He spelled it out. "She's lived down the street from us for four or five years. We're casual friends. Her daughter and ours play together. Monday evening she came over looking very worried. She pretended nothing was wrong but after jibbing around for fifteen minutes or so she asked if there were a way she could find out whether or not something were stolen without attracting official attention and getting someone in trouble."

"Did she say why she wanted to know?"

"No." Cushman rubbed his nose. "But I can guess. Tuesday afternoon her daughter was over at our house when I came home from work. She had a brand new Dyan Pennock doll. There's a sligh who visits them every Sunday. Clio once told my wife he's Tesha's father. I'd say he brought her the doll on his last visit and Clio was afraid a toy that expensive must be stolen. She was certainly relieved when the computer didn't ID anything."

His guesswork sounded good to Janna. "Where can I reach this de Garza woman?"

"She's a teacher. I think she's teaching half days in the summer session at Highland Park High School and doing special tutoring the rest of the day." He paused.

"Do you think her sligh friend is involved in this Kellener's death?"

Janna shrugged. "We're looking for leads and following them out. In case I can't find de Garza, what time does she usually get home?"

"About suppertime."

"Have you ever met the sligh?"

Cushman shook his head. "I've only seen him at a distance. I asked about meeting him once, because I was curious, but Clio said it was impossible. He's lion-shy."

Janna thanked him for his help and punched off. She sat staring at the blank screen. De Garza taught half days in the high school summer session. The summer semester at Janna's high school in Wichita had run from seven o'clock to noon, letting out before the heat of the day made the building unbearable. Perhaps Shawnee County school officials did the same thing.

She punched the directory button and asked for the Highland Park High School number. It printed across the screen. She copied it down, returned the phone to the call mode, and put in the number.

"Ms. Clio de Garza," she said to the woman who answered.

The woman that request brought to the phone was a young and attractive Hispanic. "I'm Ms. de Garza. What may I do for you?"

Janna introduced herself. Something wary came into de Garza's eyes. The woman was a bit lion-shy herself, it appeared.

"I'm calling in reference to the stolen property query you asked Officer Niall Cushman to make."

The wariness grew more pronounced. "Are those things stolen after all?"

"I don't know. I'm interested in the query because the bank record of an individual involved in a current investigation lists, among other items, the purchase of two novalon suits from Fine Threads in the Whitelakes Mall and a Dyan Pennock doll and child's computer from The Children's Bower, also in Whitelakes."

The Hispanic woman's face smoothed into the bland

mask of rigid control. Her eyes were expressive, however. They betrayed fear. Janna considered how to proceed. She did not want to frighten the woman into silence.

"Please understand that I'm not accusing you of anything, nor am I trying to trap you, but I must ask you why you were concerned about identical items."

"Coincidence, sergeant?" de Garza suggested.

"I doubt it. I'm aware your daughter has a new Dyan Pennock doll. Did your sligh friend bring it to her, and a child's computer, too?"

Her eyes narrowed. "I thought Niall was a friend."

"He had very little choice but to tell me, Ms. de Garza. I asked the questions and if he hadn't answered he would have been guilty of obstructing an investigation. Please, this is very important. Did the items come from your friend?"

Her hand moved as though wanting to stab the off button. It hovered near the edge of the screen for a long time, trembling, then slowly lowered. "Yes. The sack said, 'The Children's Bower' on it."

"What about the novalon suit?"

"He . . . was wearing one."

"Do you know how he happened to come by these things?"

She pressed her fingers to her forehead, rubbing at the creases between her eyes. "He said a friend bought them for him in return for a favor."

"You didn't believe him?"

De Garza straightened. "Of course I believed him. We have complete trust in one another. We never lie to each other."

"Yet you asked Officer Cushman to see if they were stolen."

"Because—" She sighed. "The other person could have been lying to my friend. I've seen suits like that in shop windows. I know how much they cost. And the toys were expensive, as well. I couldn't believe someone would give them away."

"It might depend on the kind of favor your friend did. Do you happen to know what it was?"

De Garza looked away. Her fingers went to her mouth, then her forehead, rubbing at the skin between her eyes. She looked several shades paler.

"Ms. de Garza?" Janna prompted gently.

She continued to look away. "He—'" Her hand went back to her mouth. She spoke through the bars her fingers made across her lips. "All he would tell me was that it was something illegal."

An electric shock trickled up Janna's spine. "Do you know who he did the favor for?"

"He wouldn't say."

From here on the questioning became harder—much harder. "Ms. de Garza," Janna waited until the woman was looking at her again before going on. "I'll have to see your friend and talk to him."

"Oh, no." Her body swayed backward. "He won't let you anywhere near him."

"I have to talk to him. Surely you can see that. If he won't agree to an informal meeting, we'll have to bring him in. You say the two of you trust each other completely. If you arrange a meeting and come to it with me, if you assure him that I'm less interested in him than in the man he did the favor for, do you think he might be willing to see me?"

"*Are* you more interested in the other man than in Ow—my friend?"

"Yes. My business is hunting wolves, not field mice. Tell your friend I need his help. Promise him that the three of us will be the only ones there."

The woman rubbed her forehead again. "I don't know. I can trust Niall Cushman because he's a neighbor, but . . . most of my experiences with the leos haven't been pleasant. I've been arrested six times for teaching in unlicensed schools."

Her special tutoring, no doubt. That was a break. If de Garza was a sligh sympathizer, it gave Janna a chance with her.

"I used to work the Oakland division. The slighs there knew me as a friendly lion. Ask some of them about me. Ask Quicksilver. Call me back at the Crimes Against Persons squad when you've decided you can trust me and have arranged a meeting with your friend."

De Garza thought it over. "And if I don't call you back?"

"I still have to talk to your friend, one way or another."

The woman sighed. "I'll see what I can do."

As soon as the screen was off, Janna went to tell Vradel what she had.

Vradel was doubtful. "I don't like the idea of your going out alone, not even to talk to a sligh. If he panics, we have no way of knowing what he might do."

"I'll have my Colt needler and I can take a K-12 spray capsule. I'll be wearing my ear button."

"All right." His grunt indicated his consent was against his better judgment. "Be careful. You get hurt and I'll break your arm."

"Yes, sir."

He looked past her. "Where's your shadow?"

"Out hunting the street dealer who sold Hazlett or Kellener or whoever the trick that killed Kellener."

His eyes glinted. "You let him go alone?"

What could she say? "Yes." She told him about the agreement between them on the Kellener case.

The lieutenant's comments were more grunts, ending with, "You're letting his imagination run away with you, but I can see holding him back isn't easy. All right, that's all." He picked up papers.

Janna returned to her worktable. A new stack of papers lay there. She sorted through quickly. They were all reports from Forensics and Pathology. Under the reports was the sheet with the activity list the watchdog program had located. There were still two items to check out. She laid the reports aside to read later.

Item number one: the group of suits recovered in a raid were part of the goods found with a fence. She talked about it with an investigator in Crimes Against Property. The Stellar Fashions suits had all born the store mark of a shop in the Gage Center. She crossed that item off the list.

The suits found in Mr. Frederick Weltmann's D-F

Kodiac were used clothing. They no longer had store marks in them. They were, however, items described in a burglary complaint made on July twentieth. Other items in the complaint—a newscanner, a microfiche viewer, and a holovision set—were also found in the Kodiac. Mr. Weltmann was currently being held in the county jail on a charge of receiving stolen property. The fact the suits were old enough for the store marks to have worn off disqualified them from Janna's interest. She crossed Mr. Weltmann's suits off her list, too.

Mama checked in just before noon and threw himself in a chair with a sigh of disgust. "I've found about half the dealers and none of them has ever seen Hazlett, or Kellener—except on the newscanner." He closed his eyes. "Maybe we can find the rest of them this afternoon."

"Maybe the computer has a better lead than street dealers."

Mama sat up and opened his eyes. He pushed his glasses up his nose. "What lead?"

She told him about de Garza and her sligh friend.

He rubbed his hands together in satisfaction. "Nova. When and where are we meeting the sligh?"

"She hasn't called back yet. *You* aren't going in any case."

He frowned.

"Don't pout, Mama. I made a promise."

He shrugged.

They spent the afternoon hunting street dealers while Janna listened to her ear button, waiting for de Garza's call. They found all but one of the dealers they wanted, for what good it did them. The dealers flatly denied selling either Kellener or Hazlett, or Liann Seaton, any trick. They did not recognize the names or pictures of any of Kellener's office staff. It was hot, sweaty, discouraging work. Janna was starting to feel dizzy from the fumes of alcohol and narcotics filling the bars where all of the dealers seemed to hang out.

Janna's ear button murmured, "Indian Thirty, call the station."

At last! Janna tapped the button. "Indian Thirty, roger." She dug a vending token out of a thigh pocket and headed for the nearest phone.

From the station, Pass-the-Word Morello said, "You had a call from a Ms. Clio de Garza. She wants you to call her right back at this number." He read it off.

"Thanks." She punched off and fed in another token. She punched the number Morello had given her.

De Garza answered on the first ring. The background behind her suggested she was using the public phone in a bar.

"Will your friend talk to me?" Janna asked.

"I can't find him. I'm in the place he works, but they say he hasn't been here for days. Sergeant, that worries me. Owan is a very dependable man. This is where he eats his meal every day. I'm about to go check his room."

The sligh was missing? That set off alarms in Janna, too. "Don't leave yet. Where are you? I'd like to talk to the people there."

"I'm at the Pioneer's Pleasure on East Seventh Street."

"I know where it is. Wait for me. I'll be right there."

She had Mama drive her back to the station, where she hung her equipment belt in her locker. It would hardly do to descend on de Garza and the sligh with a Starke slung on her hip. She substituted her little Colt needler. It was accurate to no more than two meters but was small enough to carry in a thigh pocket, an ideal off-duty weapon. She put a spray tube of K-12 in the other thigh pocket. She kept her ear button, then headed for her bicycle.

"Are you sure you don't want me along?" Mama asked.

"Two leos coming down would look like an interrogation team. If I need you, though, I'll whistle." She pointed to her ear button.

She found de Garza waiting for her just inside the door of the Pioneer's Pleasure. "They say Owan hasn't been in since Monday."

Janna looked around. "Exactly who says?"

"Alyn, the bartender."

Janna headed for the bar. "Hello, Alyn. I'm a friend of Owan. May I ask you a few questions about him?"

Alyn looked her over. "Sure, leo. What do you want to know?"

Leo. Why did people always smell lion when she walked in the door, no matter what she wore? "When did you last see Owan?"

"Monday night, like I told the other woman. He was supposed to work until the club closed but he got someone to come in for him about nine thirty and he left. He said he'd be in at the usual time Tuesday but he never showed up. He ran the dishcleaning machine. The manager was pissed about having to find a substitute at the last minute, too, I'll tell you."

The sligh disappeared the day Kellener's body was discovered. Could there be a link? "Tell me, did he work Saturday night?" The answer to that might help establish if the sligh were somehow tied to the night Kellener died.

"No, he didn't work all day Saturday."

"Was it a regular day off?"

"Day off?" Alyn shook his head. "Owan almost never took a day off."

"Then it was unusual for him to be gone Saturday and leave early Monday?"

"Like snow in July."

The smell of lion meat was strong in Janna's nose. Somehow the sligh was involved in Kellener's death. He had been free the night Kellener died and he had items charged to Hazlett's bank account. He had exhibited unusual behavior on two separate days, both days important in the case.

"Do you have any idea why he left early Monday night?"

The bartender shook his head. "He made a phone call late in the afternoon. After that he said he had to leave and would find someone to cover the last few hours for him."

"Do you know who he called?"

"No. It seemed to calm him down, though. He'd been spooky until then."

Spooky? "From the time he came to work?"

"Not that early. He was fine when he came in. The fool had a fancy new blue suit and went daydreaming around like he was in a world of his own. He didn't go nervy until I called him up to the bar to see that news story about the guy who died."

Her nerve endings buzzed. She kept her voice level. "Guy who died?"

"The colonial contractor who was found dead in his office. The news interviewed his partner. Strange thing; he was the spit of Owan. I called Owan up to see. You'd have thought Owan had seen a ghost, he went so pale. Everyone has a double somewhere, they say, but I suppose it can be a bit of a shock meeting yours."

Janna wanted to whoop in triumph. She felt de Garza looking at her. She thanked the bartender calmly instead and walked fast for the door.

De Garza followed. "What is it you think Owan's done? He's a gentle man. He'd never kill anyone. He told me that what he was involved in wasn't serious."

"I don't believe your friend killed anyone." He would not have panicked seeing Hazlett on the newscanner if he had been knowingly involved in the killing. "But it looks now as if he may be involved in the fraudulent use of a Scib Card. Now we need to check out where he lives."

De Garza's face closed. "I don't want to get him in trouble."

Janna snapped, "Talking to him is the only way I can keep him *out* of trouble. I told you, I'm hunting a wolf, not field mice."

As much as it pained her to admit it, it looked more and more as if that lunatic Mama was right. She wanted to establish a definite connection between Hazlett and Owan before she laid this in front of Vradel and the rest of the squad, though.

"I didn't get the reputation of being a friendly lion by strapping slighs."

De Garza debated, her face in a tense grimace. Finally: "All right. I'll take you there."

She drove her runabout and Janna followed by bicycle to a seedy apartment complex on the southern edge of the Oakland area. De Garza showed her to a room in a corner of the basement in the main building. There was no reply to their knock.

"He may not be here. I didn't see his bike outside."

Janna looked around the building until she found the manager. "Do you know where Owan is?"

The manager had no idea. "I haven't seen him since Monday. I'm about ready to rent his room to someone else. If he won't do the handiwork, he hasn't earned the space."

Another kind-hearted benefactor of slithyfolk. Janna kept her face expressionless. "Do you have a key to his room?"

She did. After some persuasion and a look at Janna's badge, she gave it to them. "What kind of trouble is he in?"

"No trouble," Janna said. She was not giving the manager an excuse to throw the sligh out. "We think he's the missing heir to the fortune of a western Kansas land baron. We're looking for proof of it."

They left the manager staring wide-eyed after them.

Janna unlocked the door. The room was small, little more than a cell, with only one window high in the wall, and a bed, desk, and dresser that would have been spurned in a prison.

De Garza looked around, shuddering. "I don't know why he couldn't bring himself to be idented. Imagine living like this all your life."

Janna preferred not to imagine it. She opened the closet. There were only three suits in it. Two were what she expected in a sligh's closet, a worn pioneer style shirt and trousers and a near-new but cheaply made jumpsuit. The third suit was the novalon jumpsuit glowing in yellow glory.

"That's the one he wore Sunday."

The bartender at the Pioneer's Pleasure said Owan had worn a blue suit Monday. Hazlett's purchase record showed two suits of identical price. One yellow and one blue, perhaps?

She riffled through the desk. There was nothing in it but paper and writing instruments. The wastebasket, however, had a thick layer of small paper scraps in the bottom. Janna picked out several larger pieces. Both sides of each bore writing, but no more than one or two letters each, too little to tell what had been written. One piece had a clear *ge*. On another was *zl*.

"Is it all right for you to do this without a search warrant?" de Garza asked.

"Technically, it's trespassing. Owan can raise hell if he catches us here." She dropped the pieces of paper back in the wastebasket. "But I'm not acting as a police officer," she said righteously. "I'm a concerned friend."

She opened the top drawer of the dresser. Lying on the few pair of socks inside were an envelope of the type sold by the hundreds, a small plastic tube of glue, a white card signed with Jorge Hazlett's signature, and a 2-D photograph of Hazlett, looking surprised.

"That looks almost like Owan, except Owan's hair used to be longer and tied back. Now his hair looks like that," de Garza said.

Janna returned the photograph to the drawer. Ask and ye shall receive. She had her connection between the two men. It was enough, anyway, to take to Vradel. She drew a long, slow breath and closed the drawer. "Let's go."

She locked the room and returned the key to the manager. She could see the avid questions in the woman's eyes but only gave her a card. "Call me when Owan comes back, please."

If he came back. He could have been encouraged to take a long vacation out of town.

"I'd like you to call me, too, if you see him, Ms. de Garza," she told the Hispanic woman as they left the building.

De Garza sighed. "I feel guilty about this. I hope I've done the right thing."

Without her Janna might never have discovered the possible bank record deception. "You've done the right thing." She watched de Garza climb into her runabout. "You said Owan has a bicycle. Will you describe it for me? What make and year is it?"

"No make or year. He built it himself out of Gitane and Antonioni parts, I think. He used to work at a bicycle shop. It's a ten-speed with dropped handlebars, painted gray and black. Owan said they were good colors for a sligh."

"It isn't registered and licensed, I suppose."

"Yes, as a matter of fact, it is . . . to me, but I don't remember the number."

"I can look it up. Thank you."

Janna let her go and swung onto her own bicycle, but rather than go back to the station, she rode north to Seward Street, to the Oakland division police station.

CHAPTER ELEVEN

It was like dropping three years out of her life. Stepping off her bicycle in front of the old Sacred Heart School, Janna felt as if she had never been away. Like calling the division station the Sacred Heart School. Even that came back like reflex. The concrete plaque on the front of the building had said *Oakland Division Police Station* for over fifty years but everyone in the division, leos and residents alike, still called it by its former name. The old building, bricks turned from red to black by time and grime, clung to its identity so tenaciously it even affected the local slang. Around Oakland going to work or bringing someone in was "going to school."

She climbed the concrete steps worn to a sag in the middle by generations of children's and leo's feet. He own feet remembered every step. She walked in past empty wall niches and thought, once more, of the irony of a bankrupt church school sold for taxes becoming a police station. Its convent, perhaps less ironically, was now the cell block.

It was not like losing the years, she decided after all; it was more like coming home. Sergeant Paul Davila was still the day desk officer. An old warmth woke in her at the sight of him.

"Hello, Paolo."

His head snapped up from his paperwork. His dark eyes lighted. "Welcome back, *chiquita*. Are you homesick for the war zone or just come slumming to wave your Investigator II promotion around?"

"Perhaps I came to see you."

He shook his head. "Don't tease, *querida*. The Phoenix is a mythical bird."

"Sorry. I need a man picked up."

He handed her a form and tilted his head around so he could read while she wrote. "A sligh? That'll make it harder. What's the charge?"

"He's a witness in a homicide case. Make this an APB, will you, and stress that I need him just as fast as possible? I know the watch doesn't have anything else to do."

Paul grinned. "We appreciate your efforts to keep us from being bored. Anything else I can do for you?"

His tone remained light, casual, but something serious touched his eyes. They looked squarely at each other, and for a moment Janna felt that in the midst of the people streaming around them and the incessant buzzing of telephones, they were alone. Wistful regret lay between them, and ghosts of might-have-beens. *Have you changed?* she wanted to ask, *or do you still insist the only proper relationship is in a sacramental marriage?*

Then someone at the far end of the desk called, "Davila," and Paul turned to reply to the officer's request. The moment was gone. When he came back to her, she said, "I could use a phone with privacy."

"The lieutenant's out at the moment. You can use his office."

She stepped around the corner to what had probably been one of the school administration offices long ago. She punched the Crimes Against Persons number into the phone. Maro Desch answered.

"Let me speak to Vradel," Janna said.

"I'll get him."

Lieutenant Vradel came onto the screen with raised brows. "What have you found, Brill?"

As concisely as possible, she told him about her conversation with the bartender in the Pioneer's Pleasure and what she had found in Owan's room. Vradel listened in silence, but as she talked, his face became granite and he started chewing his mustache. When she finished, he sat a minute, mustache twitching, before he spoke. "Have you put out a pick-up order on this sligh?"

"Yes, sir."

"Where are you now?"

"The Sacred—the Oakland division station. I thought I'd visit some of the sligh hangouts I know and talk to a few old friends. They may be able to find Owan faster than our people."

"If they will." He sighed. "I'd better call Kolb and have him postpone the inquest tomorrow. Why are you grimacing, Brill?"

"Sir, if we do that, it may alert Hazlett. Right now he must think his alibi is perfect. He'll be relaxed."

"Until we talk to the sligh, we'd better think of his alibi as perfect, too." Vradel chewed on one end of his mustache. "You're right about making him suspicious, but we can't very well let the inquest go ahead and risk having the jury return a verdict of suicide."

Janna was thinking hard. What could delay an inquest that would not alarm Hazlett? A witness not able to be there was one possibility, but none so far were vital enough to delay the inquest for. "Lieutenant, what if we had a street dealer who said he'd sold someone in the firm some trick? We could ask for a delay while we checked out his story."

"You don't think that will alarm Hazlett?"

"It might cause him anxiety, but it won't seem that we're after him specifically. There is always the bank record to protect him."

"All right. We'll handle it that way. Good luck hunting the sligh." He paused a moment. "What I said about being careful goes double now."

She smiled. "Yes, sir. Thank you."

She punched off and sat for several minutes mentally reviewing the sligh hangouts she remembered, planning her route. She hoped they were still there. Like jobs and living quarters, recreation locations were ephemeral things in slithyland. Three years was a long time.

She went back to the desk. "Thanks for the use of the phone."

He nodded. "I suppose you're going to rush off now. Stay long enough for a cup of caff, why don't you?"

"So we can stir the ashes? I thought you don't believe in the Phoenix."

"I believe in friendship. Let me buy you dinner some night."

"That would be nice." She blew him a kiss as she left.

She came down the steps in long bounds and swung onto her bike. There was one place she was sure would not have changed. The *Buenas Noches* was just down the street from the station, on the edge of Oakland's shopping district. It had been a favorite local bar for three generations and would probably still be serving on doomsday. The Santos family owned it. Jesus Santos, grandson of the original buyer, ran it now. Jesus ran it clean, with some gambling tables and a few girls and boys upstairs, all properly licensed and all closed for business by three A.M. Jesus deviated only in that he took barter, not just bankcredit. That way even locals on government food and housing coupons could entertain themselves. Slighs could, too.

She rode down the street, steering between the potholes and trash. From the outside, neither the faded lettering on the windows nor the begrimed, fly-specked windows of the bar seemed to have changed since she used to patrol past here. Stepping inside, she found the place had not changed, either. The wall-mounted phone near the door still had a smashed screen. The floor was still thick with peanut shells. Narcotic haze hung heavy and blue in the dimly-lighted air. A holo player cast a weak image of a jivaqueme band at the far end, playing their music on the lower threshold of perception.

The music was current, though, she noticed. It grabbed her by her biorhythms. Its flutes sang in her blood and the beat pulled her pulse into time with it. It made her want to move into the middle of the floor with the two or three people already there and dance until she folded.

Two men in earnest head-to-head conversation at a table near the door looked up as she came in. They both stiffened, then leaned back casually and pretended to listen to the music. Janna recognized them for street dealers. She knew they recognized her, too, from the time she had worked Vice.

"Still cutting your junk with rat poison, Hilding?" she asked as she passed them.

The street dealer sneered, but as soon as she was past, stood and scuttled out. She hoped she had spoiled a transaction.

Jesus' sister Dolores was tending bar. Janna ordered iced tea and turned around so she could lean her back to the bar while she looked around. The bar was almost empty. Most of the patrons would not begin coming in until after six.

Dolores brought her tea. She paid for it and carried it to a table with a good view of the door. For the next two hours she sat sipping and listening to the music of the player. Gradually the room started to fill. Some of the faces she knew. They returned her gaze with a smile or a sneer. She heard a couple of *miaows* after people had passed and were behind her.

One man called, "Hey, kitty."

She ignored the taunt and let her eyes slide past the citizens; she needed slighs. The several who came in all sat at the far back. As she expected, most were strangers. There were three who had been friends, though. One of them was Quicksilver, sallow and thin as ever. Quicksilver was something of a hero among slighs. He had run a school for fifteen years and never once had it raided.

She caught his eye and beckoned to him. He unfolded himself from his chair and made his way toward her, shuffle-walking in time to the music. She was pleased to note he did not hurry. Most slighs came to a leo in cringing-dog eagerness, if they had to come, in order not to take the chance of irritating the lion.

Quicksilver nodded. *"Buenas noches.* I was talking to someone about you just today, a Ms. Clio de Garza." He paused. "I gave you a recommendation."

"I appreciate it. Q, I'm calling in favors tonight."

His brows went up. "I owe for the warnings you passed on school raids. You hunting?"

"Not really. One of your people is a witness I need. His name is Owan. Late forties, a hundred seventy-five centimeters, medium build, brown hair graying at the temples, worn tied back or in a lion's mane, brown eyes. He may be wearing a blue jumpsuit of novalon."

Quicksilver pursed his lips. "Fine seams. It's a big favor, hunting one of my own, leo."

"I don't want to strap him, just talk to him. Have I ever lied to you before?" She made her voice velvet.

The sligh's smile was thin. "Not that I ever learned. All right. I'll take you around. Most of the places have changed since you moved downtown."

She nodded.

"Let me tell my friends over there that I'm going. I don't want them to worry about me."

Janna went on outside. Her head was spinning from the narcotic smoke and her body pulsed to the jiva-queme rhythm. She leaned against a wall, breathing slowly, waiting for the reverberations in her bones to fade.

Quicksilver came out of the *Buenas Noches.* He eyed her. "The people who know you aren't going to run away, but there are new people who will take one look and fade into the woodwork. Is there something you can do to make yourself look less like a lion?"

"I don't want anyone to think I'm trying to fool them. I have nothing to hide. I just want to talk to a witness."

"All right. We'll go as you are."

Quicksilver had no bicycle. Janna walked beside him, pushing hers. They passed a 24-hour market.

"You don't sit around in the back of that place anymore?"

He shook his head. "There's a new owner who *no es simpático*."

They continued walking. On down Seward he went around the back of a little cafe and rapped on the rear door. A woman opened it and looked out.

She stared hard at Janna. "A friend of yours?"

When Quicksilver vouched for Janna, the woman let them in. They found themselves in the cafe's smoky little kitchen. It had no dishcleaning machine, just a sink. A man she remembered vaguely was up to his elbows in water and suds. Around a table near the sink sat half a dozen more slighs, playing cards and talking to the dishwasher. Conversation stopped with the suddenness of a cut throat as Janna and Quicksilver walked in. Everyone stared at Janna.

"Davo," Quicksilver said to the dishwasher, "you remember Sergeant Brill. She caught your kid snatching in the Tiggy store and let him go with a warning."

The dishwasher nodded. Some of the wariness faded from his eyes. "What can I do for you, sergeant?"

"Forget rank; I'm off duty."

"One of our people is a witness she needs. She promises no trouble for him; she just wants to talk to him. He's named Owan." He gave them Owan's description. "Anyone know him?"

The entire group shook their heads. "Never heard of a sligh like that. Where would one of us get a novalon suit?"

"Pay for a job," Janna said.

"No one gives slighs that kind of job."

Across the table from the woman who spoke, a man

stiffened. His eyes fixed hard on his cards. "Are we playing or talking?" He spun a square of plastic into the middle of the table.

Quicksilver moved toward the door. "Let's go."

Outside, Janna looked back toward the door and sighed. "I don't know that they would have told me if they *had* seen Owan."

"You've been away a long time, slithytime, leo."

"You're sure *you've* never heard of Owan?"

Quicksilver shook his head. "I know his girlfriend from her teaching. That's all. We aren't an organized underground. You ought to know that. Organizations eventually attract official notice and we like to avoid being seen. We're mostly little islands unto ourselves, clumping together when we find other friendly islands, then drifting off alone again. Come on, there are other people to see."

The islands clumped in the kitchens of cafes, in the dimmer recesses of a few bars, and on the grass of parks. There were children in the groupings in parks. They played, running and shouting, while their parents listened to Quicksilver ask about Owan. Say what he would about slighs drifting alone, most of them knew and respected the sallow Quicksilver. It was one of the reasons Janna had cultivated him when she worked down here. The other slighs talked to him even when it was obvious they did not care to say anything in Janna's presence.

As she had times meeting slighs before, Janna noticed that eating was not part of sligh social contacts as it was in the rest of society. They talked, they sang, they complained or argued; but they never ate together. People living on the bare subsistence level did not have food enough to use it socially. Even the bar groups were few, and fewer of them were drinking anything but water. There was more likely to be food in the cafes, where the "host" sligh could feel free to offer something belonging to the boss.

They found a few slighs who knew Owan. "He's a quiet, hard-working man. What do you want him for, leo?" was the usual reaction.

171

Her insistence that she only wanted to talk to him, that he was a witness, was received skeptically. Even the people who knew Owan had not seen him recently. The most recent anyone remembered was Thursday or Friday.

After stopping in the parks, Quicksilver started on rounds of homes. He would not let Janna come in with him, but insisted on going in alone at each stop. "They'd never forgive me if I brought you in."

Homes were too personal to show to even a friendly lion. Janna had been in a few slighs' houses before, though. They made Owan's room look palatial. Most squatted in empty houses, with virtually no furniture, usually with no electricity or running water. Janna could not understand how they preferred that abject poverty to having their names and life facts recorded in a few computers. It was insane.

At one stop Janna could hear the people inside arguing hotly. Why, she failed to understand. As nearly as she could determine, everyone in it was on the same side.

Quicksilver appeared at the door and beckoned to Janna. She went down the steps into the dim, candle-lit basement. The room was as bare as she expected, but it was pleasantly cool. The debaters were in a corner. The sligh Quicksilver wanted her to see was across the room in a basket chair, a thin man, bent and twisted into crippled immobility, most likely by a childhood disease like poliomyelitis that a citizen's child would have been immunized against. His eyes were bruised circles.

"I saw Owan Friday evening. He came by for a few minutes after he finished work. He was excited and nervous about something."

Janna said, "Did he say anything about where he was going or what he was going to be doing?"

"No. He'd only say that the thing he was going to do would earn him enough to start saving for a share."

Janna did not need to ask what share. If slighs had another favorite topic besides how unfair the government was, it was talking about the imagined paradise of a colony world. The dream of almost every sligh she knew was to somehow, miraculously, come into enough property to trade in for a colonial share.

Janna asked a few more questions, but the bruise-eyed man had no answers for them. She left. The group in the corner never noticed her coming or leaving.

None of the calls they made after that provided any more information. Finally Quicksilver said, "Everyone will be going to bed soon. We all have to work tomorrow, and most of us have to start early. I'll keep asking, and if I hear something, I'll let you know."

He began fading into the shadows of the street even as she thanked him.

Janna swung on her bike and started pedaling for home. She was disappointed not to have found Owan, but not surprised. If Owan had put things together after hearing about Hazlett's partner, and if he'd panicked, he was hardly likely to be walking around socializing. The abandoned houses and stores all over the Oakland area afforded countless hiding places, if Owan were still in town. It would take a while to check them all.

She found a public phone with working sound and called the Capitol division station. No messages had come in to the Crimes Against Persons squadroom for her from either Owan's landlady or Clio de Garza. She was about to remount her bike when a watchcar drifted to a stop and hovered beside her.

"Let's see your card, bibi."

The voice was a familiar one. She turned, grinning, to face Rina Hallard and Moses Kobuzky. "So you two are still on the street together. I'd have thought that by this time the brass would have learned they need at least one officer in a team who can see out over the dash of the car."

Hallard and Kobuzky were the two shortest leos in the division.

Hallard regarded her coldly. "Your wit hasn't improved a bit being downtown. For your information, they've issued us toddler seats to use, so both of us can see out of the car now."

"Have either of you seen the sligh I issued the APB for?"

They shook their heads. "No."

"Give us something easy, like a needle in a haystack."

"You can ride with us and help search derelict houses if you like."

Janna eyed the rear compartment. "Not unless you let me ride in front, too."

"I don't know what your objection is. Only two winos have thrown up in it tonight," Hallard said.

"Three," Kobuzky corrected.

"She wasn't a wino; she was a ulysses."

"Details, details."

The air from the fans felt hot against Janna's ankles. She moved the bike a little farther from the watchcar. "What street did you have in mind?"

"How about a few blocks of Jacquot? There can't be more than forty empties along there."

Those crumbling houses, at night, in this heat? They were probably joking. She was not about to bite on one of their stunts. "I'll pass. I think I'll go home. I've given the company more than its share of my time today."

She did turn the bike down Jacquot on her way, though. She looked at the houses in passing, when she could spare the time from steering around holes and weeds. Some of them would make good hiding places. For that matter, so would the houses along a dozen other streets.

She passed a boarded-up corner building that had once been a 24-hour shopper when she worked the area. So that place was gone now, too. Had the owner, a friendly man who always had free tea and caff for leos, made enough to buy the share in the colony ship, as he was always talking about doing—or had he been robbed so often he just gave up and closed?

Everyone wanted to go out to a colony, it seemed. Only some of them would ever manage the price. She sighed. She was being given the chance to buy a share. She could leave this jungle any time she wanted. She would even have friends waiting for her when she arrived on the new world. Might she be smart to grab the opportunity?

She must decide just as soon as this case was wrapped up. This case. What a headache. She rode home thinking about it. It bothered her that not only had no one admitted to seeing Owan since Saturday, no one appeared to be lying when they said they had not seen him. No one she had talked to seemed to be helping hide him. He might have left town, of course. On the other hand, something worse might have happened. A man who would kill once could certainly kill again.

Janna sucked her lower lip. She hoped they found Owan soon, and found him in good health.

CHAPTER TWELVE

Janna appeared in the squadroom early to write up her reports on the evening's work before rollcall. As she talked into the dictyper's mike, the machine's laser mechanism silently printed her words onto the report form.

Mama banged in as she was finishing. "There's a notice on the M.E.'s hearing room. Kellener's inquest has been postponed pending new evidence."

Janna pulled the report out of the dictyper. "That's right."

"What new evidence? What have I missed?"

"Nothing. We're just buying time by telling people we have the dealer who sold the trick used."

His eyes lighted behind his glasses. "Buying time?

Then there really is new evidence. What did that sligh tell you yesterday?"

"I didn't see him." She handed her reports to Morello.

He handed her another in return. "This came in late yesterday afternoon."

She glanced through it. It was from Forensics, the handwriting analysis on the signatures. The discussion of slant and loops and stroke pressure was going to take close reading to determine what the report was actually saying. She dropped the report on her table to read later.

The rollcall room was filling with the day watch. The investigators lounged in the chairs, yawning and exchanging friendly insults. Some held cups of caff and tea. Vradel walked in as the wall chrono read: 8:00. Conversation and the scraping of chairs died away.

Vradel nodded at them. "Good morning, leos."

"Roar," someone in the back said.

Vradel studied the notes in his hands. "It was a night of fun and games, as usual. You may all take a moment to mourn the passing of that illustrious fence Jet Horlas."

There was light applause.

"Some unhappy supplier or customer helped Jet beat the heat by ventilating him with a knife. Too bad we can't award a medal."

The list went on. It was long. It always was in extended periods of hot weather. Janna took notes, but scarcely paid attention to what she heard or wrote. Her mind was busy trying to think of places a sligh might hide, or something that might flush him out. Surely a sligh in a novalon suit would be a combination easy to notice. There was the possibility, of course, that in the suit, Owan would no longer look like a sligh.

"Here's a beauty," Vradel said. "Last night three pedestrians had legs broken just below the knees where they were struck by the airfoil skirt of a late-model red Hitachi Bonsai. The runabout was reportedly driven by a Caucasian female. She didn't stop, of course. In fact, she missed the third victim on her first

176

try and had to come back for a second run at him. Let's find this bibi.

"The weather report for today is continued hot with temperatures in the mid to upper thirties. There's a chance of cooling and showers tonight. Keep your fingers crossed. All right, let's sail. Brill and Maxwell, I'll see you in my office."

He strode out of the rollcall room. The rest of the squad followed.

Morello said, "Call for you, lieutenant."

"I'll take it in my office."

Janna and Mama followed him into his office and closed the door behind them.

The caller was Liann Seaton. "Someone from the medical examiner's office called me just now and said Andy's inquest has been postponed. Something about new evidence. Will this help prove my husband didn't kill himself?"

Vradel did not look directly at the screen. "We don't know, ma'am."

"Well, I feel confident that this new witness or evidence will not only show Andy didn't kill himself, but clear him of the charge he was responsible for these poor people on the *Invictus*. Thank you, lieutenant." The screen went blank.

Mama sighed. "I envy that Kellener. None of my wives ever had that kind of faith in me."

Vradel glanced up at him. "They didn't? Strange. Don't start rearranging my desk, Maxwell."

Mama jerked back the hand that had started to reach for an untidy stack of papers on one corner.

Vradel looked at Janna. "Have you told him about the sligh?"

The phone buzzed. It buzzed only once. A moment later Morello stuck his head into the office. "It's for Brill."

She punched the button. Jorge Hazlett's image appeared on the screen. She hid her surprise. "Yes, sir?"

"The medical examiner's office called. It is true the inquest has been postponed?"

Janna kept her face expressionless. The trick was to

keep him from learning she suspected him. "Yes, Mr. Hazlett. We have a witness who may be able to help us locate the source of the trick that killed your partner."

Jorge felt a hot-cold wash of excitement and fear. Had Serena suddenly remembered the drug he took away from her? Had she told someone else? The game was becoming more serious—more serious and consequently more worth playing. That she-lion was so careful to keep expression off her face it must mean she thought they had something important. Still, whatever they had, it should not seriously be able to implicate him. He still had his bank record alibi.

"I'm glad to hear that, sergeant. Good luck with the witness." He could not keep the mocking note out of his voice. He wondered if she noticed it.

Janna noticed. She punched off with a stab of her finger and scowled at the blank screen. "That bastard is laughing at us, lieutenant."

Mama stiffened. His head snapped toward her. He pushed his glasses up his nose. "Hey, bibi, does this mean—"

"It means," Vradel said, "that we're exploring the possibility that Hazlett somehow used the bank records to build himself an alibi. And if you let loose that whoop I see in your eyes, Maxwell, you won't have a day off for six months."

Mama dropped into a chair and sat with fingers laced tightly together. "So you realize I'm right."

Vradel's eyes glinted icily. "We have evidence to that effect now, yes. Note that, Maxwell . . . *evidence*." He told Mama what they had.

Mama's mouth kept opening, as if he had comments, but Vradel did not give him time to speak. "Just listen, Maxwell. You had an inspiration, or made a lucky guess. It wouldn't mean a thing without facts to support it. We have some facts now. Unfortunately we need more." He picked up his pencil and started sketching on his memo pad. "I want to know how Hazlett found himself a double. If he did it, so can others.

178

Think what that will do to the reliability of bank records as evidence of whereabouts."

Janna had a worse thought. What if others already had? There was no way ever to find out. It made her feel dizzy and insecure. Hopefully, she suggested, "Maybe the two of them have known each other for years."

"We can always hope. If they have, some of Hazlett's other friends must be aware of it. Talk to them."

"Except," Mama said, "that Hazlett's a chess player. He thinks a long way ahead. If he thought he might use the sligh this way some day, he would probably have kept the acquaintance a secret."

Vradel frowned. "Can't you contain that imagination for a while? In any case, if what that sligh in Oakland had to say about Owan's behavior Friday is correct, Hazlett set everything up then. Check out his calls for that day. Find out everywhere he went and everyone he saw." He stopped sketching and toyed with the pencil. "This scares the hell out of me. Investigation can be hard enough without having one of our best information sources taken away from us. So until this is settled, until we know for certain whether Hazlett did or did not use a double—and how he managed it— I'm taking you off all other casework. Live, eat, and sleep with this. Bring me back irrefutable evidence. Pretend I'm the D.A. and make me a case that will look so good in court, I'll be sure to be reelected in November." He laid down the pencil and picked up some papers.

It was obviously a dismissal. Janna and Mama filed out. It gave her great satisfaction to pick up the complaint sheets from her worktable and return them to Pass-the-Word Morello. Then the two of them headed for the garage.

"We don't need it for court, but it would be nice to establish a good motive for killing Kellener," Janna said.

"We have one, bibi. Hazlett killed him to put the blame for the *Invictus* and the other frauds on him."

"You're forgetting the papers weren't signed by Hazlett."

"Hazlett could have forged them so they'd look like Kellener did it."

She stopped to stare at him. "Forged his own signature to look like someone else was forging his? That's pretty complex. One time I might be able to believe, but those records go back almost twenty years."

"I told you chess players think a long way ahead. I think complexity ought to be expected, too."

She snorted and walked on. "We'll see what the handwriting people in Forensics have to say about the signatures. I say your idea is too complex. This is real life, not a holo-v program."

"All right, we'll just see what the handwriting experts do have to say, but wouldn't you think that in twenty years, Kellener would have learned to forge his partner's signature better?"

They had almost reached the garage when she remembered that the handwriting analysis was lying on their table right now. She would have to be sure to read it when they returned.

The Santa Fe Building was the first stop.

Riding up in the elevator, Mama said, "Let's have a chat with Hazlett. Let's ask him what he's done with everything he bought Saturday night, and see what he says."

Janna sighed. "Let's not. I'd still like to avoid making him aware his alibi isn't as secure as he thinks."

"He's going to wonder when that prettyboy receptionist of his tells him we wanted to know all the calls and all the visits he made on Friday."

She sucked her lower lip. Mama did have a point. She considered how to get around it. There was a way.

She asked the receptionist for all *Kellener's* calls between Wednesday and Saturday.

She did not have time to warn Mama ahead of time, but if he were startled by her request, he hid it well. He added, "If he left the office during working hours, we'd like to know where he went, too."

"I have the phone log, but you'll have to ask Mr. Peddicord about meetings."

The receptionist pulled the log book from under his desk. In it were pasted strips of tape from the phone's automatic logging attachment that recorded all numbers called through this phone the previous week. On a facing page were listed incoming calls. The outgoing calls did not differentiate between callers, simply listed every number called. Janna wrote down the numbers for Friday. Then she had a thought. The news about the *Invictus* came Wednesday. She wrote down Wednesday's and Thursday's numbers, too. The incoming calls were differentiated so she could list only those coming in to Hazlett.

"Robert, close that book," a crisp voice said.

Janna quickly copied down the last number before the log snapped shut, then looked around at the thin secretary. "Good morning, Mr. Peddicord."

"You will be good enough to obtain a warrant before trying to look at any more of our records. You won't find us willingly helping you and that government agent make Mr. Kellener into a villain."

Mama pushed his glasses up his nose. "Hey, jon, we're not trying to make anyone a villain; we're just gathering evidence."

Peddicord switched his icy stare to Mama. "Is that so? Agent Talous made his position quite clear. He's passed judgment and all he wants is enough evidence to convince a hearing committee of his opinion."

"Well, we aren't Department of Justice agents and we aren't working for—"

Janna stepped between them. "We're doing our best to be impartial, Mr. Peddicord. It might help if we were to know all Mr. Kellener's movements the four days before he died."

"I've had to tell Agent Talous. Ask him." He swung on his toe and marched out of the reception room. They heard his door shut firmly.

The receptionist smiled in apology. "Mr. Peddicord worshipped Mr. Kellener."

Janna nodded. There were several people who had,

apparently. "What about Mr. Hazlett's meetings on Friday? May we speak to his secretary?"

"Ms. Abram isn't here today, but I can tell you that Mr. Hazlett had just two meetings on Friday, both with clients."

"Did he leave the office at any time during the day?"

"Yes, once for lunch and once about two o'clock."

"Was he gone long?"

"About half an hour, I think. He was back in plenty of time for his three o'clock appointment."

"Do you have any idea where he went?"

"He walked some clients to the elevator. They kept him there answering more questions." The receptionist smiled. "He acted out the more comical parts for us when he got back. He's a very good mimic, you know."

Janna thanked him and they went back to the car.

"He could have been setting up Saturday with the sligh in that half hour," Mama said. "He could have just said he was talking to the clients when he was actually using the public phones downstairs to call the Pioneer's Pleasure."

That was a distinct possibility. They needed to ask the Pioneer's Pleasure's bartender if Owan had taken a call Friday afternoon. "But will you do me a favor, Mama? After this, if you can't say something polite, act strong and silent. You didn't help the department's public relations any by that scene with Peddicord."

"Am I supposed to let him be abusive? You'd think Kellener was a saint we were trying to accuse of being in league with the devil."

Who was to say Andrew Kellener might not be as close as mortals came to sainthood? There were a few genuinely fine people in the world. Not everyone was a deek or a toad, though it did seem that the few nice people she met were always victims of the normal representatives of society. Wim and Kellener had been victimized by the deeks, and though she knew little about the sligh Owan, from his girlfriend's regard for him, Janna thought he was probably another nice jon used destructively. Thinking about the class of people she usually saw, she could understand why Wim wanted to go off to a new world. Maybe the good people would be in the majority in the colonies.

They headed back for the squadroom. There they divided the call log between them, then they started the phone work.

"This is Sergeant Janna Brill of the Shawnee County Police. You received a call from Hazlett and Kellener, Colonial Contractors, on Wednesday, July twenty-seventh. May I inquire the nature of that call, please?"

She repeated the message over and over, varying only the day of the call. Usually she received a prompt reply. The call was to arrange for colonial supplies, or to set up medical examination for colonists who were to travel in the sleeper sections of their ship. One call Wednesday was to a club making dinner reservations for two on Friday evening.

"Did you see Mr. Hazlett when he came in that evening?"

"No, but the book is marked *reservation used*."

"Would there be any way to learn who his companion was?"

"I suggest you ask Mr. Hazlett, sergeant."

If Hazlett had come in with a double, some word of it would have spread around. She really doubted Hazlett would have allowed himself to be seen in public with a double, but the question had been worth trying.

The newscanner murmured a public service announcement, urging citizens to buy drugs only from licensed drug stores. "Street drugs are cheaper, but they are not government-inspected. They can be contaminated or below quality."

Janna called the next number. A handsome afroam woman answered. "Lambeth Rentals."

Janna introduced herself. She asked her question.

The woman replied, "I didn't get a call from Hazlett and Kellener as such. Jorgie called me, though."

"May I ask why? This may be relevant to an investigation we're conducting."

"Into why his partner died? I don't think this has

anything to do with that. Jorgie and I are friends. It was just a social call."

"And your name, please?"

"Colla Hayden."

"What did you talk about, Ms. Hayden?"

Hayden looked surprised. "On a social call? Nothing in particular. We traded sexual innuendos and chatted about some of my past parties."

He had called her up at work in the middle of the day just for that? It rang alarms in Janna's head. "He didn't have a reason for calling you?"

"No." She frowned. "Is there something wrong with that?"

Yes, Janna thought. As Mama would no doubt have expressed it . . . it smelled wrong. "No, I suppose not. Does he often call like that?"

"Not often." Hayden's reply was short.

Janna tried to think of a question whose answer might explain the incongruity. Her mind was blank. She thanked Hayden and punched off before the woman's irritation could become hostility.

The next number was a furniture store. The person answering could not recall having talked to Hazlett or Kellener, nor could anyone else she asked around the store at that moment. The number after that was also a furniture store, and they did not remember Hazlett or Kellener, either.

After the sixth furniture store Janna began wondering what was going on. Which of the partners had made these particular calls and why? This puzzle did not quite replace the nagging worry about why Hazlett made a purely social call in the middle of the day, but it pushed it down to a deeper stream of thought.

"Are you getting a lot of furniture stores, Mama?"

He nodded. "Looks like whoever it was, was calling every one in the city. I've also reached one interior decorator. Do you suppose some client wanted a very homey interior in his ship?"

Janna had visions of a ramjet decorated in neo-Victorian or Eighties Depression. She swallowed a giggle. "Just keep calling."

184

Her next number was answered by a pouting beauty of a woman with chestnut hair and sapphire eyes. "Many Mansions, Marca Laclede speaking."

She looked familiar. Janna introduced herself. Halfway through the conversation, she placed the woman. Laclede was one of the buffs who hung around Tuck's place. She had been there on Friday, in fact. She was the one with the sligh jon.

"Hazlett and Kellener?" Laclede said. She looked thoughtful. "Yes, we had a call from them. Rather, I talked to a Mr. Jorge Hazlett."

At last! "What about, please?"

"We're interior decorators. Mr. Hazlett wanted to find a chair to match one he has in his study at home."

Disappointment stabbed like a knife. That would explain all the calls to furniture stores. "Did you find it for him?"

"Oh, yes. There was no trouble at all. I had it by Friday."

Janna held back a sigh. So much for that call. She thanked the decorator.

Laclede smiled. "Any time, sergeant."

Mama craned his neck to see her screen as she punched off. "From the sound of the voice, I wish I'd gotten that one."

"I had the impression she would have adored helping a he-lion," Janna said dryly. "All of which is interesting but no help regarding Kellener's murder. Do you have anything?"

"Nothing."

The phone buzzed. Janna punched it on.

The caller was Clio de Garza, looking upset. "Look what came in the mail today." She held up an official-looking letter in front of the screen. Janna could read nothing of it but the Traffic Division letterhead. "It says I left a bicycle parked in the Sunco lot at Thirteenth and Jackson without a ticket. The bicycle has been impounded and if I want it back, I have to pay the parking fee, impounding charges, and a recovery fine."

Bicycle? Janna straightened. "The one Owan had registered to you?"

The notice came down from the screen. De Garza nodded. "Sergeant, what was Owan's bike doing in a downtown lot?"

Particularly *that* lot. "The impoundment number should be given in the notice. What is it?"

De Garza read the number.

Janna wrote it down. "We'll check on it. Thank you for calling." She punched out and came up out of her chair heading for the door. "Mama, forget those calls for a while."

Impounded vehicles were held in a warehouse in north Topeka, just across the Kansas River in the Soldier Creek division. At the warehouse, Janna showed her badge to the attendants and read off the number Clio de Garza had given her. They were shown to the bicycle.

It was as de Garza had described it, custom-built of Gitane and Antonioni parts. It was a beautiful machine. It did not look cobbled together at all. Owan obviously spent time caring for the bike, too. The gray and black paint had the patina of careful waxing and painstaking hand rubbing.

"When did it come in?" Janna asked.

The attendant checked the tag wired to the handlebars. "It came in Tuesday morning."

"Tuesday? This is Friday. Why did it take three days to notify the registrant?"

The attendant shrugged. "Don't blame me. We just keep them here. Traffic's computer is supposed to print out the notices and after that it's up to the post office to deliver them. Complain to the turtle express."

Mama ran a finger over a gleaming fender. "Would he have abandoned a machine like this, do you think?"

"Not if he could take it with him. Hey, don't auction off this bike. If it isn't claimed, here's my card. Call me. I'll pay the fees on it." She gave the attendant her station card. Interesting it should be in the Sunco lot. Let's pay their librarian another visit."

186

Sunco's librarian smiled at them. "You're getting to be familiar faces. What can I show you this time?"

"Monday night, late. Start about ten o'clock."

She ran the tape. Owan's bike appeared on the tape at the ten-oh-six mark. Owan himself, or his back, at least, was also visible.

"How about Saturday night, too?" Mama asked.

"Right. Give us Saturday night, keyed to the bike's number."

On the Saturday tape, Owan's bike came in at seven-oh-nine.

"Nine minutes after Hazlett sailed in," Mama said. "When does he leave?"

The tape showed no bike of that number leaving by the *Out* ramp.

"He may have lifted the bike back over the *In* gate. I wonder if he knows about the monitor. We can only have summonses issued on bikes we catch coming and going," the librarian said.

"The *In* monitor won't catch him going out?"

"No. It's triggered by weight outside the gate, so by the time the monitor is activated, the bike is already out of camera range."

Janna sucked her lower lip. "Then there should be a space in the tape where the camera runs but there's no vehicle. Run it from about a quarter to ten on through ten thirty."

At ten-oh-five the tape ran with no vehicle in its frame, only empty *In* ramp.

"That's it, bibi. It must be. He got back in time to return the card so Hazlett could catch the bus and be home by ten thirty."

Janna rubbed a crease between her eyebrows. "What was Owan doing back Monday night? Run Monday again, will you, only start twenty minutes earlier?"

At nine fifty a road car with the license number SHH 41348 entered the Sunco lot.

Mama pushed his glasses up his nose. "Hazlett!"

"Together again." Janna said it lightly but she did not feel light-hearted. Something cold and uncomfortable was tweaking her stomach. "Show us when he left, please."

The tape ran . . . and ran.

The librarian frowned. "The car doesn't seem to have left Monday night."

"Run Tuesday."

They ran Tuesday, and Wednesday. At no place along either tape did the computer recognize the Vulcan's license plate and stop the tape.

"I don't understand this," the librarian said. "Could he still have his car there?"

One phone call to the attendant at that lot established that no Vulcans were on the lot, and had not been in the attendant's memory. She would have noticed and remembered a Vulcan, she assured them.

Janna sighed. "Too bad you don't have attendants in the evening, too."

"It's the worker shortage, sergeant. We just don't have enough people to keep someone on the lot evenings."

"Just run the entire Monday night tape, then," Mama said. "Let's see every vehicle that leaves."

They ran the tape three times. It showed no SHH 41348 on the *Out* ramp.

Janna raked her fingers through her hair. Damn. What had happened to Hazlett? "Would it have been possible for him to have left by the *In* ramp, say if someone triggered the gate from the outside?"

"Except then we'd see blank tape like with the bicycles," Mama said. "I didn't see any blank places. Did you?"

They ran the tape once more to be sure. It had no sections showing only empty *In* ramp. They gave up the search for the time being and went to lunch at the Lion's Den.

"What do you think, bibi?"

Janna took a bite of sandwich and washed it down with iced tea. "What do *you* think?"

"I asked you first."

They brooded over their sandwiches. All Janna's alarms were clanging. "I don't like it, Mama. He tricked his way out of that lot somehow. If he went to that much trouble—"

"His game is more than chess, and it stinks clear to Port Bradbury."

"How could he get out of the lot? He had to pay his parking fee before the *Out* gate would open. If he went out that way, the monitor should have seen him. Now we can use one of your blue sky inspirations."

"The oracle doesn't work in the presence of unbelievers."

Janna was searching for a suitably sharp retort when Fleur Vientos, manager of the Doll's House, stuck her head into the Lion's Den. "Hey, she-lion, I could use you upstairs for a few minutes, and your skinhead friend, if he can help toss an obnoxious customer."

Mama sat up straighter. "Come on, bibi. Let's give the lady a hand and earn ourselves some hospitality."

"You can have mine." She finished her sandwich in two big bites. "Let's hope the customer is only unruly, not mean."

He was both unruly and mean. He was holding a boy prisoner in one of the bedrooms, his thick arm a vise around the boy's throat. The boy, a ho about Janna's age—in his profession he would be a "boy" until he retired—was crying. Both his eyes had been blackened and an ugly bruise was forming on his jaw.

"I'll kill him if you don't let me out," the customer yelled.

"You shouldn't have touched him in the first place, jon," Mama said. "Bruising the merchandise doesn't come with the price of admission."

"He's unclean. He's possessed by the devil. I was trying to drive the demon out of him."

"Oh, god, not another." Fleur's mouth was tight. "That's the second Bible cultist this month. I wish they'd content themselves with just praying for our souls. Get rid of that animal. I'm preferring charges against him!"

Janna stepped back out of sight and unsnapped her holster strap. She drew the Starke.

The jon was a big man. One needle might not be enough. She would give him two.

She leaned around the door and depressed the trigger. The red dot of the laser sight appeared on the man's forearm, where it came around the boy's throat. Janna fired twice and started counting. She hoped the percurare would work fast on this deek.

The jon looked shocked, then outraged. "I warned you." His arm started to tighten on the boy's neck.

Then it was as if he were a marionette whose strings had been cut. He collapsed in his tracks. He also quit breathing.

"Damn." Now she would have to breathe for him. "Call an ambulance. Tell them we have a percurare apnea."

She pulled the boy loose from the paralyzed man. Rolling the jon over on his back, she knelt beside him and began resuscitation. She refrained from grimacing at his foul breath. He could not move, but he could still feel and hear everything. She continued breathing for him until the ambulance medico arrived.

The medico measured the jon with her eyes. "How many needles?"

"Two."

The medico injected the percurare antagonist with a hiss of hypodermic spray. In a few minutes the jon was not only breathing normally, he had control of his muscles again. He glared accusingly at Janna. "You tried to kill me."

Tried to kill him? The stupid deek. "It was a temptation to let you suffocate. Maybe I should have." She turned away, disgusted by the sight of him.

"I'll see you're reported for this. I'll have you fired."

He was still threatening as the ambulance attendants took him out. He was going to be even more unhappy when he not only found himself riding to the hospital with Fleur's boy but also discovered that the next stop after Memorial's emergency room would be the Capitol division jail.

"I suppose he'll call Internal Affairs, and then the peeps will be around making my life miserable, trying to find a punishable offense in this." She hissed through her teeth. That grubby planet of Wim's was beginning to look like heaven itself. Could he really buy her a share with his pension?

"If the peeps come around here, every boy and girl in the Doll's House will testify to what happened," Fleur said.

Janna grinned. "That would make the hall here a little crowded, don't—"

She stopped, staring. Fleur was standing against the open door of the room, her head obscuring most of the number on the door. Only the last half of the final number was visible.

"Are you all right, leo?"

"Don't move, please, Fleur. Mama, tell me what number that is."

He looked at it. He turned to regard her with tolerant amusement. "A three."

"All right, Fleur, now you can move away."

She did. The room number was four eighteen.

Mama's dark eyes met Janna's in shock. "My god. Hazlett's license."

"Yes. Let's go back to Sunco."

CHAPTER THIRTEEN

Hazlett's car had to be license 11313. It was a number that could be made by covering parts of 41348 and, according to the gate monitor tape, no vehicle with the number 11313 had ever come into the lot. But license 11313 had left the Sunco lot at ten ten. Janna and Mama left the Sunco offices deep in thought.

"Four minutes after Owan arrived," Janna said. "I wish we could have seen enough of the car to tell whether there were one or two people in it when it left."

"I'm betting there were two. The question is whether Owan met him for blackmail, to ask for help getting out of town, or—something else."

"Let's bring Hazlett downtown and ask him."

Janna frowned. It was tempting. "Is that your answer to everything, drag Hazlett in for interrogation? This isn't the twentieth century, you know. You can't harass respectable citizens. Besides, no one ever laid an effective ambush by taking shots at someone over the next hill. Wait until you can see the whites of his eyes."

Mama pushed his glasses up his nose. "You can't clear cases by waiting for nothing but blue-ribbon, tied-with-bows evidence, either. I know this kind of snake, bibi. You have to kick over his rock and drive him out into the sunlight."

The metaphors were thick today. Janna allowed herself just one more. "What if he only finds a deeper hole? No, we don't bring him in. We don't go near him until we know enough of the answers to ask the most uncomfortable questions."

Mama jerked off his glasses and began polishing them on the pantleg of his jumpsuit. "They really have you braintrained, don't they? You investigate like John Dias prosecutes. When you let your gut lead yesterday, look what you accomplished. Now you're right back in your old set."

She rolled her eyes. He was back in his obnoxious set, too, and just when she had been starting to feel she could get along with him. She noticed clouds building up in the west. She hoped they held rain. Something needed to break this heat.

They went back to the station and resumed checking phone calls. It was discouraging work. The numbers Janna reached were usually connected with equipping and preparing colonists. There were a few miscellaneous calls. One was to a girlfriend of the receptionist. She begged Janna not to tell anyone

"Roberto" had made personal calls during business hours.

"Roberto's boss doesn't approve of personal calls," the girl said.

"Which boss, Mr. Hazlett or Mr. Kellener?"

The girl did not know. It would be interesting if the disapproving boss were Hazlett, in light of his call to Colla Hayden. Janna began wondering again why Hazlett made that call.

Another number she reached was that of the woman Hazlett took to dinner Friday evening. That was the last on her half the list. Janna punched off with a sigh. Not one number could be tied to the sligh Owan.

She started on the incoming calls. She was not surprised to find one on Friday afternoon from Many Mansions. The Laclede woman had said they located the chair Hazlett wanted by Friday. The call was probably to tell him about it. Nevertheless, Janna looked back through the list for Many Mansion's number and punched it.

Laclede appeared on the screen with a mechanical smile. "Hello, you've reached Many Mansions interior decorations. I'm Marca Laclede. Mr. Adrian Cabot and I are out of the office just now, but if you'll leave your name and number at the sound of the tone, we'll call you back as soon as we return."

A recording. Before the tone sounded, Janna disconnected. She grimaced. That was the lot, outgoing and incoming alike, and none of them seemed to be connected with the sligh. The only call she could at all construe as suspicious was the one to Hayden. That one gnawed at her. People did not usually punch up other people at work for casual chatter. Hazlett must have had some kind of reason for calling. What could it have been?

She voiced the question to Mama.

He squinted through his glasses at her. "Ah. Are you intuiting something?"

She scowled back. "No, I'm not intuiting. I have a sound reason for wondering about that call."

"Then don't just sit there wondering. Investigate."
Janna reached for the phone one more time.

Colla Hayden was surprised to see her again. She also appeared slightly annoyed. "You're still worried about Jorge's call? But I told you all about it."

"Ms. Hayden, this may be important," Janna said patiently. "Try to remember *exactly* what you talked about."

Hayden sighed. "It was nothing, just chatter. He asked me when I was going to have another party. I told him he didn't need a party, that I'd party with him. We made sexual jokes and after a bit, he punched off."

"Before you said you talked about past parties. What about them?"

Hayden shrugged. "Really, sergeant, I can't remember. It was just talk." She ran a hand through her kinky mane of hair and grimaced as she tried to remember. "I think we may have talked about some of the people that come."

Janna pounced on it. "What people would those be?"

"Just . . . people. I remember we talked a little about the Tabers."

"Who are the Tabers?"

"A bi couple who are married but pretend to be twins so people will think they're committing incest. Michael and Michal Taber." She spelled the names.

Janna wrote them down. "Did you talk about anyone else?"

The other woman scowled in thought, then shook her head. "Not that I can remember."

"Do you have the Tabers' phone number?"

"Yes." She disappeared from the screen for a few minutes and reappeared with an address book. She read off the number. It was a local exchange.

"Did Hazlett ask you for the number?"

Her eyes widened in puzzlement. "Of course not. I told you, they're bi. Jorge is strictly het. Besides, he likes his companions with more intellectual capacity than a pair of butterfly brains like the Tabers."

"Can you think of anything else you may have talked about? Anything at all?"

Hayden could not. In addition, she started looking at someone or something beyond the range of the screen. "I'm talking to the police," she said. After that she displayed an eagerness to end the conversation.

Janna let her go. She took the number Hayden had given her and compared it to those on the outgoing call list from Hazlett's office. There was no match. She sat back in her chair and stared at the number, lips pursed.

"Are you going to call it?" Mama asked.

"Would you?"

"Sure, but I'm always wild blue yondering, as you well know." He grinned.

She bit her lip.

"Without a record of Hazlett having called the number, do you have a sound reason for calling it?"

"Yes." She smiled. "I'm desperate for something to connect Hazlett to Owan." She punched the number.

The red-haired young man who answered reminded Janna of the boys at the Doll's House, so flawlessly handsome he looked like a store mannequin. His eyes widened as she introduced herself. "Police? Suns. What do you want with me?"

"A week ago Wednesday did you have a call from Mr. Jorge Hazlett?"

The mannequin shook his head. "I was out of town all last week, but maybe my sister talked to him. Michal!" he yelled.

He was joined by a young woman just as red-haired and equally beautiful. Janna could see why they were able to pass as twins. Michal Taber's eyes widened as Michael's had at Janna's introduction. "Suns," she said.

"A week ago Wednesday, did you have a phone call from a Mr. Jorge Hazlett?"

"A week ago Wednesday." Her eyes wandered as she thought. "Hazlett? Oh, Hazlett. Here I thought his name was Walnut. Yes, he called. He wondered if I knew the name of a man at one of Colla Hayden's parties last year. Do you know Colla?"

"I've met her." Janna wondered why Hazlett had not asked Colla. A man. That sounded more promising than anything else she had heard today. "Did you know the man's name?"

"Not exactly." Michal Taber grimaced. "I'm terrible about names. What do they matter when you're putting three with beautiful bodies?"

Personally, Janna liked to know who she was bending the mattress with. "So you didn't exactly remember the name. Does that mean you remembered something of it?"

"I remembered what it was like. It was something like Adriatic taxi." She paused. "Why are you asking? It wasn't important, just one of those nagging things that drives you off your tick until you remember."

"Adriatic taxi," Janna repeated.

Across the table, Mama was slithering down out of sight in his chair, laughing soundlessly.

"Was Hazlett satisfied after you told him that?"

The bibi shrugged. "Well . . . no. He wanted the name, after all, but I told him everything else I could remember, like the man had a body past pluto and his tongue was nova!"

Mama started to make wheezing sounds.

"And he had a furniture fetish," Michael Taber said. "Don't forget that."

Mama choked. Janna kicked at him under the table. "Furniture fetish, sir?"

"He knew the style names of every chair and lamp and table."

"Did he seem anxious to find the man?"

"He didn't want the *man,* just the *name.*" The bibi's voice was scornful. "He did remember it just before he punched off."

"Did he tell you what it was?"

"No, just that he had remembered it."

Janna sat for several minutes after the screen went blank, listening to Mama giggle but hearing Michal Taber's words repeating in her head. Adriatic taxi with a furniture fetish. Adriatic taxi. There was no way that could suggest Owan's name. Furniture fetish. She must not forget the furniture fetish.

"Well, that wasn't very relevant, but it was entertaining," Mama said.

Janna sucked her lower lip. "Not relevant? When Hazlett spent a good part of the rest of the day calling furniture stores?"

He stopped laughing. "He was looking for the Adriatic taxi, you think?"

"One of the decorators at Many Mansions is named Adrian Cabot." She paused. "Cab boat."

He stared at her. "I'll be damned. Maybe we should talk to Mr. Adrian Cabot."

"That's what I think."

She punched Many Mansions' number.

Laclede answered, in the flesh this time. She was showing a good deal of it, too. Off to the side, out of view of the screen, Mama drooled.

Laclede smiled at Janna. Her color brightened. "Back so soon?"

The undercurrent of excitement in the woman's voice made Janna wonder if Laclede were tripping. "I'm afraid so. Did you call Hazlett Friday afternoon?"

She nodded. "I wanted to tell him I'd found the chair."

"Did he come over to see it?"

Laclede wrinkled her nose. "No, as it happened. By that time he'd changed his mind and didn't want the chair any longer."

Janna wrote on a memo sheet: *Call Hazlett's office and see if Roberto will give you the name of the client Hazlett supposedly walked to the elevator.* She shoved it at Mama.

He read it and nodded.

"I wonder if I might speak to Mr. Cabot for a moment."

The improbably blue eyes widened in surprise but Laclede said, "Of course. I'll get him."

The screen became blank—she was on hold. When

it came back on, Janna felt as if someone had put a foot under her diaphragm. Her breath stopped. The man on the screen was—at first she had thought it was the sligh they had seen with Laclede on Friday, but a moment later she realized this man was too elegant. This man was only a physical double for the sligh. A double!

"Yes, may I help you?" Cabot said.

Janna fought for her voice. "Have you ever met a Mr. Jorge Hazlett, or a Colla Hayden, or a couple named Michal and Michael Taber?"

The bluntness of the question worked. Cabot's face became gray. Panic flooded his eyes. "No, no, I haven't. Never. What are you bothering me for?"

Abruptly, the screen went blank. Janna did not care that he had punched off on her because she was on her feet running for Vradel's office. She pounded once on his door and burst in.

Vradel looked up in annoyance from his conference with an assistant district attorney. "Brill, when that door is closed—"

"I'm sorry," she apologized hastily, "but this is important, sir. Do you remember the civilian couple we saw in the Den on Friday?"

Vradel nodded. "It would be hard to forget a woman like that."

"Do you remember the sligh with her?"

"Yes." He frowned and his mustache twitched. "What's this about?"

"I just saw her on the phone. She called Hazlett Friday afternoon and, lieutenant, that sligh and her boss look like twins."

Vradel stared. He came half out of his chair. "The link to Owan?"

She felt breath on her neck. Behind her, Mama whispered, "Jackpot. Bibi, I couldn't get Hazlett's client's name, though."

"One sligh double might be able to find other sligh doubles," said Janna. "Sir, can you make me a sketch of that sligh in the Den?"

Vradel tore off the marked top sheet of his memo

pad. On the clean sheet he drew a sketch in short, quick strokes.

The assistant D.A.'s brows were hovering near his hairline. "Sligh doubles? What are you talking about?"

"Nothing to do with you or Dias for a while." Vradel handed the sheet to Janna. "Will that do?"

It was amazing to Janna that so few lines could convey so much. The sligh's angry face looked up at her from the paper with startling vividness. "It'll do beautifully. Thank you, sir. Sorry to have interrupted you."

"It's all right." His forehead furrowed. "Do you think she's making a business of this kind of arrangement?"

"It would certainly explain how Hazlett found what he needed so fast, wouldn't it?"

Vradel shuddered. "If she is, strap her, Brill . . . fast."

"Yes, sir." She backed out, closing the door. "Well, Mama, now we need to find out if Laclede and her sligh friend are indeed providing doubles for citizens."

"Let's send someone around to Many Mansions to apply for her services."

She nodded agreement. That was a fine idea. "Why not go yourself? You don't look like a leo." She pointed to his shining scalp and lavender-and-blue patterned jumpsuit. "Morello can set you up with one of the false identities in the undercover file."

He looked surprised but agreed. "And what will you be doing in the meantime?"

"Meanwhile—" she folded the sketch lengthwise and slipped it in a breast pocket of her romper— "I'll go look up some friends in Oakland and see what they know about Mr. Adrian Cabot's alter ego."

Marca Laclede felt as if the black man towered a kilometer into the air over her. He had to be one of the tallest, thinnest people she had ever met, but he wore a suit with a stylish pattern and he was a simply lovely Dutch-chocolate color. His bare scalp shone with the gloss of wax. She was fascinated.

"Won't you sit down?"

Once he folded himself into the chair on the other side of her desk, she could talk to him without straining her neck. She smiled at him. "What can I do for you?"

He smiled back at her. It was dazzling in the darkness of his face. "I looked around my apartment the other day and thought it had to be the worst example of twenty-first century drab I've ever seen. My last wife decorated it. I want to do it over, make it more my style."

She loved his voice. It pulled at her blood almost like jivaqueme music. She noticed he was studying her with interest through the transparent top of the desk, counting every square centimeter of skin not covered by her romper. She was wearing body paint to fill in gaps, of course, but she had the feeling he could tell exactly where cloth ended and paint began. She also noticed he made no pretense of not being interested. She leaned forward to give him a better view of her cleavage.

"Exactly what do you feel your style *is*, Mr.—?"

He paused a moment before answering. "Maxwell . . . Mahlon Maxwell. Everyone calls me Mama, though. My style is . . . unconventional. Show me something you think might interest me."

He rested his arm on the desk. She leaned across and put her arm beside his. "I see you surrounded by ivory. I'd paint your walls ivory, hang ivory curtains, furnish in molded foam covered with ivory plush. I'd finish by laying an ivory and brown fur rug so thick you could get tangled in it. Don't you think ivory would look good next to you?"

He moved his arm until it touched hers. His skin was as warm as its color. "I think you're right, bibi."

She sat back and reached into a desk drawer for a pad of forms. "Before we go any farther, we ought to talk price. Many Mansions can create you a fine decor, but our services cost what they're worth."

He nodded. "Of course. I expect to pay well for any service you provide."

She enjoyed the warmth the sound of his voice and his words sent down her back into her thighs. She crossed her legs, and watched him watch her cross them. She smiled. "What do you do for your bank-credit, Mama?"

He looked up. "I'm a police officer."

The warmth changed to a sharp tingle, something of the same feeling she got making arrangements with Tarl under lion noses in the Lion's Den. She crossed her legs the other direction, letting the romper ride higher as she did so. "And you can afford Many Mansions?"

He smiled. "A police officer can develop useful connections so he doesn't have to live on what the taxpayers allow him. You could be one of the useful connections, bibi, and it could be to both our advantage."

The air around him lighted red with danger signs. The tingle in her sharpened. "A decorator's assistant can be useful? How?"

He leaned forward on the desk. His voice dropped. "I'm not talking about a decorator's assistant. I'm talking about sligh doubles."

She felt a spasm of fear so intense it was almost ecstasy. "What do you mean?"

"Your business is small-time now. With my connections, you could develop an empire. Why go for small card when you could be collecting megacredits?"

"How—" Her breath felt short. "How did you find out?"

"I told you, bibi . . . a lion can develop connections." He smiled. "Don't worry. No one else knows. Your secret is safe with Mama."

Some of her breathlessness was subsiding. She started thinking. Marca stood and went over to the door. One push shut and locked it.

She turned to him. "Strip down."

He stared at her. "What?"

She made her voice hard. "Strip down. I'm not saying one word more to you until you prove to me you're not broadcasting."

His surprise changed to amusement. He grinned. "Whatever you say, bibi."

He pulled at the pressclose of his suit. The strips parted with a tearing sound. Marca felt foolish. Anyone who agreed to a search that willingly was either carrying a radio so well hidden he knew she would never find it or else he was clean. She did not feel she could back away, though. She let him strip to the skin and as he handed her his clothes, she went over them carefully. When he was down to his skin, he pirouetted in front of her, flexing his sinewy muscles.

Marca quit feeling foolish and started enjoying herself. How many people could make a lion strip naked in a public building? She handed him back his clothes. "All right. I don't find anything. You can get dressed."

He made a show of it. She enjoyed watching. As soon as the game was over, though, she came back to business.

"What are you claiming you can do for me?"

"I'll expand your clientele. What do you have now —ordinary people, citizens with an illegal kink, maybe, or guilty consciences, men with wives they don't want to lose but who won't let them play away from home, women with similar problems. You collect, say, a couple of thousand from each for setting them free." He sniffed, passing off the amount as a trifle. "Bibi, I know people who really need alibis, alibis they're willing to pay handsomely for."

Criminals, he meant. She thought about that. Yes, they probably could pay. The possibilities made her lick her lips. Visions of riches shone in the air before her. She smiled at him. "I'd like to hear more. Come back when I get off work. Five o'clock. Take me to dinner and dancing. Talk to me, and we'll see what happens."

Janna could not find Quicksilver, but was not surprised. He would be teaching his school. The best Juvenile officers in the department had never been able to find Quicksilver's school. She checked stockrooms and the backs of Oakland's stores until she found some other slighs she knew.

One of them was an Oriental-Hispanic who called himself Amber. He did not freeze up at the sight of her, but he did eye her shoulder bag as if trying to see if she were carrying a gun and strap in it. He did not stop attaching price tags to the shirts in the box he was unloading, either. "Are you still looking for that Owan?"

"Yes, but that isn't why I'm here today. I need to know if you've seen this man around."

She pulled out Vradel's sketch of Marca Laclede's companion.

Amber paused long enough to look at it. Looking up from it to her, his eyes were inscrutable Oriental eyes. "I've seen him. I don't know his name, though, or anything about him."

"What has he been doing when you've seen him?"

"Talking to people." He went back to tagging. "What else would he be doing?"

"Oh, maybe looking for someone. Maybe he gives a description or shows a photograph and asks where he can find a person who looks like that."

Amber bent his head over his work. "No, I don't recall that he ever did anything like that."

She regarded him in silence. He was lying, she felt sure. How much was the question. It would be hard to find out. Accusing him of lying would accomplish nothing useful. In the slithy world, leos and other officials of government and society were meant to be lied to—whatever it took to preserve the anonymity of slighs.

She thanked him for his help, her voice heavy with irony, and left.

Visits to other slighs yielded much the same results. It was frustrating. Many were people who used to be valuable Eyes and Ears. She had been away too long. She could see by their faces that they recognized the sketch. Some even admitted having seen the sligh around Oakland. Beyond that, she found little help.

No one would specify a length of time he had been living there and no one would give her a name.

In two slighs, one a man, one a woman, the sketch provoked a marked pupil response. Those two flatly denied ever having seen him anywhere before. The vigor of their denials told Janna as much as an honest admission would have. It suggested strongly that the sligh had approached them with a proposition like the one Owan accepted. If only she could find one who would talk to her about it.

She finally located Quicksilver in Ripley Park. He sat on the grass in the shade of a tree, surrounded by a circle of children. In the rising wind—Janna hoped it was not spawning tornadoes—Quicksilver was pointing out trees and birds to them, naming each and telling something about them. Seeing Janna, he sighed and stood up.

"You hunt for four-leafed clovers, kids." He came to meet Janna. "I haven't found Owan yet."

"I think this man may be able to help me." She handed him the sketch.

He studied it. "He does seem to move around enough to have met every sligh in Oakland, perhaps even all of Topeka."

"What can you tell me about him? Do you know his name? Where he lives? Where he works?"

Quicksilver frowned. "I smell blood. You're hunting, aren't you?"

"It's important I find this man. Have you ever seen him behaving . . . oddly?"

The sligh looked past her. "You're using up all your favor credit, leo. Behaving oddly how?"

"Does he spend much time looking for one person or another?"

"Sergeant, of course he asks for people. We all do. I wish I could help you more than that, but—"

"Come on, Q; don't go polite on me! Help me! Believe this, what he may be involved in could hurt slithytown. It could bring legislation against slighs."

Quicksilver's frown deepened. "How? You want me

to trust you, leo, try trusting me. Tell me what's happening."

Janna bit her lip. Informants gave information; it was not given to them. What she had passed on in the past was bribery, to keep Quicksilver in her debt. Police business was not something to be discussed with outsiders.

He started to turn back toward the children. "Sorry, sergeant."

She reached for his arm. "Wait."

As briefly as possible, she told him what they thought Owan had done, and what Marca Laclede and her sligh friend might be doing. "We don't know how they do it, though. That's why I have to talk to some of the other slighs who may have done what Owan did."

Quicksilver's mouth tightened. "Stupidity. I can see their point. It sounds like a chance to make a fool of the System, but exposing themselves to prosecution that way . . . stupid. You're right; this business could hurt every sligh. I can see the politicos in the Statehouse panicking and passing legislation making identation mandatory, just so no one could double for another citizen without leaving a noticeable gap in records somewhere." He looked around at the children combing through the grass for clover. "His name is Tarl. I don't know the rest. He doesn't spend much time looking for people. Usually he asks for them by name when he does. He spends most of his time socializing, just drifting around meeting everyone possible. Doesn't talk about himself and of course no one asks. I don't have any idea where he works. Maybe he doesn't. He must collect something for hunting doubles."

Janna thought of the jewelry Owan had bought. If Marca Laclede and Tarl had found Owan for Hazlett, they would have asked a price. How much of that jewelry went to them?

"Do you remember the names of any people he's asked for?"

"Yes, but I won't tell you. You'd want to know who

205

they were and most of them are terrified of leos. They'd never talk to you."

"Tell me this: are there many of them?"

He shook his head. "Not many."

That was something of a relief. There would be just a few falsified bank records around, then. Perhaps none of the others had involved criminal activity. She could always hope.

"Do you suppose some of the children might know where he works?" Children had a way of knowing things no adults did. Children were a great untapped market of information. She herself had discovered them just four years ago.

Quicksilver's mouth quirked. "You can ask them."

Janna took the sketch to the group. "This man's name is Tarl. Can anyone tell me where he works?"

They eyed her in silence. She reached into her pocket for a handful of vending tokens. "These to anyone who can tell me."

A girl said, "I'm very sorry, officer, but I've never seen that man before. I can't help you. I wish I could."

Janna refused to let herself sigh. It was said like a true sligh, so polite, so earnest she could not be accused of being uncooperative, but giving no information. She heard a chuckle behind her. She looked around in time to see a grin disappear from Quicksilver's face.

"Thank you, Q."

He bowed with elaborate courtesy.

It was almost four o'clock.

She went back across the park to Indian Thirty and headed downtown to the station. It was in the usual organized turmoil of changing watches. Mama Maxwell was not there, but Pass-the-Word Morello had a message from him for her: *I'm counting coup on the doppelgänger queen tonight. I'll give you the prurient details later.*

Janna gnashed her teeth. What was he up to now? "What identity did Maxwell check out of the undercover file?"

Morello blinked at her. "He didn't check out any identity. Was he supposed to?"

"Damn!" She crumpled the slip and hurled it to the floor. "Double damn."

Whether she was cursing Mama or herself she was not sure. Why, *why* was it impossible for him to do anything the established way? She must have been an idiot to let him go out to decoy Laclede. It gave her hot flashes and cold chills just trying to think what a strange mind like his might be planning. If he stunted around and bombed this case, so help her she would needle him and inflict long, painful tortures on his paralyzed body.

She retrieved the message slip to throw it in the trash, then stalked down to debriefing. Just let Schnauzer Venn ask her what was bothering her tonight.

As it happened, he did not ask. Everyone was volunteering complaints and problems. A couple of rookies were seriously disturbed by the discovery that good, "law-abiding" citizens resented them. They were upset at what they saw supposedly civilized people doing to each other. Janna had no chance to talk. She left debriefing looking for a shoulder to cry on.

Wim, she thought . . . but as soon as she walked into his room at the hospital she could tell he was a poor choice. His shoulder was not still long enough to be cried on. The doctors had taken off his bandages that afternoon and removed any tissue staples which had not been absorbed. Wim was high as a tripper because of it. There remained just the splint across his nose, protecting the nasal bones while they healed. The scar around his head was a thin one and as soon as his hair finished growing back in, it would be almost invisible. Only his eyes looked strange, banded horizontally in red.

"The doctors tell me I can leave in a few days. They just want to make sure I'll be ready to cope with the world out there."

"How are your rehab lessons coming?"

He grinned. "I can find peas with my fork now. And look at this."

He made a wide circle around the room. Janna held her breath, waiting for him to collide with the beds or chairs. He avoided every obstacle, though. Every time he went around something, Vada smiled proudly. Finally Wim stopped and dropped into a chair with no more than a backward feel with his leg to locate it. "Janna, you'd have to go through this to know what it's like. I never knew the world was so full of sounds and smells. Everyone smells different. I think I could almost tell where you and Vada are by tracking with my nose. I'm turning into a bloodhound. Just think, on Champaign there will be a whole new catalogue of smells and sounds. I can hardly wait to learn what they all are."

He seemed to be adjusting to his handicap very well. Janna knew she should be relieved and pleased, but it gave her a strange feeling she could not name —something like loneliness, or being shut out. For the first time, she was able to appreciate how Vada must have felt all these years as she listened to Wim and Janna talk about the alien world of their work.

She tried to bring the conversation back to something she knew. "I wish this Kellener case were going as well as your rehab."

"How is it doing?"

She thought he would never ask. She started to tell him.

After a few sentences, Vada said, "Our company almost went to that firm." She shuddered. "I'm glad now they didn't."

"I knew it was only a matter of time before someone found a way to beat the bankcard system," Wim said. "It's a war and the escalation never stops. Are you about ready to resign, Jan?"

Outside, thunder boomed. Wim stopped, head tilted, listening. "I knew it was going to rain today. I could feel a difference in the air of the sunroof. My teacher says it's due to static electricity. It's going to pour tonight, but it doesn't quite feel like a tornado breeder.

I wonder if the air will change the same way on Champaign." His scarred eyes looked dreamily into nothingness.

After a minute he shook himself and turned his face toward Janna. "Oh, I talked to the pension office. They say they can't give me a lump sum. The pension comes from tax payments and there's just so much budgeted per year. However, they referred me to the bank. I called the main branch of Topeka National and they'll loan me as much as I want, then they'll take over the pension until the loan is repaid."

Janna stared at him. "Wim, you didn't need to—I mean, not already. I haven't decided yet."

"You have to soon. Our ship leaves in a little over two weeks. I know you want to come. You've been telling me how miserable the job's been lately. Come on and join the future."

"It isn't always bad. Sometimes I almost like Mama, but then—" Then he went off blue skying. What *was* he doing with Laclede tonight?

"If this Laclede woman really has found a way to counterfeit a thumbprint, it's going to play hell with investigations. She'll have wiped out the usefulness of bank records and fingerprinting in one chop. A lion's life will be no fun anymore."

Janna appealed to Vada. "Help. Your husband is twisting my arm hard tonight."

"I'll help him if he wants me to—whatever it takes to convince you to come along with us."

"Enough," Wim said. "The arm-twisting is over for now. Listen. It's starting to rain."

The first tentative drops hit the windows. Janna looked out. The sky was black and boiling. Beneath it, the sunlight had a peculiarly luminous quality, making the colors of the city almost fluorescent. There was a sharp crack of thunder, and then the deluge began. The light and world disappeared beyond sheeting rain.

"Let me tell you what I learned about sound today, Jan. Did you realize that a human can't tell if a sound is directly in front, behind, or overhead? A dog can

209

distinguish many separate points of sound origin. So to compensate, a person has to—"

Janna heard him repeat the tricks for localizing sound, but she was not actually listening. Mixed emotions churned in her. She had come wanting to talk, not listen, but Wim wanted to talk, too, and for the first time in their association, neither was interested in what the other had to say. Their interests were a barrier between them rather than the unifying force they had always been. The realization of that hurt. Janna did not like it at all. If she were to go out to Champaign, they would be sharing experiences again.

She made an effort to listen to Wim, but could not. Her mind kept sliding back to Mama Maxwell, wondering where he was and what he was doing.

She stood up. "I ought to go. I have to find Mama."

"Let him hang himself. If you're not around at the time, you won't be caught in the noose, too."

"I don't care if he hangs himself, but it does concern me what he might be doing to our case."

"You can't go yet," Vada objected. "It's pouring."

Janna lied. "I came in Sid's runabout."

Riding in the rain was not bad. By the light of street lamps coming on, Janna could see the hot pavement steam where the rain struck it. The cars and runabouts appeared to be riding on a cushion of smoke. Janna was careful to stay well inside the bicycle lanes, out of the path of larger vehicles.

She had no destination in mind. No telling where Mama might be. She just wanted to ride, to enjoy the coolness of the rain and forget everything else. It was with some surprise, then, that she found herself swinging down the ramp into the Capitol division's garage. She started to turn around, then shrugged and rode on down to the bike racks. As long as she was here she might as well see what was going on. She wrung out her romper and hair in the locker room before walking up to the squadroom.

Crimes Against Persons seemed quiet. The night watch supervisor Lieutenant Chris Candarian and three investigators were drinking tea and watching the newscanner. A candidate for Congress was delivering her carefully polished pitch for votes.

Candarian's brows rose as she saw Janna. "Overtime? Vradel didn't tell me he'd authorized any."

Janna shook her head. "I'm on my own time, not wrecking the budget. I was just passing by."

One of the investigators looked toward the window slit. "How is it out?"

"Wonderfully wet. You're looking empty. Everyone on the street tonight?"

"Here and there," Candarian said. "That bibi in the red Bonsai broke four more pedestrians' legs this evening. She's getting skillful." Her eyes narrowed. "What are you tracking? I can't believe you came in just to dry off and you're no rock jock rookie."

"Has Sergeant Maxwell called in since the watch change?" Of course that was what brought her here, she realized all at once.

The lieutenant shook her head. "Is he out on something dangerous without back-up?"

"He isn't supposed to be."

The phone buzzed. Candarian punched the button. "Crimes Against Persons, Lieutenant Candarian."

The screen carried the image of a uniformed officer with sergeant's bars on his collar. "I'm looking for Sergeant Janna Brill. Can you give me a number where I can reach her, or take a message for her?"

Candarian looked up at Janna with arched brows. "It is luck or are you prescient, sergeant?"

Janna moved up to the screen. "I'm Brill. What is it?"

"Hallard and Kobuzky asked me to get in touch with you. If I can find you, you're to meet them at Atchison and Jacquot. They think they may have found your sligh."

CHAPTER FOURTEEN

Jacquot Street was even more depressing than usual in the rain. The downpour absorbed what little glow came from its few operational streetlights, leaving it a black tunnel. The headlights of the jane car Janna had borrowed from the station lighted sodden, drooping weeds growing up through the steaming pavement ahead of her and reflected off turbulent pools made by trash damming the gutter streams. Beyond the reach of her headlights, the houses squatted dark and dere- lict in the dripping tangle of their yards. The only visible life on the street was at the intersection with Atchison, where it looked like a carnival was in prog- ress.

Police cars parked in a cluster before the boarded-up store on the corner were a light show. Red, white, and blue bands chased each other around the light rails on top of three watchcars and the pop-on cherry of a jane car flashed like a ruby strobe from inside the front window of the car. The play of lights caught rain-slickered leos moving around the building and intermittently illuminated the Forensics insignia on a fifth car.

Janna's lights crossed one officer as she swung in to the curb, marking the leo with fire where they hit the reflective stripes on the slicker. Janna ran down a win- dow a crack. "I'm looking for Hallard and Kobuzky."

The leo looked around. "Hi, Brill." It was Rina Hallard.

Janna set the jane car down on its parking rollers and pulled on the slicker she had brought from her locker at the station. She put up the hood and slid out over the airfoil skirt. She hardly noticed when she sank in half an inch of mud. Her attention was riveted on the abandoned store.

"He's in there?" She hoped not.

"Yeah."

She grimaced. Even without the strained note in Hallard's voice, Janna's stomach would have lurched. A fugitive might hide in a place like the old store, but it was not as likely as other places. Buildings like this were often launching pads for winos and trippers. They were too public for good hiding. If Owan had been found here, he had not been found alive.

Hallard leaned against a watchcar. The rain streamed down her helmet and slicker in rivulets alternately red, white, and blue. She leaned her head on her arms. "I never thought I got that Criminal Justice degree just to wade through shit falling over deaders. I could have used it to qualify for the Moon colony, or Mars."

In quadrasonic sound, the radios of the watchcars and jane car murmured of screaming women and traffic accidents and bar disturbances. Janna regarded Hallard with a tired sigh. "How did you happen to find him?"

Hallard did not raise her head from her folded arms. "Usual body count of the known abandoned buildings." Her voice was muffled.

Body counts were one of the less loved parts of patrolling in Oakland. It was either look through the buildings or wait until the stench or some nervous citizen announced the demise of winos and trippers.

"It was my turn to walk tonight. I knew I had one the moment I got near the door. A few more days and we'd have been able to smell him halfway down the block. Christ." She swallowed audibly.

Bloody damn it to hell. Owan had been Janna's witness. Despite all her fears and pessimism, she had been counting on him for testimony against Hazlett. "What makes you think it's my sligh?"

Hallard lifted her head. "How many people down here wear blue novalon suits?"

Janna looked at the building. "Mose inside?"

"Around back, helping secure the area until the forensic team finishes. Secure the area." Hallard snorted. "What hasn't washed away by this time will be fun picking out of that filth inside."

Janna sighed again. "I'd better go take a look."

"Excuse me for not joining you."

She circled the building. A she-lion from one of the other watchcars shined a light in her eyes. "You must be Brill. What's your interest in this case?"

The faintly this-is-not-your-division-what-are-you-doing-here attitude annoyed Janna. "The man's dead, isn't he?"

"First time I ever saw Crimes Against Persons come out for an OD."

Janna regarded her a moment in silence. "What makes you think it's an OD?"

"Hey, I saw the body. Trick OD's are hard to mistake."

Trick! Janna plunged past her on around the building.

The stench of death hit her about the corner, even in the downpour. She set her jaw and started cautious breathing through her teeth.

Moses Kobuzky and several other leos stood outside the open rear door of the store, watching the forensics team finish holotaping the door and interior of the building. Kobuzky waved at her. "Sorry we had to find your sligh this way."

One of the forensics techs played a light over the ground around the door and shook his head. "No way of picking up prints from that. It was like concrete before, but now the only footprints are those of the officer who found him."

"Any footprints inside?" Janna asked.

"Smeared ones. Can't help sliding in that stuff. It's the local public latrine."

Janna eyed the door with distaste. "Do you have another mask? I need to go in when I can."

"You can go now. We're about finished." He

pulled a crumpled paper mask out of his pocket and handed it to Janna.

She slipped the elastic over her head and settled the cup over her mouth and nose. The material looked thin but it did its job well. The air reaching her through the mask was almost odorless.

She went into the building.

Most of the interior was lost in the shadows beyond the small pool of Forensic's lights, but the prime exhibit was brightly illuminated. The deader lay in the middle of the light pool, twisted and bloated. Janna fought her stomach. Rats had been chewing on the exposed face and hands. The half face that remained was so distorted it was unrecognizable. The jumpsuit he wore was distinctive, though. By some bizarre irony, the rats had not touched it.

One of the advertising claims for novalon was that the material resisted soiling and wrinkling, so that however hectic, however long the day, clothing made of novalon remained fresh-looking. For once, the commercial propaganda was accurate, though Janna doubted the manufacturers would appreciate hearing of this particular example. In the midst of the building's filth, the suit sheathed the contorted limbs of the corpse in clean, unwrinkled, gloriously iridescent blue.

Janna could see why the she-lion outside had called this an OD. The position of the body was nearly identical to the one in which they had found Andrew Kellener.

"Is he your sligh?" Kobuzky called from the doorway.

Janna shrugged helplessly. The deader had brown hair with gray at the temples. The remaining eye was brown. He was a medium build. He had a superficial resemblance to Jorge Hazlett. Beyond that, identification was uncertain. She could not judge what height the deader had stood, and the face was in no condition for comparing it to Hazlett's image in her mind. There was that suit, though. That suit. It looked right. It also made her nerves twitch seeing a human turned into a

215

grotesque pretzel and his clothes still as neat as if just taken from a closet.

The twitch reached her stomach. She retreated outside and stood with her hood back, letting the rain pour down over her head. She took deep breaths.

Kobuzky grinned at her. "Glad you're downtown out of the body-counting business?"

The rain on her face made her feel cleaner. "I still count bodies, only for every division in the county."

Someone said, "Here comes the M.E."

A figure shuffled around the end of the building. Janna's brows went up. It was Dr. Sandor Kolb himself, looking even worse than usual. Now his hair and suit were wet as well as unkempt.

He looked around with a vaguely surprised expression, as if he had been light-years away in mind and was startled to find himself where he did.

"Good evening, Dr. Kolb," Janna said. "Are you working nights now?"

He peered at her as if she were an alien speaking an unintelligible language. Suddenly he straightened and ran his hands through his hair. The wrinkles disappeared from his jumpsuit. His eyes focused on her. "Good evening, Sergeant Brill." His voice was crisp. "No, I just happened to be in the office and since it was clear everyone was anxious to let someone else come out, I volunteered." He swung toward the door of the building. "Well, show me what you have."

Janna shook her head in wonder. In two motions, he had gone from being the Mad Doctor of Shawnee to Mister Medical Examiner. She had seen the transformation many times, in the field, at inquests, and in court, but it never failed to amaze her. The man who reputedly slept on autopsy tables and forgot to eat or go home became a distinguished scholar who remembered the name of every police officer he ever met, every corpse he ever examined, and the names and signs of countless causes of sudden death.

Kolb entered the building without a mask. From the doorway, Janna watched him squat beside the body and go over it with the same careful attention Sid had given Andrew Kellener's body. Kolb peered, probed, and straightened limbs. He appeared not to notice the odor and decomposition.

"Fractured left humerus, left tibia and fibula, and right radius and ulna. Cyanosis indicative of anoxia." He looked up at Janna. "You've had a couple of trick deaths now, haven't you?"

"That's your judgment of the cause of death?"

"Oh, certainly, certainly. Couldn't be much else. That's unofficial, of course." He lifted a brow. "Your interest must indicate you don't think it's a simple OD."

"No." She pressed her lips into a thin line.

Kolb cocked his head. "Ugly way to commit a murder. It's a less traceable weapon than a knife or shooter, though, I suppose."

"Did he die here or was he brought in afterward?"

"Judging by the post-mortem lividity, he died in this position. Those could have been caused by an agonal struggle." He pointed to smears in the filth on the floor.

"How long do you think he's been dead?"

Kolb shook his head. "I wouldn't care to speculate. The heat in here will have speeded putrefaction. I'll have to see what he looks like on the table. Oh, and I'll let the computer give me a guess, too."

"Could he have died Monday night?"

"Monday?" He considered with his forehead furrowed in a thoughtful frown. "That's within the limits, I'd say."

Which meant he could have died Sunday, or Tuesday. Janna sighed. "I'd like that suit as soon as you get him out of it."

"Pick it up at the office any time. Come on, come on." He beckoned to ambulance attendants. "He's not going to bite. Let's wrap him up."

The attendants hung back, looking unhappy at being soaked by the rain outside but equally unhappy at having to come inside. Kolb came out and dragged them in. Janna moved aside to give them room.

As she moved outside, she found Rina Hallard beside her looking up. "What do you want to do now?"

Janna considered the building. She looked up the black street. "I need to knock on doors, I'm afraid. The locals aren't going to be happy, but if I wait until tomorrow, no one may be home. Want to go back on patrol or would you like to help me do some real police work?"

"Help interview a population of blind deaf-mutes?" Hallard snorted. "That's masochism, not police work."

She and Kobuzky helped anyway. They took one side of the street while Janna covered the other. They knocked on every door of the blocks stretching up Jacquot and Atchison from the store's intersection. The houses behind many of the doors were empty. Others might just as well have been. The residents were not interested in being helpful. They resented being visited by the police so late at night.

"Do you know what time it is? Come back in the morning."

In a country club district Janna would have smiled politely and begun every statement with "sir" or "ma'am." Here she leaned on the door to keep them from shutting it and said, "We can talk here or at the station. It's a long trip for just one question. Did you see or hear anything sometime after ten o'clock Monday night, perhaps near the old store on the corner?"

They were Hallard's blind deaf-mutes. They had never in their lives seen or heard anything unusual, certainly not at night, most emphatically not on Atchison or Jacquot Streets. Monday night was a complete blank in their minds.

Janna toyed wistfully with daydreams of picking up a few of them and bouncing them off walls. She could have done it. She was taller than most of them. She also envisioned the glee of the peeps in Internal Affairs when citizens reported a leo playing heavy in the middle of the night over routine questions. She contented herself with leaning on the doors.

She walked across another door stoop shaking rain off her slicker, and knocked on another door. The resident was a man stripped down to undershorts, tak-

ing full advantage of the cooler temperature brought
by the rain. He regarded her suspiciously through
the crack the guard chain permitted the door to open.

Janna held up her badge and ID. "I know the
hour is inconvenient but there's been some trouble
at that abandoned store on the corner. Are the people
in this house the same as those who were in it Monday evening?"

He hesitated. Behind him there was a scuffle and a
muffled giggle. The man said quickly, "Yes . . . me."

For the twelfth time that evening, Janna asked,
"Did you see or hear anything unusual in the street or
near the old store after ten o'clock on Monday night?"

He did not even stop to think. "No."

Another muffled giggle behind him.

Janna put a hand against the door. "May I come in
so we can talk about it?"

"I didn't hear anything, I tell you."

"Did you see or hear anything at all that was different from the usual neighborhood routine?"

"Just the car."

Electric shock shot up her spine. She eased her
hand to her pocket and tapped on the microcorder.
"You say you saw a car on the street Monday night?"

Beyond the crack, the female giggle was higher.
The man started to shut the door. "No, there was no
car. Good night."

Janna shoved her weight against the door. "Jon,"
she said easily, "I don't know what you have going
in there and if you satisfy me with answers to questions about Monday night, I won't care."

The man stopped trying to close the door. "I don't
have anything going. I'm alone. I'll answer your questions because I'm a conscientious citizen. Yes, I saw a
car Monday night."

Janna smiled at him. "What time did you see it?
What make and color was it? Could you read the license number?"

"Read the license number?" His laugh was a short,
sharp bark. "By what light? I couldn't even see the car

well enough to tell you what it was. I think it was a road car, though, and it was a sportster model."

"Why are you so sure of that?"

"Its fans had that whine that sportsters do. It came by about ten thirty, I guess."

"Jon, you're being really helpful. Is there anything else you can remember about it?"

The man considered, frowning. "Yeah. There was some jon in it yelling."

"Yelling what?"

He shrugged. "I couldn't tell. It didn't make any sense."

Someone with his tongue trick-tangled, perhaps?

She tapped off the microcorder. "Thank you very much, sir. I appreciate your cooperation. Good night. Have an enjoyable evening."

She had two more houses to visit. One was empty. She heard sounds of human occupancy in the last, but no one came to the door and when she circled the house, stumbling through the wet tangle of weeds around it, the one gleam of light inside disappeared. They were probably squatters, in which case they would never even talk to her, let alone admit anything they knew which would indicate they had been in this house Monday night.

She walked back to the old store. The carnival was over. Forensics and the jane car were gone. All the watchcars but Kobuzky and Hallard's had left, too. The two leos sat in their car waiting for her.

"We found a couple of people who heard some shouting about ten-thirty Monday," said Kobuzky. He reached out through the car's window and handed Janna a microcorder chip and a notebook page with two names and addresses. "One of them even lives near a functional street light. She doesn't know car makes but she's sure it was a road car, not a runabout. It was small. The light wasn't bright enough to see the color well. She thinks it was a light orange or blue, maybe gray."

Or maybe sundust gold? Janna took the chip and notepage and slipped them inside her slicker before the rain could soak the paper. "Thanks, Mose, Rina. I appreciate this."

"Well, it's a change from carrying drunks and toxy trippers home and breaking up fights," he said.

Hallard added, "Next time you get ready to ridicule our size, just remember that if you're nice to the little people, they'll be kind to you."

Janna slipped the chip into her microcorder and listened to it while she drove back downtown. The two witnesses Hallard and Kobuzky had found said substantially the same thing as the man Janna had questioned. There was a road car on Jacquot street Monday night. It was probably a sportster. A Vulcan? No one had seen the license number. It was all suggestive, but not very definite, not what she could call real evidence.

She parked the jane car in the garage and went around to the morgue section of the building. She found the forensic and medical personnel taking fingerprints from the fingers the rats had not bitten off. That gave them a thumb and the little finger of the right hand and the last three fingers of the left hand. The corpse lay stripped and draped on a plastic alloy cart. His clothes were folded on a nearby table.

Janna waited outside in the corridor before entering, peering in through the windows until the cart had been wheeled off to the coolers. Even so, her stomach flipped and churned. The stench of decomposition remained strong in the room. In particular, it clung to the clothes. She swallowed hard and tried not to recoil as she reached for the jumpsuit. Her nose wrinkled involuntarily.

A technician grinned. "Don't you know that real lions, the four-legged African kind, like their meat a bit ripe?"

"Just run those prints through the computer, will you?" Janna shook out the suit and checked for the label. The suit had been made by Stellar Fashions. She laid it aside and picked up the other pieces of clothing. In contrast to the suit, the underclothes, socks, and shoes were of cheap manufacture. The soles of the shoes were wearing thin and the plastic uppers were brittle and starting to crack.

She sucked her lower lip as she put down the shoes and picked up the suit again. She handed it to a forensics tech. "Let's see what the label looks like under UV. There may be a store marking."

The technician held up a small blacklight. "I already checked it. There is a store marking. It looks like this." She handed Janna a notepage. On it was drawn what looked like a square capital A, but with the top bar extending beyond the second leg and the lower crossbar not quite reaching the second upright.

Janna returned the page to the tech. "Let's see who uses that mark."

She washed her hands thoroughly before going up to the computer keyboard in Forensics with the technician. The tech drew the symbol on the screen with a light scriber and ordered the computer to run. The answer came back in seconds. Janna read the screen with a sigh. The store marking belonged to Fine Threads in Whitelakes Mall. She realized she had been hoping the deader would turn out not to be Owan. If the deader were wearing Owan's suit, though, he was probably Owan. Damn.

There was one more chance, though. What if the fingerprints belonged to someone else? She trotted down the corridor to the fingerprint computer.

The technician there presented her with a printout. "There you are, hot out of the printer."

The prints that had been fed in matched, the printout said, the corresponding prints of a child idented forty years ago in the Oakland division following a school raid. There were no further records and no application for a Scib Card recorded for anyone with those prints. The name given at the time of the school raid was Owan Desfosses. The still-applicable parts of the physical description were the brown hair and brown eyes.

She handed back the printout. "See it gets to me

tomorrow, will you?" Damn and double damn. It was Owan, definitely. "I'm going home."

The rain had settled to a steady drizzle but there were still rivers in the street, mostly in the bike lanes. Janna left her bike parked in the police garage and took the bus home.

She and Sid shared the second floor of a twentieth-century stone house near the west side of the division. Sid was sitting reading a medical journal when she sloshed in. He peered over his glasses at her as she peeled out of her slicker. "You look like you've been soaked and wrung out."

"At least a couple of times." She dumped the slicker over a chair. "Make me some hot tea, will you? I have a hard call to make."

She punched Clio de Garza's number on the phone.

De Garza knew something was wrong the moment she came on the screen. While Janna was wondering how to begin, the Hispanic woman guessed. "You've found Owan, haven't you?"

Janna nodded. "And he—"

"And he's dead." De Garza's mouth trembled. "All day I've had a feeling of dread. Now I know why. How did it happen?"

In as brief and unemotional sentences as possible, Janna told her. De Garza's face reminded her of Liann Seaton's. Both held their grief. Both controlled their faces until they were like porcelain masks.

"I'm sorry," Janna said.

Something bleak blew through de Garza's eyes. "So am I, sergeant. Thank you for calling me."

Janna punched off. "God, I hate making calls like that."

She turned to find Sid with a bath towel. "I'm heating the tea water now and a bath is running. Go climb in. I'll bring the tea when it's ready."

She hugged him and planted a kiss on his forehead. "And people wonder why I live with you. You're superlative, Sid."

The bath was lovely. She soaked in the water sipping tea, and Sid sat on the edge of the tub listening to her talk. She reflected that she should have come home to Sid for that shoulder to cry on tonight, instead of going to Wim. Sid was nodding, encouraging, and commiserating in all the right places.

"That's rotten luck to have your most valuable witness killed. What will you do now?"

Janna shrugged. "Dig for physical evidence." She drained the last of the tea and handed him the empty cup. "I wonder if I can talk a judge into giving me a search warrant to go over Hazlett's car and clothes. All I need is some matching soil, a weed, some threads ... something to tie him to that building."

"Would you like your back scrubbed?"

"I love you, Sid." She leaned forward and let him scrub. "I want to strap this deek. Lord, how I want him. What kind of person just stands by and watches two other human beings die that way?"

"What kind of man puts lye in his wife's douche? That's what happened to one of my customers today. We've both had enough experience to know there's no limit to what people will do to one another. How come we're surprised when a new cruelty turns up?"

"I suppose we keep thinking we've seen the limit. Hand me that towel, will you?"

She climbed out of the tub. Sid dried her back for her. She smiled over her shoulder at him. "You make a great mother, you know that?"

"Speaking of mothers, where do you think your partner is?"

She sighed. "I haven't the faintest idea."

"Do you think you ought to ask the watch units to look for him?"

"After the Night of the Caged Lion?" She grimaced. "No. Worrying about Mama is probably as pointless now as it was when he went into that apartment house after the sniper. He's thoughtless enough not to call in. I'll wait and see if he shows up for roll-call in the morning." She yawned. "I'm going to bed."

She was asleep almost before she finished crawling under the sheet. A pounding dragged her back to consciousness some unguessable time later. She struggled up through the fog of sleep groping for orientation. What was happening? It took a couple of minutes to register that someone was at the front door.

In one blink she was fully awake. She swung out of bed, reaching for both a robe and for the .22 shooter in her bed table. She padded to the front door on silent, bare feet.

"Who is it?" She cocked the shooter and moved to the side of the door rather than stand directly in front.

"Mama. Let me in."

Mama! She peered at a table chrono. "It's three o'clock!"

"I know." His voice reverberated with rich, self-satisfied tones. "But this can't wait. Let me in."

She uncocked the shooter and dropped it in her robe pocket. She unlocked the door.

Mama pranced in wearing copper knee boots and a sleeveless copper foil suit that looked sprayed on. Gold and silver star appliqués spangled his arms. A cloud of narcotic fumes followed him. "It is a splendid night, bibi." He bumped into a chair.

Janna rolled her eyes. "You're toxy."

He dropped into the chair and lay back, giggling, arms and legs outflung. "Mostly I'm blind. I'm not wearing my glasses, you'll notice. And I'm toxy, too, yes, I admit. The Laclede bibi likes her pleasures and I had to keep up with her." He closed his eyes. "It wasn't easy, especially when she wanted to finish off with some of the most strenuous mattress bending I've ever been a party to."

"But you rose to the occasion, somehow."

Her dry tone opened one of his eyes. He peered myopically at her and giggled. "Yes, I rose to the occasion." He closed the eye again. He sang, *"Let's you and me put two, bibi/Let's count coup*. On her stomach she had: *Feel safe tonight; sleep with a leo.* Let's *do* put two, bibi, and both feel safe tonight." He giggled again.

"Do you want help throwing him out?"

Janna looked around to see Sid in the hallway leading to the bedrooms. His round face was pink and cherubic with sleep. He blinked at her through his glasses. "I'll see. Mama, haven't you had enough of mixing partners and passion? And what makes you think I'm interested in you as a sexual encounter?"

With obvious effort, Mama opened both eyes. "This isn't passion, bibi; it's celebration."

"What are we celebrating?"

Mama giggled. "What Laclede told me." He made a weak effort to sit up straighter. "Do you have some caff, bibi? I'm so far in orbit I can't keep my mind going one direction for more than a minute at a time."

She sighed and headed for the kitchen. "I think I can handle this. You go back to bed, Sid."

She made the caff strong and managed to pour six cups of it into Mama, forcing him to walk up and down the living room between cups. Finally his steps steadied and he stopped giggling. Only then did she let him sit down again.

They stayed in the kitchen, where Janna could pour him more caff. Mama propped his elbows on the tabletop and leaned his head in his hands. "Thanks, bibi."

She sat down opposite him. "You can thank me by telling me about Laclede. You contacted her this afternoon?"

"I contacted her."

"You told her you wanted to use her services?"

"Not exactly."

She poured him another cup of caff. "What did you tell her?"

"I told her I was a police officer."

"You *what?*" Janna came up out of her chair.

He extended a long arm and caught at her elbow. He pulled her down in her chair again. "Don't get excited. I knew what I was doing. This bibi is brainbent. You said she took her shade friend to Tuck's place at a time when they must have been arranging for Owan to meet Hazlett. So it seemed to me she gets a boost out of playing with fire. I went to Many Mansions pretending I wanted to redecorate my apartment. She was ad-

226

vertising herself every minute. I took a chance and told her who I was. That really lit her fuse. When I told her I wanted to go into business with her, that almost short-circuited her."

Janna poured some caff for herself and took a big swallow. "And then?"

He told her about being searched. He told her in some detail.

She raised a brow. "Laclede lit your fuse, too, didn't she?"

Mama grinned. "A man ought to enjoy his work. When she saw I was clean, she invited me to take her out this evening and talk about what we could do for each other. So I did. I wined and dined and danced her at the Ad Astra Club. Then we danced some more. I think we visited every place in the city with a jivaqueme band."

"Where you drank and smoked as well as danced, further enjoying your work."

He peered at her with reproach. "I sacrificed for this. I left my glasses home so I wouldn't keep playing with them. I had to pay a fortune in taxi fares because I couldn't see well enough to drive and I spent an entire evening with one of the flashiest bibis in the city without ever really being able to see her."

"I'm bleeding for you. What did you do after the dancing?"

"She took me to her apartment and counted coup on me. Lord! That bibi is high voltage. It was worth it, though."

"I'm beginning to doubt letting you in here was worth it."

He leaned toward her. "It was worth it because then she told me how she works the doppelgängers. That's what she calls the sligh doubles . . . doppelgängers."

At last, something relevant. "Are you able to remember what she said?"

He winced at her sarcasm. "I'm not that toxy. Furthermore—" he reached into his pocket and pulled

227

out a microcorder—"this evening I was *not* clean. I have everything she said recorded."

He tapped the corder on. Marca Laclede's voice said, "Reveal all my secrets to a lion, even if he is a partner? I couldn't do that."

"Can't you tell me something about the set-up? You ought to trust your partner. Talk to Mama. How do you find your doppelgängers?"

"I can tell you that. I have a sligh friend who hunts them for me. Oh." Her gasp was sharp, ecstatic. "That's nice. Do some more of that."

Janna regarded Mama speculatively. "Do what?"

"Hush and listen."

Janna listened. As she did, a reluctant admiration blossomed for Mama. In half an hour, between groans and cries of delight and much heavy breathing, he had wheedled every detail of the doppelgänger operation out of her.

"Where did you have the corder?"

"In a boot, but with a remote control and mike taped to the inside of my wrist chrono."

"Clever."

He preened himself. "It was, wasn't it?"

She rolled her eyes.

The explanation of faking the thumbprints left Janna with a chill. It was a frightening thing to hear. She had always believed in the infallibility of fingerprints. This was like giving a Bible cultist irrefutable proof of God's death.

"Did I read her right, bibi?"

"You read her right. Nice work."

"Will your sligh object to having another partner?" Mama's voice asked on the tape.

"Tarl has no ambition, no sense of destiny." Laclede's voice was a purr of satisfaction. "Telling him about you will only disturb him. Let's let you be my secret."

Janna rolled her eyes. "She's incredible." She tapped the corder off. "Let's make sure Vradel hears this right after rollcall. Then maybe we can start wrapping up this case."

CHAPTER FIFTEEN

Marca Laclede took her time dressing. Let Adrian complain if she came in late. Soon she would be quitting to set up her own decorating business. She did not plan to do much decoration, but it would still be a good front for her real business.

She lingered in her bath and brushed her hair two hundred strokes. She paused frequently, while slipping star and planet appliqués on her arms and legs, to look around her and imagine her apartment as one of those semiunderground townhouses out near the governor's mansion. She wanted one like Jorge Hazlett had. Soon the clothes in her closet would be only the most modish and made of the finest materials. Thanks to the clients Maxwell would soon bring her, she would be able to afford anything she wanted. The black man was going to be useful, just as he claimed. He was not a bad bounce, either.

Marca inspected the appliqués critically in the mirror. Were there too many? Not enough? She did not like the bare patch on her left shoulder blade. Contorting, she added a quarter moon and a tiny star. She examined the results. That looked better.

She wiggled into a pair of hose and her dress. It bared her left shoulder and hung to her ankles in steamers. Every movement revealed the entire length of her legs. She checked it in the mirror. Nice. She blew her image a kiss.

She was putting in her contact lenses when the doorbell chimed. Marca's brows rose. She glanced at her dressing table chrono. It read 9:10. Who could be coming to see her at this hour?

She checked the security screen before opening th
door. A Dutch-chocolate face grinned up at her.

Marca opened the door. "Well, Mama, back agai
alread—"

She broke off as she saw the lean, smoky-haire
woman with Maxwell. That woman was a lion, too
Marca remembered. It was the officer who had calle
her yesterday afternoon, and the she-lion was *not* smi
ing. Sudden fear, unalleviated by any excitement thi
time, washed through Marca. She started to slam th
door.

Maxwell's arm came out and caught the edge
"Sorry, bibi." The she-lion put a paper in his othe
hand. He held it up before Marca. "We have a war
rant for your arrest, for solicitation and conspiracy t
fraudulently use a Scib Card."

"I beg your pardon. Did you say solicitation?" De
spite her fear, she was able to keep her voice icy
"What nonsense."

"Solicitation," the she-lion said, "is the counseling
procuring, or hiring of another person to commit
crime."

Her fingers were bloodless on the edge of the door
"You have no evidence against me."

The two leos exchanged glances. Maxwell said, "
have a recording I made in your bedroom last night."

Imagining all that was on that recording was to
much. Tearing the door open all the way, Marc
launched herself fingernails first for the black leo's fac
and eyes. "You goddam filthy black motherbouncer."

Janna caught her before she managed to rak
Mama's face more than once. She spun the smal
woman across the corridor, bouncing her off the wal
and onto her knees on the floor. Before Laclede coul
get up, Janna had both the woman's hands behind he
back and a wrap strap around her wrists. She use
the bound wrists to haul Laclede to her feet.

"That isn't a nice way to treat Mama."

"Bastard." Laclede spat at her. She turned or
Mama with her lip curled in contempt. "You, too.
should have known any afroam who was such a stink-

ing bounce couldn't be a real man. He'd have to be a kittylion. Miaow."

Mama straightened his glasses and wiped at his cheek. A few flecks of blood came away on his fingers. "You have the right to remain silent. If you give up the right to remain silent, anything you say can and will be used against you in a court of law," he said evenly. "You have the right to an attorney. If you want an attorney and cannot afford one, the court will appoint one for you. Do you understand what I've said?"

"Go count coup on your mother again."

"Do you understand?" Janna repeated. "We can go over it again, until you do."

Sullenly, Laclede started to parrot the rights statement. Janna stopped her. "Not in the same words. Tell me in other words what it means."

"It means I don't have to say anything to you about anything, but if I do, some toad prosecutor will take it to court. It means I can hire a lawyer, or take what the court gives me."

"Good girl." Janna shoved Laclede ahead of her into the apartment. She pointed her at a tip-over style chair. "Sit and stay. Where do you want to start, Mama?"

"How about the bedroom?"

"You can't search my apartment!"

Janna pulled the search warrant out of her thigh pocket and waved it at Laclede. "I'll take this room."

Janna found nothing significant in the living room. Mama found some jewelry in the bedroom. They compared it to the list of purchases on Hazlett's bank record.

"That recording last night is worthless," Laclede said from her chair. "I was just playing a game. I don't know any sligh named Tarl."

Janna looked around at her. "Then how did I happen to see you with him in the Lion's Den last week? He looks just like your boss, only with none of that elegant polish."

"He's just a friend. He never doubled for Adrian in his life."

None of the jewelry in the bedroom matched anything on Hazlett's bank record.

"I'll try the bathroom," Mama said.

Janna headed for the kitchen. On impulse, and prompted by a vague memory of something heard during one of her courses, she opened the freezer. Through the open door of the kitchen, she saw Laclede half rise from the chair, then sit back, biting her lip. Janna sorted through the plastic-wrapped packages. Most were solid, but one seemed to be made of small, moving pieces. She took it out and broke the seal.

Laclede screamed.

Janna returned to the living room, where she tipped over another chair, making it into a small table. Onto it she poured the contents of the package. "Mama, come look at this."

While Laclede swore at her, Janna compared the jewelry she had found to their list. A sapphire bracelet, some diamond earrings, and a jade pendant appeared to match.

Janna held them up before the other woman. "How did you come by these?"

Laclede glared. "My lawyer will tell you."

Mama came in from the bathroom carrying two small bottles. "These aren't marked but look what happens when you mix a little from each." He gave Janna a small oval of soft, rubbery material.

He was also carrying a pair of shoes. He handed the bottles to Janna and knelt to put the shoes on Laclede. A foot lashed at his chin. Mama ducked just in time to avoid contact.

"Bitch!" His hand drew back.

Janna caught his wrist. "Let her go without shoes. That sidewalk out there is heating up. Let her burn her feet."

Mama dropped his hand. Laclede glared, then jammed her feet into the shoes. She launched a few more choice profanities at both of them.

Marca Laclede had not always been such a flash bibi, Janna reflected. That language spoke of more inelegant beginnings.

They did not take her directly downtown. They stopped at the Santa Fe Building first. Janna stayed in the car with their prisoner while Mama went up to Many Mansions. He came back ten minutes later with two more little bottles, a compact with a jelly substance in the bottom, and an address book. Under the names and addresses of each entry were stars. Adrian Cabot's name had seven. Jorge Hazlett's entry had one. By holding the compact at an angle to the light, Janna could just see a fingerprint in the jelly.

"Nice." She scratched her identifying mark on the compact and returned it to Mama.

Laclede looked pale enough to faint.

Then they took her on to the station.

Lieutenant Vradel had an interview room ready for them when they brought her up after booking her and tagging the evidence. Marca Laclede sat in the straight hardboard chair at the hardboard table and rubbed her wrists as if still feeling the wrap strap around them. She stared tight-lipped at the jewelry, compact, and bottles set on the far edge of the table. She also stared at two jumpsuits, a white card, and a photograph of Jorge Hazlett lying beside them.

"The rights the arresting officers repeated to you still apply," Vradel said.

A gleam came in her eyes. "Rights? They didn't tell me any rights."

Janna took out her microcorder and tapped it on. Mama's recorded voice delivered the words repeated to every arrested citizen since the famous Miranda decision more than a hundred years before.

"Bitch," Laclede spat at Janna.

Janna tapped off the corder.

Vradel said, "Do you want an attorney, Ms. Laclede?"

Her face was hard in the lights of the interview room. She looked up at Vradel, not knowing the leos were standing so she would have to look up, not know-

ing she was facing straight into a hidden camera taping the entire interrogation. When the questioning was
through, experts would go over the tape, measuring
stress in her voice, noting pupil response to the questions asked, determining when she was telling the truth
and when she was lying. The experts' thoughts would
not be admissible evidence in court; but they could
determine the course of any subsequent investigation
of her case.

Unknowing, Laclede said, "I don't need a lawyer.
I haven't done anything wrong." Her voice was sullen.

"Then you'll answer some questions? You don't
have to answer any you don't want to."

"You're so kind." Her pouty mouth looked more so
than ever.

"Where can we find your friend Tarl?"

"I don't know any—" She broke off, looking at
Janna. "He's just a friend. He hasn't done anything
either."

"Do you know where we can find him?" Janna repeated.

Laclede shrugged. "No. Slighs never stay still for
long."

"You're going to be prosecuted," Mama said. "Do
you want to go to trial and maybe jail alone, while
Tarl is free to spend what he's made, and maybe set
up a new business with someone else? He's the one
who finds the doppelgängers. He doesn't need you to
find citizen customers. Any ambitious, unscrupulous
person can do that for him."

She started to spit at Mama, but stopped. Janna
watched the relays close in her head. The room was
silent while they let Laclede think. After a few minutes, their prisoner smiled. It was a thin, malicious
smile. "Tarl works at the Goodway Market on Sardou
Street, in the back."

Vradel glanced toward Janna and jerked his head
at the door. Janna felt for the warrant for Tarl in her
thigh pocket. She and Mama left the interview room.
They opened the door of the watchbox next to the interview room. Assistant District Attorney Ward Prior

234

sat watching the room next door on a screen leading off the video camera.

"Interesting case."

"You will prosecute, won't you?" Janna said.

"I'll see what you have after the lieutenant finishes interrogating the suspect."

Mama wrinkled his scalp. "You be careful now. Don't make any impulsive decisions." He closed the door of the watchbox, grimacing in disgust. "A Dias clone."

They headed for the garage.

They found the Goodway Market without difficulty. In its parking area, they climbed out of Indian Thirty and stood studying its clouded windows papered with bargain notices. The air was like a sauna, humidity so high it created a visible haze. Janna felt as if she were being steamed.

"Do you want to go in or watch the back?" Mama asked.

"I'll watch the back. You may be able to walk right up to him without him smelling lion."

She watched Mama start in the front, then she circled the building. She stopped in sight of the market's freight door and stood with her hand on her gun, ready to draw and shoot if Tarl came out the back. With her other hand she lifted the hair off her neck. Last night's rain had only made the weather worse, not better. Her jumpsuit was starting to stick to her and she could feel sweat trickling down between her breasts.

Inside the market, a man yelled. A moment later a woman screamed. Janna was in motion even before the sound quit. She raced for the front of the market.

The sligh she had seen with Marca Laclede came running out of the market as Janna came around the rear end of the building. He saw her and bolted away, across the street. Janna pulled her gun.

"Halt! Police!"

He ran faster. She fired after him, arms stretched before her with elbows straight, left hand steadying her right. The needle missed. She saw it hit the ground and skid into a crack in the paving. She aimed again but Tarl was running such a bobbing, erratic course that she could not keep the laser sight on him. Swearing, she jammed the Starke back into its holster and concentrated on chasing the sligh.

She did not like the choice. There could be something exhilarating in running down a suspect, but not here in Oakland. She always listened to what the watch officers at Department Exchanges had to say about local conditions, but there was a difference between hearing and experiencing. Practically speaking, she was three years out of touch with the streets down here, three years out of field experience with the lion traps being set. She had to spend almost as much time being aware of where she was putting her feet and on checking the space ahead of her for neck wires as she did watching the fleeing man. Too, she kept wondering uneasily what had happened to Mama.

Tarl cut across a lot where the scattered pieces of a razed house made an obstacle course. She followed using exactly the same path her quarry took. He was no runner, and she was gaining on him fast. Her main worry was not whether she could catch him but if she could do it before she drowned in the saturated air.

Only a few meters ahead of her by then, he cut around the end of a crumbling wall. Another few strides and she would have him! She forgot about following in his path and vaulted the wall.

"Oh, shit."

There was no ground on the other side. The wall was part of the foundation of the house which had stood there. Below her was the gaping hole of the basement, turned into a pool by last night's rain. Janna fell full length into the muddy water.

Tarl had long since disappeared by the time she found a corner where she could climb up out of the basement. She stared in the direction she had last seen him heading, swearing at him and at herself. After several minutes, she gave up the chase and headed back to the market.

Mama was leaning against Indian Thirty, brushing at dirt stains on his red and yellow suit. He looked up in surprise at her. "If that's all due to sweat, it must have been one hell of a chase. Where's the sligh?"

"In Jefferson County by this time." She eyed him. "And what, may I ask, happened in there?"

He jiggled his glasses, pretending to adjust the temple pieces behind his ears, and focused somewhere on infinity. "He dropped me."

"How?"

He shrugged. "When I told him who I saw, he acted resigned. He came right along, all cringing smiles and careful sligh politeness—you know the pattern. When we had almost reached the door, though, he came around with a yell and kicked me in the groin. I've spent the last ten minutes getting up off that floor in there." He rubbed at a stain. "Lord, it's filthy."

Janna shook her head. She raked her fingers through her wet mane. "For a couple of Oakland veterans, we've made a damned poor showing today, Mama."

The manager came out of the market. "My girls just told me what happened. I'm terribly sorry." He was almost bowing in his obsequiousness, but a mocking note lay under it. "I want you to know I never realized that sligh was involved in anything illegal. I just gave him a bit of work from time to time because I feel sorry for those people."

The manager had given Tarl work to save himself money and paperwork and they all knew that, but Janna did not call him on it. "We don't know that he is involved in anything illegal. We just want to talk to him."

"You wouldn't know where he lives, by any chance?"

The manager shook his head.

Janna said, "You let us know if he happens to come back here."

"Certainly. Where can I reach you?"

Janna reached into a sleeve pocket for a card. She found them all soggy. "Mama."

Mama handed one of his to the manager. "Brill or Maxwell."

The manager nodded.

It was a silent, uncomfortable ride downtown. Janna kept berating herself for vaulting the wall when Tarl went around it. She ought to have known better than that. She supposed—hoped—Mama was treating himself to similar flagellation for accepting Tarl's surrender at face value and not putting a wrap strap on him. They were even more uncomfortable later telling Lieutenant Vradel how they happened to let the sligh escape.

The lieutenant listened in pained silence, his mustache twitching. At the end he sighed. It was a bone-weary sound. "Have you put out an APB on him?"

They nodded.

"Didn't put a strap on him." Vradel sighed again.

Janna was afraid the next sigh and remark would be directed at her. She changed the subject. "How did Laclede's interrogation go?"

"She's made a complete statement. She doesn't want to be an accessory to murder, so she's being very cooperative. She told us she arranged for that sligh to double for Hazlett, and told us where and when they met to switch."

Mama whooped. "When do we get a warrant for Hazlett, then?"

"We don't get one." Vradel's mustache twitched. "Laclede's statement gives Hazlett opportunity, but there's still nothing that definitely places him in the Sunflower Federal Building Saturday night, or in that abandoned store in Oakland, either."

"Oh, come *on,* skipper."

"You come on, Maxwell. Keep digging for evidence."

Mama looked thoughtful. "Maybe there's another way. The British have a polite term for it. Let's invite Hazlett down to *assist* us with our inquiries."

Vradel sketched Hazlett's face on a corner of his memo pad. "What exactly do you have in mind?"

"Asking him some nasty questions and seeing how he reacts."

"Hoping he'll give something away?"

Mama nodded.

Vradel doodled meaningless faces while he considered the plan. He drew a pair of frowning eyes. "Do it."

Janna looked up Hazlett's office number. Mama punched it into the phone. He was wearing his most charming smile when the receptionist put him through to Hazlett.

Hazlett nodded courteously at Mama. "Good morning, sergeant. How is your investigation going? Have you found that witness yet?"

"The investigation is almost over." Mama's voice was smooth and deep. "There are just a couple of points to be cleared up. I don't want to impose, but I wonder, Mr. Hazlett, can you come down and help us settle some details this morning?"

Across the table from Mama, out of sight of the phone's screen, Janna smiled and nodded approval.

Hazlett looked doubtful. "I have a very busy schedule today."

"We need half an hour of your time . . . no more."

"Well." Hazlett shrugged. "I can give you half an hour. I'll come early this afternoon."

"Thank you very much, sir."

He punched off and reached across the table to punch Janna's shoulder. "Cross your fingers, bibi."

They bought sandwiches in the snackbar and chased down the post-mortem report on Owan while they were waiting for Hazlett. Janna read the report with a frown.

"Trick killed him, too, and it was a massive dose, like Kellener's. Kolb thinks it was administered in some Scotch whiskey." She looked up at Mama. "The whiskey, according to the good doctor, was bottled gold, not the kind a sligh would be likely to be drinking."

"I don't suppose he offered any opinion on the brand and year."

Janna sucked thoughtfully at her lower lip. "If we could get a search warrant for Hazlett's house, we could compare the stuff found in Owan's stomach with what Hazlett has in his liquor cabinet."

"I like your thinking, bibi."

"Let's hope Hazlett helps us get the warrant."

Circumstances had an air of conclusion about them, Jorge reflected, definitely an end-game feeling. When that afroam lion started being polite it had to be because he recognized he was not going to be in a position to be impolite much longer and get away with it. Jorge walked into the Crimes Against Persons squadroom feeling expansive and generous.

"I'm only too glad to do what I can to help settle this," he told the smoky-haired she-lion. "This has been very upsetting for everyone, especially for Andy's wife and children."

"Naturally," Brill said. She held open a door for him.

Jorge's good humor faded. It was the interview room. His eyes narrowed. They wanted him to help them clear a few points by talking to him in the interview room? The end game suddenly had a new feel about it. Who was about to be mated was less certain. He felt the throb of his pulse in his throat, half fear, half excitement.

"Am I being arrested?" He made the question casual.

Brill's eyes widened in surprise. "Why should we arrest you?"

"Then why are we talking in here?"

She smiled. "Just routine. Please sit down."

He sat down in the chair. His eyes moved past her to the perforated acoustical tiles on the wall opposite him. Behind one of the holes the lens of a camera was aimed at him.

"I'm familiar with police procedure, sergeant. The interview room is used for interrogating suspects." He was careful to keep all alarm out of his voice; he left in a slight indignation.

"Not always," Brill said.

Behind her, the black lion polished his glasses on a trouser leg. He blinked myopically at Jorge. "You don't have a guilty conscience, do you?"

Brill frowned around at him then turned back to Jorge. "I'm sorry if this makes you feel threatened." Her voice was earnest, apologetic. "We just need to ask a few questions and I thought it might be more comfortable in here, away from the general confusion. Would you feel better outside?"

Jorge made himself meet her eyes. "It isn't important. This is fine. I just like to know what's going on. What questions do you need to ask?"

"Well, to start with, I need to have you look at something." She pulled a carton from under the table and began piling its contents on the table. "It's in here somewhere."

Jorge sat back in his chair and made his body relax. That last sentence rang flat in his ears. Its note of absent-mindedness was at complete variance with everything else he had seen in the she-lion. She was trying some new gambit on him. He had better go slow while he studied it and decided whether to accept or decline.

The pile on the table included two beautiful suits that begged to be fingered, some jewelry, and a metal compact. Jorge allowed himself to touch one of the suits, as anyone might.

Brill flipped a square piece of stiff paper onto the table. Jorge stared at it. It was a photograph, but lying face down. He was pricked by the urge to pick it up and turn it over. For one moment as the she-lion was removing it from the carton, Jorge had caught a glimpse of the front. He thought the face was his. It looked like an instant photo, the kind the Laclede woman had taken of him. If it were, they must have found out about the doppelgänger, and they were not likely to have done that unless they were investigating him.

Brill grimaced. "It isn't here. Mama, do you know where it is?"

"Not if it isn't in the box, I don't."

She sighed. "Damn. I'm sorry, Mr. Hazlett. I can't seem to find what I need."

"Find what?"

"It doesn't matter, I guess."

The photograph was so close to him. It would take only a second to turn it over, to see if it were of him or not.

"Perhaps you can answer me this. Do you know where all the merchandise you bought Saturday night is?"

They must know. Why else ask that kind of question? He felt the eye of the camera on him, felt his pupil responses and words going down on tape for the later scrutiny of experts. He casually removed his hands from the top of the table where they were folded and used them to rub his eyes as he feigned a stretch.

"Why do you ask?" He kept the question casual, innocently curious.

"Well, some of it—"

"Some of it's been turning up in places we never expected it to be," Maxwell interrupted.

They had been checking his bank records! They *did* suspect him, then.

Brill said, apologetically again, "We've checked the bank records of everyone connected with your partner."

Indecision prickled at him. If they had been investigating him with the idea of finding evidence against him and found out about the doppelgänger, why should the she-lion bother apologizing for the investigation? Maybe they did not know after all. He dropped his eyes to the study of his fingernails. "Of course." If only he could see the face on the photograph. That would tell him whether they knew or not. If only—but he dared not touch it. He was careful not even to look at it.

Brill repeated, "Do you know where your merchandise is?"

He could not tell the truth, obviously, but he could

not lie, either. That was just as bad as the truth. He kept his eyes down, away from the gaze of the camera. "I don't understand what that can have to do with deciding why Andy died." He kept his voice low, too.

"Would you mind speaking louder, Mr. Hazlett? I can hardly hear you."

She, or the recorder?

"I know these questions don't seem relevant to your partner's death, but . . . it's just one of those little things that turned up and we felt we needed to settle it."

Her tone was almost slighlike in its anxiety not to offend. If he were sure they suspected him of killing Andy, he could simply refuse to answer any questions without an attorney present; but if they did not know anything, refusing to answer would be suspicious. And her manner did not help him. If only he could see the photograph!

She sighed. "If only I could find that—" She turned away. "Maybe Morello took it out. Mama, let's go ask him. Would you mind waiting here a few minutes, Mr. Hazlett? We'll be right back."

They left the interview room, closing the door behind them.

The muscles in Jorge's hand ached with the urge to reach out for the photograph. He felt the gaze of the camera, however. Someone would be monitoring the camera, too. They may have left, but he was hardly alone.

With everything in him screaming to look at the photograph, Jorge made himself sit back in the chair with arms folded behind his head and stare at the ceiling, yawning now and then in pretended boredom. He closed his eyes.

In the watchbox Janna looked from the monitor screen to Assistant D.A. Prior and Lieutenant Vradel. She shook her head. "He isn't going for the skin. Come on, deek, look at the photograph, damn you."

"I don't think he needs to," Mama said. "I think an

243

innocent person would be curious enough to take a look. He's been so carefully ignoring it that I think that proves his guilt. You notice the other things haven't affected him that way. He looked at them when they first came out. He didn't recognize any of the stuff, either, which means he never bought it."

Prior brushed at a spot on the brown paisley of one knee. "That goes toward proving fraudulent use of a Scib Card, nothing more." He stood and picked up his briefcase.

Mama frowned. "Skipper, did you show him everything we have so far? Did you tell him about the Sunco tapes and the sligh's murder?"

Vradel's mustache twitched. "I told him."

"I can't see that you can even establish the sligh was murdered, let alone that this man had anything to do with it. The physical evidence indicates nothing more than a simple OD," Prior said.

"Oh, come *on*," Mama protested.

Prior's eyes were cold. "Come on where, sergeant? You have a law degree. You know what constitutes evidence. I admit that everything taken together indicates Hazlett probably did kill his partner, and possibly the sligh, too; but there's nothing a competent trial lawyer couldn't demolish in front of a jury in five minutes. What you need are self-incriminating admissions from Hazlett."

Mama swore. Janna sighed gustily. She recognized that Prior was right and she hated him for it. If they had to wait for Hazlett to incriminate himself, they were going to have their twenty years in and be ready for their pensions before the case ever went to court. Hazlett was not even going to be cooperative enough to give them some lies they could work on.

She looked at the screen. He was sitting where they left him, apparently dozing. He was not touching any of the evidence left enticingly before him. He was not even looking at it. When he left they would be able to check his recorded voice for stress, but there would be no pupil response to study, no unconsciously committed incriminating actions. Damn it to hell.

"Give us a couple of hours to work on him and we'll bring you something incriminating," Mama told Prior.

"If you can do it, fine." Prior stepped out the door of the watchbox and headed for the squadroom door. "Good luck."

The door closed behind him.

Vradel chewed a corner of his mustache. "You two decide what you want to do."

Janna watched the man on the screen of the watchbox. "He's an iceman. I don't think we're going to touch him."

"We can try, bibi."

She looked up at Mama. He had successfully defended a number of leos against charges brought by Internal Affairs. Maybe he could do something with their suspect, too. Janna freely admitted that the idea of letting Hazlett go stuck in her throat. It violated her sense of justice.

"All right, let's try."

Jorge allowed himself a look at his wrist chrono. The leos had been gone a long time. What, exactly, was their gambit? The debate started in his head all over again. How much did they know? About the doppelgänger? About the murder? Both of them? Or did they know anything at all? Perhaps they just knew about the doppelgänger. In which case they might be trying to see if it related to Andy's death. They might just be fishing for anything suspicious. There were so many possibilities, and each needed a different response. If he only knew where he stood. If only he dared turn over the photograph.

The door opened and the two leos stepped back in. Brill's forehead was creased in anxiety. The black lion moved with the sinuous stride of a stalking leopard. Jorge still did not know what they knew, but he could recognize the beginning of a Mutt and Jeff act when he saw it. The real questions were about to start.

Something in Jorge unwound. It no longer mattered what they knew. He could anticipate them now. He would decline their gambit and counter with one of his own. They were going to push. Well, he would just push back and see how strong their position was.

"You didn't find it, whatever *it* is?"

"Not yet," Maxwell said, "but we won't give up. We'll find it yet."

"Unfortunately, I don't have time to wait until you do." Jorge stood up. "Saturday is a busy day for me. I have to leave."

"Not just yet, jon," Maxwell said, moving between Jorge and the door.

Now was the time to challenge them. Jorge raised a brow. "How do you intend to prevent me from leaving? You might try arresting me, of course. Do you have the grounds to do that?"

They stared at him. Brill reacted first. "You're an ass," she snapped at Maxwell, then turned to Jorge. "I apologize for the department on behalf of my partner. We don't intend to arrest you or otherwise hold you by force. We need your help. I appeal to your civic conscience and regard for your late partner in asking you to inconvenience yourself by giving us just a few more minutes of your time."

An excellent move by the Queen. He applauded her silently. Now for the King's answer. He smiled. "I wouldn't need civic conscience or the regard for my late partner to persuade me to give you a very great deal more of my time, my dear sergeant, but no duty on this Earth can compel me to subject myself to the abusiveness of your partner. Good day to you."

He pushed past them out the door of the interview room. He did not look back as he crossed the squadroom. He longed to turn and see their expressions. Shock? Frustration? Rage? Looking back was a fatal fault of humans. Look what happened to Lot's wife, and that harpist of Greek mythology who was leading his girlfriend out of Hades. Jorge determinedly kept his eyes front. Inside, he laughed.

Janna did not know what her expression was. What she felt was dumbfounded anger.

"He's laughing at us, bibi," Mama said. His fist crashed down on the top of the interview room's table with such force the hardboard shivered all the way down its legs to the floor.

"Why not?" Janna said bitterly. "He just walked right through us and there wasn't a thing we could do to stop him."

"That's what burns. It's another round to the deeks of the world. The good guys lose again." He slumped against the wall.

Janna sucked on her lower lip. Something Mama had said not long ago was working its way up through her mind. It broke the surface. She studied it with care. She knew that another time she would have refused to entertain such an idea, but right now, it looked good.

"Do you remember saying that in order to catch snakes like Hazlett, they have to be driven out into the sun?"

Mama lifted his head. He pushed his glasses up his nose. Behind them, his eyes were expectant. "I remember."

"Let's go kick over some rocks."

CHAPTER SIXTEEN

Jorge thought this had to be one of the most satisfying days of his life. No matter that the air steamed and the air-conditioning in his offices could barely keep the temperature at a reasonable level. He did not care that the Sunchild Company's ramjet was far behind schedule at Beach-Cessna and over half the Aurora Company still had not taken their physicals with launch just a month and a half away. Jorge felt he was wrapped in a cloud of euphoria, girded in sweet triumph. They had not arrested him because they could not. Whatever they might suspect, they did not have evidence. They had wanted him to say something that would help them find the evidence they needed.

He took pride in knowing he had given them nothing. If only criminals would realize it, lying was the second worst response to a police question, surpassed only by the danger of truthful responses. Any admission, true or false, could be used by the leos. Statistics showed that suspects who refused to say anything at all were very rarely convicted. Physical evidence was only circumstantial. The police needed a damaging admission by the defendant himself to make their case. Silence was not only golden, it was sanctuary.

It would be comforting to know exactly how much they suspected, but not vital. Jorge sailed peacefully through the afternoon. When the problems of the office began threatening to spoil his mood, he decided to cut the day short. He walked out of the office about three o'clock and went to a local bar for a leisurely drink before climbing into the Vulcan to drive home. He mentally reviewed his favorite girlfriends. He felt like company. He would call Senta. She was a good companion for a celebration.

Not until he was halfway home did he realize a bright green Monitor had been visible on his rearview screen for some time. He turned up the magnification on the screen until he could see the driver. It was that black leo Maxwell. Brill was in the car, too. Jorge returned the screen to normal scan. What could they want? He did not for a moment believe it was coincidence they were on his tail. For a heartbeat, he felt fear. Had they found some definite evidence and were coming to arrest him?

Jorge slowed the Vulcan. The Monitor slowed, too, maintaining the same distance behind him. Jorge speeded up again. The other car did likewise. Jorge's fear evaporated, replaced by annoyance. They just wanted to follow him. Moreover, they must want him to know they were doing so, or they would not be so obvious about it. Well, that at least answered his question about where he stood. They must certainly suspect him of killing Andy.

When he turned in at his house and floated the Vulcan across the yard into the garage, the Monitor pulled up across the street and settled to its parking rollers. Jorge paused at the top of his steps to look across at them. Brill waved. That confirmed it; they wanted him to know they were there.

He hurried down the steps into the house. Did they think following him would unnerve him to the point he would incriminate himself? Probably. The police mind worked that way. He smiled thinly. Very well, if they wanted to think that, let them. They would see whose nerves went first.

The tops of the windows were above ground level. By standing on a chair, Jorge could see what was outside. He looked out twice over the next hour. The Monitor remained where it was.

Jorge decided to show them how little they were affecting him. He climbed the steps and crossed the street to the police car.

"Good afternoon, sergeants. It must be uncomfortable out here. May I offer you something cold to drink?"

Brill smiled. "No, thank you. That would be fraternizing with the enemy. We couldn't do that."

Jorge stopped his frown before it appeared. He made himself shrug instead. "You're the ones sitting in the sun. I'm just trying to be civil."

Maxwell was slouched in his seat with his head leaned against the back. His eyes were closed. "Sure, just like you were when you offered that sligh your whiskey Monday night. I don't like the additives in your drinks, jon."

Jorge went back into the house chuckling. They really thought they were going to frighten him by telling him how much they suspected. He did not give a damn how much they suspected, nor even how much they knew. It only sweetened his triumph of knowing how helpless they were.

He looked out the window again about five o'clock.

The Monitor was still there. He frowned in annoyance. Surely they did not intend to sit there all night? They must be off duty by now. He would be leaving to pick up Senta in just an hour. He did not at all welcome the idea of having leos in attendance at dinner and wherever else he and Senta decided to go this evening. He crossed the street again. Brill poked her sleeping partner. Maxwell sat up and the two regarded him quizzically.

"May we help you, Mr. Hazlett?"

"Is it fraternizing with the enemy to come inside my house for a few minutes? I'd like to talk to you."

The two exchanged glances. Brill said, "We're always willing to talk to you."

They followed him back to the house. He took them to the study. There he sat down behind his desk and stared up at them. They were in almost the same relative positions as in the interview room. What a difference in circumstance, though. He was in command of this interview.

"Just what, may I ask, do you two want?"

"You, Mr. Hazlett."

"You murdered two men, jon, and we don't think that's very civil. We think you ought to be punished for it."

"Two men? Who was the second?"

"Don't play innocent, jon. You know it was the sligh who doubled for you Saturday night."

He leaned back and smiled. "You're dreaming. Do you have evidence of this?"

"No," Brill admitted.

"Not yet." Maxwell made it a grim promise.

Jorge lifted his brows. "You expect to find some?"

Maxwell nodded. "You think you're safe, that you've gotten away with it, but the truth is, you're human, jon, and humans make mistakes. Even the perfect murderer will slip sometime."

"We plan to be here when you slip, Mr. Hazlett." Jorge chuckled. "How? By camping on my doorstep? I doubt your superiors would approve, even if it were physically possible to follow me twenty-four hours a day. It will all be in vain anyway. Surely you realize two Knights alone can never capture a King."

Janna was regretting having come. They did not seem to be driving Hazlett out into the sun. On the contrary, he appeared to be enjoying himself immensely, at their expense. His smile made her hand itch for a night stick. There was so much that could be done with one of those and never leave a mark. She reminded herself they were here to disturb Hazlett, not assault him.

"Our superiors have no love for unpunished murderers, either, Mr. Hazlett."

The infuriating, arrogant smile did not waver. "I may call them and ask about that."

In Janna's ear, the Capitol dispatcher's voice whispered, "Indian Thirty, call the station."

Mama's eyes flicked toward her. One brow hopped. She understood the unspoken request. He wanted her to roger the call. She tapped her ear button.

"Indian Thirty roger. Excuse me, Mr. Hazlett, do you have another phone I can use?" She did not want to use the one on his desk.

"There's one in the kitchen. It's down the hall to the left."

"Thank you."

She started to leave, then stopped, feeling a chill. Mama was eyeing Hazlett so intently. She wondered if it were wise to leave the two of them alone.

"Mama."

He looked at her.

"Keep Mr. Hazlett in good health while I'm gone."

She did not like Mama's answering smile. Still, she walked out, looking for the kitchen.

She found the kitchen, and the phone. She punched the station's number. The board put her through to Lieutenant Candarian.

"Don't you two ever go off duty?" the night watch supervisor asked.

"We're tracking down new evidence."

"I feel sorry for Vradel, having to justify all this overtime."

Janna sighed. "What do you want, lieutenant? I'm on a hot lead that may go cold if I don't chase it fast."

"A Milo Talous has been looking for you most of the afternoon, he tells me."

"Talous?" For a moment, she could not remember anyone named Talous.

"Of the Department of Justice."

Janna felt foolish. Of course. How could she have forgotten him? "What does he want?"

Instead of answering, Candarian lifted her brows. "You had trouble remembering him? Suffering from a little tunnel vision, Brill?"

Janna bit her lip.

"Does that mean you haven't kept him up to date on the investigation? Maybe that's what he wants. He left a number for you to call: 233-4111."

Janna wrote the number down on a pad by the phone. "Thank you."

"Any time." Candarian smiled. "Good luck hunting new evidence."

Jorge wished the she-lion had not left. The door closing behind Brill appeared to be some kind of release for Maxwell. He flexed his shoulders and seemed to grow even taller. Jorge found him towering over the desk, and smiling very unpleasantly.

"Well, jon, it's just you and me. Let's have a real exchange."

Jorge maintained his smile. "Man to man, as it were?"

"It'd only be man to man if you were, but you aren't, jon. You're a toad. We'll have a man to toad exchange."

Jorge felt his face freeze. Anger flared in him. Just who did Maxwell think he was? "We won't talk at all, sergeant. I find your tone insulting."

The black leo snorted. "I haven't even started. My partner is very polite. She's a conscientious officer who's going to make Investigator III and even Lieutenant some day. She works by the book. I'm different, though, so let me put it my way now." Maxwell leaned across the desk toward Jorge. "We're going to live with you, toad. You're not going to be able to breathe without us counting it, toad. You won't be able to count coup without our company. You might as well make us partners in your business because we're going to be there for every transaction, toad."

Jorge forced himself to a wintry smile. "That's called harassment. I can bring charges against you for that."

"Harassment?" Maxwell snorted in contempt. "You don't even know the meaning of the word, toad. Harassment is a cold shoulder compared to what we're going to do to you. You're going to find us sticking to you tighter than ticks. Our faces are never going to be out of your sight. It isn't going to be harassment; it's going to be like becoming a Siamese triplet."

Jorge started shaking with fury. He stood up. "I think I've tolerated enough of this. You have one minute to leave my house before I call—"

Maxwell sneered. "The police?"

"Get out of my house!"

"Not until we can prove you murdered your partner and that sligh. When we go, we intend to take you with us. After that it won't be long before some prison doctor draws up a syringe of T-61 and in the name of the State of Kansas, shoots it into your veins to send you on the longest odyssey of them all."

Red haze clouded Jorge's vision. He could hear his pulse thundering in his ears. The black man could not do this. People ordered out were supposed to go. The game was over—and he, Jorge, had beaten them. How dare Maxwell not obey the rules!

Janna met Milo Talous's tired clerk's eyes sheepishly. "I'm sorry we forgot to keep you informed, Mr. Talous. We've been busy with our line of investigation and it didn't seem to have much to do with yours."

The Justice agent frowned. "Information ought to be shared routinely between different agencies as well as between different departments in the same agency. For all you know, I might have had information that could help you."

"Yes, sir. Now, what can I do for you?"

"You can help me arrest Jorge Hazlett."

Jorge yanked open the desk drawer and pulled out the .22 revolver there. He pointed it at Maxwell. "I said get out of my house. I refuse to be subjected to any more of this abuse. You've lost. There is no evidence I killed anyone. There never will be. You've lost . . . *lost.*"

Maxwell looked at the .22. "I know: two Knights alone can never capture a King. But what if one of them isn't a Knight? What if one is a Rook?"

Jorge stared at him. He caught the pun. A rook was also a black, crowlike bird. Could a Rook and a Knight capture a King? Any end game implied that each side had at least a King left, and of course it was possible to checkmate with a King and a Rook.

His mind snapped back to attention just in time to find Maxwell launching across the desk to take away the pistol.

Janna stared at Talous. "Arrest Hazlett? I'd love to, but what for?"

Talous winced. "My god, you not only don't talk to people you need to; you don't even read all your forensic department's reports. The handwriting analysis—"

The handwriting analysis! She thought of the report lying on her worktable right now, the one she had never quite had time to read.

"—indicates Hazlett signed the contracting papers for the Laheli Company account and ten others. This afternoon the U.S. District Attorney handed me a warrant for—"

The flat crack of a pistol shot interrupted him.

Janna whirled. The sound had come from the direction of the study! She charged out of the kitchen and down the hall.

The shot was not loud, nothing like the sound of gunfire on holo-v programs, but in the confined area of the study, it sounded to Jorge like the thunderclap announcing the end of the world. Jorge had not intended to pull the trigger. He was horrified to find Maxwell collapsing across the desk.

Panic overwhelmed him. He had shot a police officer! He dropped the pistol and bolted from the room. He heard the she-lion shout at him, but he did not pause. He dived for the front door, jerked it open, and flung himself up the steps.

Behind him, Janna was wrenched two ways at once. The running man woke all her chase instincts at the same time that fear pulled her toward the study. She debated in the last few steps before she came even with the study door. She decided and dashed into the study.

Mama was slowly sliding off the desk onto the floor, clutching at his chest. Crimson was staining the bright yellow of his shirt.

"Mama!"

She caught him and helped ease him the last few centimeters to the floor.

"Mama, what happened?"

He coughed and whispered, "Got him on attempted murder."

She tried to yell at him that they did not need another charge. They could get him on Tescott violations. Her throat was too tight for yelling, though. Her vision seemed to be blurred, too. Surely she could not be crying, not for Mahlon Maxwell.

He closed his eyes with a soft sigh.

Outside, a sportster's fans wound up.

Janna came onto her feet. She tore out of the house and across the street toward Indian Thirty. She rapped her ear button. "This is Indian Thirty, requesting assistance and an ambulance. One officer down. Brentwood and Danbury."

She reached into the car through the open window and jerked the shotgun from its rack. Pumping a shell into the breech, she spun and raced back for the house. She wiped her eyes so she could see to shoot.

The Vulcan was backing across the lawn toward the street. It turned as it backed, ready to start forward at the first possible moment. Janna fired into the nearest

fan vent in the airfoil skirt. She pumped another shell
into the breech and fired again. The fiberplastic of the
skirt shattered.

The fans' whine flattened in sound. As it did, the
right rear quarter of the car dropped. The skirt plowed
into the lawn. The fans screaming, the Vulcan bucked
in anguish. It struggled to stabilize and move, but it
could only pivot around the damaged fans.

Janna pumped in another shell and circled the
Vulcan to the front. "Set her down, Hazlett!" She
aimed the shotgun at the open window of the driver's
side, straight into Jorge Hazlett's white face. "Checkmate. The game's over. Now climb out of the car . . .
slowly. Make one move I consider too fast and you'll
be a candidate for total thoracic transplant."

In the distance, she heard the *whew-whew-whew* of
police sirens.

Hazlett climbed out of the Vulcan with infinite care.

CHAPTER SEVENTEEN

The waiting room outside surgery was well appointed
with comfortable chairs and numerous microbooks and
current periodicals. Janna sat down in none of the
chairs and read none of the books or magazines. Like
some great cat, she paced the carpeted area in endless
circles and on each round, paused to stare at the surgery doors. She cursed herself. What a stupid waste the
shooting was. If she and Mama had held back . . . if
she had read the handwriting analysis when it came
up from Forensics . . . if she had not left Mama alone
with Hazlett while she called the station. The "if's"
went on endlessly. She blamed herself. She was the
senior partner and she was By-the-book Brill. She

knew procedure. She had to bend it, though, had to suggest they go stick pins in Hazlett. The lapse might cost Mama his life.

She had certainly bombed eight years in one spectacular bloody splash. The only thing that kept her from writing out her resignation now was the knowledge that the peeps would probably see to it she was fired. Well, there was always Champaign. Wim might be able to find something constructive for her to do out there.

From the doorway of the waiting room, Vradel said, "He's still in there? How long has it been?"

She could not bring herself to look at him. She kept pacing. "Three hours."

"You look like you think it's your fault."

She twitched her shoulders.

"Brill, you and Maxwell are partners, not each other's nursemaids. What happened?"

Now she really could not look at him. "It's all in the report."

"Hazlett resisted arrest, it says in the report. Do you know what Hazlett says? He says you two were threatening him and he shot Maxwell in self-defense."

She made herself turn around and look straight into the lieutenant's eyes. "Mama never threatened him. I could hear every word they were saying while I was on the phone."

Vradel chewed his mustache. "You'll swear to that in court, and to the peeps?"

She swallowed. Look at her. She was doing just what Wim had warned her about. She was jeopardizing herself by lying to superiors for Mama Maxwell. Why? She had no clear idea.

"Of course I'll swear to it."

He regarded her speculatively. "You have a good record. They may believe you."

She started pacing again. He walked with her. They both stopped to stare at the surgery door.

"There's no trace of that sligh Tarl yet."

She shrugged. She was not surprised.

They paced another circuit.

"I can assign you a new partner now, if you still want one."

She was staring at him, trying to understand the sudden confusion in her, when Wim and Vada Kiest walked into the waiting area.

"Wim."

He came toward the sound of her voice and put his arms around her. "One of the nurses told me what happened. You're sure having bad luck with partners lately."

She leaned her cheek against his forehead. "Luck is a bitch."

"You're looking well, though, Kiest," Vradel said.

"They're letting me out tomorrow." He let Janna go and stepped back to reach for Vada's hand. "It won't be long before we'll be leaving Earth. Which reminds me, Jan. The *Invictus* incident scared a number of people on our ship. They're looking for people to buy out their shares. We could set up the loan and you could come out on this ship. We could all go together."

Go now? If fate ever spoke, it must be like this. It sounded like a fine idea. So why did she have this hollow in her gut? "Leave in two weeks? Is that possible?"

"Sure. All you have to do is buy the share and get your physical."

Vradel's mustache twitched. He said conversationally, "I'm putting together a special squad to find that banzai bonsai. People aren't safe on the street until we strap that bibi."

Janna looked at him. "The hit-and-run driver?" It was about time they concentrated on her.

"Don't let him skin you, Jan. Don't forget that could just as easily be you in there being put back together. It's a bad job. You can do better."

She sucked on her lower lip. The world was full of Hazletts and Lacledes preying on the Kelleners and Owans. Leos stood between the two and the crossfire could be deadly. She thought of the jon who shot at her the day Wim was injured. She had been only millimeters from death then. There had been that sniper, too. The reward for the last job had been an apartment manager's insisting they pay for damage to the building. Who needed that for twenty years?

The surgery doors opened. Green-clad OR personnel guided a gliding stretcher out. Mama lay on it, tubes running from his chest to bottles hanging over the edge of the stretcher. Other tubes ran from bags of solutions down into his arms. Still others led from an oxygen tank to his nose. The life-function indicators on the side of the stretcher were a muddy color.

Janna touched his hand. He did not open his eyes. She looked at the nearest person in green. "Will he be all right?"

"You'll have to ask Dr. Teeter that."

Janna searched their faces. "Where is Dr. Teeter?"

Dr. Teeter stood behind the stretcher, a handsome woman in her fifties. "Are you a relative?" she asked.

A moment later she shook herself. Her eyes went from Mama's Dutch-chocolate color to Janna's smoky hair and fair skin. She sighed. "Excuse me. It's been a long night."

"She's closer than a relative," Vradel said. "She's his partner."

"I understand. His condition is serious, but it's stabilizing, I think. The next few hours are the most critical. Fortunately the bullet was a small caliber and only nicked the aorta or he would most certainly be dead. I'd say his chances of surviving are fair. Now, excuse us, please. We need to get him to Intensive Care."

They glided the stretcher on down the corridor.

Janna stood looking after it. "If he dies, what has it all been for? We could have strapped Hazlett anyway."

Vradel said, "Could we? Hazlett has an attorney who's been demanding that a handwriting expert of his own examine the signatures on those records. If Hazlett were arrested for the Tescott violations alone, he could be out on bail. As it is, the judge has set bail so high, your snake is in lock-up. He might beat the Tescott conviction, but he'll have a much harder time convincing a jury he didn't shoot or was justified in shooting Maxwell."

"It still seems useless," Vada said. "I'm glad you're going to get out and come with us, Jan."

The stretcher was nearing the corner. Janna did not take her eyes from it. Strange. She felt a piece of herself going with it.

Maybe not so strange. She took a close look at her feelings. A piece of her was with him. He was her partner. There was more to it than that, too. Different as she and Mama were, they shared something of the same soul. Vradel shared it, too. "No, I'm not coming."

"Oh, Jan."

"Why not?" Wim demanded.

"Not everyone can leave. Someone has to stand between the sheep and wolves that are left or there really won't be any hope for this planet."

"It doesn't have to be you standing between. Don't be noble."

She smiled at him, as if he could still see her expression. "I'm not noble. That's just an excuse. The truth is, it does have to be me standing between. I'm a leo, Wim, blood and bone. Rotten as it can be, I love the job. I gave up law school for it, and maybe a husband and family. I'm doing what I want to do."

Vradel grinned.

"I couldn't be a farmer, never in this world or any other. I'm glad you're getting what you want, though. I wish ramjets weren't one-way trips or I'd come visit you after you're settled." It was strange to think they might just be arriving on Champaign when she was an old, dying woman. "I wish you both the best of luck." She looked around at Vradel. "Would there be room for me on that special squad?"

"I expect so. I need something to keep you busy until your partner heals up."

"Thank you, sir." She looked at them, then off in the direction the stretcher had disappeared. "I'll see you all later. Will you excuse me right now? I'd like to see if they'll let me sit by his bed until he wakes up."

About the Author

Lee Killough is a 5'7" redhead who began her love affair with words and tales very early in her Kansas childhood. She started on science fiction in junior high school, after reading Leigh Brackett's *Starmen of Llyrdis* and C. L. Moore's "Shambleau." First published in 1970 in *Analog,* she has since appeared in a number of science-fiction magazines.

She supplements her writing income by moonlighting as a radiographer at KSU Veterinary Hospital in the College of Veterinary Medicine, Kansas State University, in Manhattan, Kansas. She shares her life and home with a big-eyed cat named Merlyn and a charming fellow named Pat, a lawyer turned business-law instructor, at whose insistence she first began submitting stories for publication.

She has taught riding—hunt seat—and ridden and trained horses. She is a compulsive book buyer, an insatiable reader, and a devoted Sherlock Holmes buff. She and Pat like to attend science-fiction conventions when their work schedules permit.